MIND OF A KING

MIND OF A KING

A NOVEL BY DUECE KING

This novel is dedicated to the two people that I hold dear to my heart.

My mother and nephew; Annette and Tevin Morris.
May 'The Most High' grant you peace in paradise and I pray that I continue to make you proud.

Love Always,

Duece

INTRODUCTION

THOUGHTS FROM A JAIL CELL
JUNE 2010

"Damn! I don't believe this shit!" were the words that escaped my mouth once I entered a freezing holding cell that I was all too familiar with. As far back as I can remember my life has been a constant roller-coaster ride, up and down, round and round. When I'm down, it feels like my luck cannot get any worse and when I'm up, it feels like things could be better; but who am I to complain? I'm just another black man from the streets of Buffalo, New York, making moves to stay ahead. Along this journey that we call life, I've come across several obstacles and made many decisions that have caused plenty of people pain. Costing some people their life and others their freedom. I'm not proud of all the choices that I've made but in the same breath, I don't regret them. The life that I've chosen has molded me into the man that I've become, so I refuse to be apologetic for my shortcomings. Sometimes, 'The Most High' allows us to go through adversity and suffer the hardships so that we can become the person that we're destined to be.

As I sit here, staring at the walls of silence, the demons of my past come to life, haunting me night and day. I envision my friends lying dead on the pavement with their eyes wide open, looking deep inside of my soul. I can still picture the courtroom while standing in front of a Judge, awaiting the verdict that would alter my life forever. I've witnessed the betrayal of the closest comrade, during the darkest moments. The women that you think are innocent; the ones that you thought would ride with you to the end of the earth will eventually switch sides, whispering your most confidential secrets into the ear of the enemy. Crack heads and junkies roam the ghetto aimlessly all night in search of that next fix with a look of despair and hopelessness in their eyes. Yeah, I have seen it all. Imagine having to watch your back twenty-four seven, studying every vehicle that passes by or sitting with your back to the wall, eyes locked in on everyone who enters the room. I've put myself in the presence of my adversaries without realizing that they were the competition. While coming up in these streets, I kept a gun in arms reach, especially around the ones who claimed to love me. I thought that I had seen everything with my eyes wide open, unconsciously walking through life blind. I'm at a stage where I have to step outside of myself to receive clarity. I've spent my entire life running towards the problem in search of a solution without realizing that the answer was in my presence the entire time. Since an adolescent, I've traveled a road to destruction, of drugs and violence, trapped in a world where disputes are settled in war, ending in bloodshed. Shackled down with the ball and chain of my past makes it difficult to move forward but I refuse to give up, I refuse to lie down, I refuse to allow these prison walls to swallow me up and seize my mind. Over the years, I have learned to trust no one. In this profession, I can't trust a soul because the first sign of weakness could cost me my life. As I dig deep within myself, confronting my fears, I go back to a place that I forgot existed. A place where dreams were broken, families shattered, and lives were lost. The memories that I buried into the abyss of my mind were now being brought forth to the surface of my soul.

This story that I am about to share with you isn't about some poverty-stricken kid that went from rags to riches. It's about a young man who could have been anything that he chose yet somewhere along the way became a product of his environment.

CHAPTER 1

THE BEGINNING
1987

I was born January 1, 1977, during one of the worst storms to hit Western New York. I was much too young to remember the blizzard that held most residents captive in their homes but I've been told stories on more than one occasion.

My name is King Jones. My birth place is Buffalo, New York. Some call it the forgotten city; others know it as the 'land of the snow' but I refer to it as The Town. I can recall, running up and down the block at the tender age of ten, playing sports until the street light came on. My friends and I caused all types of mischief around the neighborhood from throwing rocks, breaking windows to groping the young females. Yeah, those were the days!

I was the youngest of five children. The baby boy! My siblings and I had the same father but different mothers except for me and my brother Damon. We had different fathers but the same mother, so we were the only ones that grew up in the house together. I looked up to Damon and being that I was his younger brother, he exposed me to things that the average kid my age wasn't privy to. He took me under his wing early, molding me to be tough from day one. It seems like it was yesterday when he was calling my name to prepare me for my daily exercise.

"Yo King!" Damon yelled from the basement. "You ready for your training!"

"Yeah, hold up a minute, I have to go and put on my boots," I shouted back before running off to my room.

As I strapped up my boots, I could hear the chatter of teenage boys, coming from the basement so I knew that it was show time. When I entered the area where Damon usually entertained his company, I was engulfed with a cloud of marijuana smoke mixed with the scent of jasmine incense burning. Bo, Gee, and my cousin Nino sat around a circle shaped table across from my brother, drinking Old English and smoking weed. I dapped everyone up around the table then stopped at Damon.

"Are you ready for your training?" he repeated.

I scanned the faces in the room and nodded.

"Then show me where your heart at!" he instructed, raising his hands.

I got into my boxing stance and began throwing hooks and jabs into his palms for the next couple of minutes. Every so often, he would pop me upside the head, forcing me to defend myself. After ten minutes of going through this routine, I became tired. Out of breath, I took a seat in a chair next to my cousin Nino.

"This lil nigga is going to be ready when he gets older," Gee stated.

"What the fuck you mean when I get older?" I cursed. "I'm ready now!"

Laughter broke out throughout the room."

"That's right little cousin, let that nigga know what's up!" Nino said, blowing out a ring of smoke.

"Aye, Nino where Vanessa at?" I questioned.

"She should be at the house, why?"

"Do you think that she'll let me spend the night?"

Nino passed the joint to Bo then grabbed the 40 bowl from Damon.

"Yeah, she should let you spend the night," he took a swig of the beer. "She doesn't do anything else but talk on the phone all day anyway. Just check with my moms to make sure that it's cool."

It was a luxury being around my brother and his crew. I learned a lot by listening and watching closely, trying to imitate everything that I saw them do. While most kids were idolizing some fictitious character that they had seen on television, I was getting a one on one lesson from my brother.

Rumor has it that Damon was the leader of a young crew that terrorized the eastside of Buffalo in the late eighties. They were known for fighting other neighborhoods and extorting local hustlers. I once overheard a story about the nephew of an infamous hustler that they'd tortured and left for dead because he refused to pay. As the years passed Damon's reputation grew throughout the town and the streets respected his gangster. I was extremely too young to be involved but I did receive some of the love, being that I was his brother.

"Let me hit the weed," I reached for the joint.

"You can't hit shit," Damon barked. "Now take your ass back upstairs before Ma Dukes get home from work."

"That's some bullshit! You called me down here, talking about some mutha fucking training now you want to run me back upstairs. Fuck y'all, I'm out!"

"Hold up!" he stopped me in my tracks. "Sit your little ass back down."

"Damn, make up your mind!"

Amused with my performance, Damon laughed. "You really want to hit this shit?"

"Yup," I grinned.

"Yo Bo, let me see the weed."

Bo released a ring of smoke then passed it to Damon.

"Open your mouth," he said.

As I followed instruction, Damon gave me a shotgun and I immediately began coughing. More laughter broke out amongst the teenagers as I desperately tried to catch my breath.

"That's what you get, trying to be grown," Nino patted me on the back.

"Yo, don't King remind y'all of my lil cousin TK?" Bo questioned.

"Yeah, both of them little niggas is off the chain," Gee agreed.

Damon turned to face me. "Aye bra, do you know lil TK?"

"Does he be up at the park?"

"Yeah, his bad ass is at the park all the time," Bo confirmed. "Y'all two got to be around the same age."

"I think that I know who you're talking about."

Gee rolled another E-Z Wider and added fire to it.

While the marijuana circulated throughout the concrete room, I sat silently, pretending to be cool as the THC took its effect on my young mind.

"You need to get back upstairs before Ma Dukes gets home," Damon suggested. "You already know that she's going to start bugging out if she catches you down here."

I quickly gathered myself and dashed up the steps into the bathroom. Splashing a hand full of water onto my face, I attempted to shake off the high that had taken control of the better part of my brain. An hour later I was awakened by the voice of my mother shouting at Damon.

"Damon if you don't get out of my house smoking that shit, I'm going to kick your ass!"

Ma, why are you trippin?" Damon contested.

"I'm not tripping," she replied. "You're the one who must've been tripping when you brought this foolishness under my roof. I don't understand why you think that it's all right for you to bring that nonsense here. I don't want to smell that stuff when I come home from work."

"Alright ma, calm down."

"Boy don't tell me to calm down!" Ma Dukes roared. "Now where is your little brother? Have you been keeping an eye on him or has he been watching himself?"

At the mention of my whereabouts, I rushed into the kitchen where all the commotion was taking place.

"What's up Ma?"

"Don't say what's up to me like I'm one of your little friends," she responded. "What were you doing and why are your eyes so red?"

"I just woke up," I answered quickly.

"Have you been down in the basement with your brother today?"

"No, not today!"

She studied me suspiciously for a moment then turned to face Damon.

"I don't want King down in that basement while you got company Damon. My baby doesn't need to be around that garbage. He already emulates everything that he sees you do so you need to set a good example."

Ma Dukes managed a smile, but I could see the aggravation all through her brow. She was the epitome of what a strong black woman stood for. Her charcoal skin was flawless, and her eyes radiated with intelligence. When she was seventeen, she had gotten pregnant by a smooth hustler six years her senior. With the support of her parents, she was able to complete college while working two jobs. Over the years, Ma Dukes constantly stressed the importance of education and hard work, but nothing was more significant to her than family. Although she was firm, she was fair. Ma Dukes wanted the best for her children and she made sure that we didn't go without.

Knock... knock... knock...

"Who is it?" Ma Dukes screamed.

"It's Junior Ms. Jones," a voice answered back. "Is King home?"

She turned to me. "Go ahead and see what your friend wants."

I grabbed my jacket and hurried outside before she could ask me anymore questions or find something for me to do.

"What's up Junior?" I gave him dap.

"I'm chillin. What's up with you?"

"It's the same ole thang. Ma Dukes, bugging out on my brother again. Let's hurry up and bounce before she comes out here talking crazy."

Junior lived up the block with his mother and two older sisters. We had literally come up in the sandbox together. Ever since we were in diapers, we'd been playing and fighting one another. As we rode up the street on Junior's BMX, I spotted Shawn and his younger brother Shakim heading towards the corner store.

Shawn was a heavy-set kid from the neighborhood who was always talking loud and cracking jokes. Shakim was the complete opposite. He was quiet and serious.

What's the deal with y'all boys?" Junior rode up on the sidewalk.

We're on our way to get my mom's a Pepsi," Shawn replied.

I hopped from the handle bars and greeted them both with some dap.

"Give me the money that y'all about to spend for the Pepsi and I'll creep it instead." I told them.

Shawn was contemplating what he should do as Shakim eyed me questionably.

"And I'll get y'all some shit too," I assured him.

"That's a bet!" Shawn handed me two singles.

"Meet us around the corner in five minutes," I instructed. "C'mon Junior."

Stealing wasn't a necessity for me; it was more like a hobby. I was enthralled by the adventure of committing a crime. Junior stole because he was hungry and there wasn't any food at his house. His mother received a check once a month from the government, but she spent it on drugs and alcohol. She even exchanged her food stamps to get high, leaving Junior and his siblings to fend for themselves.

When I entered the store, I headed straight to the counter while Junior walked towards the cooler in the back. For the next couple minutes, I distracted the cashier, giving Junior enough time to make his move. As he began stuffing sodas and chips inside of his jacket, I was at the counter, acting as if I was undecided about what to purchase. The Arabian clerk was beginning to get frustrated as a small line began to build up behind me. It was obvious that he wanted me to hurry up and buy something from the expression on his face. Once Junior exited the store, I bought fifty cents worth of penny candy and walked out the door smiling. Around the corner, Shawn and Shakim were impatiently awaiting our return.

"What took you so long?" Shakim questioned as we walked up.

"Did y'all get the stuff?" Shawn asked all excited.

"Damn, chill out!" I told them. "Y'all acting like we weren't coming back."

Junior pulled the Pepsi from his jacket and handed it to Shawn then gave him and Shakim a bag of chips.

Take your moms her pop and then meet us at my crib," Junior suggested.

In less than twenty minutes, we were all at his house, playing Nintendo while listening to music in his room. The super sonic boom box, sitting on Junior's dresser blasted the sounds of Run DMC. Captivated by the rhythm exploding from out of the speakers, I bopped my head to the beat. I listened closely to every word, wishing that I could orchestrate rhymes into a sentence like them.

"Aye Junior, let me borrow this tape until tomorrow?" I asked.

"That's my sister's and you already know how Terri is about her stuff," Junior replied.

"Well I'm going to bring you a cassette, so you can dub it for me."

"I got you!"

Junior had beaten everyone in the room at least once on the videogame and was about to defeat Shawn for the second time.

"Next!" he screamed once the game was over.

"Junior, you're garbage as hell!" Shakim passed the joystick to Shawn. "The only reason that you keep winning is because you're using the best team on the game. Play with somebody else and I bet that I win."

"I'm not trying to hear that," Junior sneered. "Talk to me when you get back on the sticks."

"This dude really thinks that he did something too." Shawn stated. "You need to comb that nappy ass head instead of playing games all day. That shit look like the back of a sheep's ass."

"I know that your fat ass ain't talking. You so fat when you stepped on the scale it read to be continued."

Shakim and I laughed in unison.

"That shit was corny as hell," Shawn replied. "And I don't know what you're laughing at King? You so black, you sweat tar."

"Watch your mouth fat boy," I stopped laughing. "I'm not with all that joking shit."

"Chill out! I'm just playing with your sensitive ass."

"Yeah, whatever!"

There was a knock at the door as it eased open. Junior's mother stepped inside of the room smoking a cigarette while holding a glass of beer.

"Why are y'all making so much noise in here?" her words were slightly slurred.

"C'mon mom, don't come in here embarrassing me in front of my friends," Junior protested.

"Who do you think you talking to boy? This is my house; I pay the bills up in this muthafucka!"

"Alright ma, go ahead with all of that."

"Don't tell me what to do!" she waved him off. "King your mother just called here looking for you. She told me to tell you to come home."

"Okay," I replied.

As she was leaving the room, Ms. Shirley kicked aside some of Junior's dirty clothes.

"And clean this shit up. I don't know how you could bring anyone into this pigpen," she closed the door behind her.

"I'll be back in a minute," I told them. "I'm about to go and see what Ma Dukes is talking about."

"We'll be right here," Junior said.

"Alright, I'm going to ride your bike to the building!"

"That's cool! Just make sure that you bring it back!"

As I peddled the bicycle down the block, I could hear the engine of a motorcycle from a distance. Turning up into the driveway, I noticed that it was Gee speeding past my street on a Ninja Kawasaki. On the back, there was a light skinned female, holding him around the waist. He acknowledged me with the horn as he zoomed by. I responded with a peace sign as I dropped the BMX onto the steps and went in the house.

"Ma!" I screamed up the stairs.

"Boy, stop all that yelling," Ma Dukes appeared in the hallway. "I can hear you!"

"Ms. Shirley said that you were looking for me?"

"Yes, I was," she stood there with her hand on her hip. "Can you explain to me why you left this house without informing me that you were leaving?"

"I don't know," I shrugged my shoulders.

"Do you think that you're grown or something?"

"No!"

"Evidently, you do because you didn't even ask me if you could go anywhere."

"I was only up the block at Junior's house."

"I don't care if you were down the street at the Pastor's house; you better let me know where you're at. As long as I'm the one putting food on the table and clothes on your back, you'll abide by the rules. Do I make myself clear?"

"Yes ma'am!"

"Did you do your homework and clean your room when you got home from school?"

"Oh, I forgot," I sighed. "I'll do it right now."

"See what I'm talking about? You're all up the street at your friend's house and you haven't handled any of your responsibilities around here. Boy you better get in there and do your homework before I whoop your behind."

CHAPTER 2

JEWELS PAST DOWN TO AN INNOCENT CHILD

Awakened in the middle of the night to use the bathroom; I heard voices coming from downstairs. After recognizing the laughter of my pops, I crept down the steps to see who he was conversing with. When I stepped into the shadows of the living room, I witnessed something that would have an effect on me forever. Pops was at the kitchen table, counting large sums of money with a man that I had never seen before. Between counts, they sniffed a white powdered substance that was spread across a dinner plate. Before I could return to my bedroom without being heard, Pops grabbed his pistol and turned in my direction all in the same motion.

"Who is that?" he spoke in a threatening tone.

"It's me Pop's," I quickly emerged from the dark. He lowered the 357 Revolver.

"Get over here boy," Pop's motioned me over. "Why aren't you in the bed?"

"I was thirsty, so I came down here to get something to drink."

"Do you think that I'm stupid or something son?" he laughed, grabbing me by the head. "You came down here being nosey."

"Nuh uh, I came to get some water," I defended.

"Hurry up and get some water then get in the bed. You have to get up early for school tomorrow."

Pop's was a hustler who was originally from Harlem, New York. He began his life in the streets, running numbers at the age of fifteen and advanced to drugs the following year. Once he discovered that the drug market was wide open upstate, he connected with his cousin Frank and moved to Buffalo. In the late 60s and throughout the 70s, they distributed heroin on the city's eastside and it was believed that Pops would kill anyone who played with his money. Feared by men and adored by women, he built a reputation that extended out to the west coast. He was still mentally sharp at the age of forty but years of living life in the fast lane was beginning to catch up to him. At 5 feet 11 inches, with a medium build, Pops had begun to grey at the temples.

When I opened the refrigerator, I stole a glimpse of the guy sitting across from Pops. A cigarette hung from his lips as he counted the bundle of cash in front of him. At his feet there was a duffle bag, holding the same white substance that they had been snorting; only it was wrapped in plastic. Once I finished drinking my water, I told Pops good night then hurried up the steps. As I lay in the bed, I thought about what I'd just witnessed before dosing off to sleep.

♟ ♟ ♟ ♟

The next morning, I awoke to Ma Dukes, yelling from the doorway of my bedroom.

"King it's time for you to get up!"

"I don't feel good!" I groggily replied.

"You better get up and get ready for school King. There isn't anything wrong with you."

"I don't want to go to school today."

"You don't have a choice in the matter," she spoke with authority. "You should've taken your behind to bed last night instead of watching television. Now get up and get dressed, I'm not about to go through this with you this morning."

As I dragged myself from the bed, images of what I had seen the night before were still vividly clear in my mind. Stepping into the hallway, I heard loud snoring coming from Damon's room.

"Why he dont have to get up and go to school?" I mumbled under my breath.

After brushing my teeth and washing my face, I dressed quickly then joined Ma Dukes for breakfast. When I entered the kitchen, she was sipping a cup of hot tea while reading the newspaper.

"Good morning handsome," she cheerfully greeted. "Good morning, Ma," I replied in a dry voice. "Why are you so irritable this morning?"

"I don't know," I picked over my grits and eggs.

She placed the palm of her hand over my head, checking to see if I had a temperature.

"You don't have a fever. Maybe you'll feel better after you put something in your stomach."

Once I completed my breakfast, Ma Dukes handed me the keys to the Cutlass Supreme. Every morning, she would allow me to start the car and warm it up before we left. When I stepped outside into the cold, I spotted Junior, sprinting past the house in an attempt to catch the school bus.

"You better not miss that cheese," I laughed in his direction. "Ya moms is going to beat that ass if you do!"

Even in a hurry, Junior still managed to flip me the middle finger. I cranked the ignition and turned the radio station to 93.7. My mind drifted to the previous night, thinking about what I had witnessed. I wondered about the man who was with Pops, counting all that money; and what was that powder they were sniffing? I was brought back to the present moment once the car door opened.

"Do you have everything that you need before we pull off?" Ma Dukes asked

"Yes Ma," I responded.

I'm not trying to hear that you forgot something once we're halfway across town."

"I said that I got everything. Dang Ma give me a break!"

Ma Dukes reached across the seat and back handed me in the mouth.

"What you hit me for?" I held my face.

"For your smart ass mouth!" she admonished. "You talking about give you a break. I'll give you a break alright; when I break your damn neck. You better check yourself before you get hurt little boy."

"Sorry Ma!"

"Don't be sorry, be careful. I told you before that I'm not one of your little friends. Now when you get out of school, you're to go directly to your grandparent's house and wait for your father. He should be there to pick you up between three and three thirty. Once he drops you off, you are not to leave this house until I get home. Do you understand?"

"Yes Ma."

"Good. And make sure that you clean your room after you do your homework."

There was nothing but silence for the rest of the ride. Ma Dukes accentuated respect, especially towards women and elders. She engraved this principle into the mind of both Damon and myself and so I knew better than to fly off at the lip. Every day she groomed us about the wicked ways of the world. It was imperative for her to instill ethics and morals inside of us, so we'd know the difference between right and wrong. Once we arrived at school, Ma Dukes pulled behind a row of yellow school buses and parked. I snatched my book bag from the back seat before opening the door to leave.

"I'm sorry for being disrespectful Ma but I didn't feel like coming to school today," I apologized.

"I accept your apology," she grinned. "I know that it may seem like I'm being hard on you King but I'm only trying to prepare you for situations that may occur in life. I'm not always going to be here to take care and protect you. An education will present opportunities for you to fend for yourself."

"I understand what you are saying Ma but sometimes I feel like school isn't that important."

"Knowledge is power King! That's one of the only things that no one will be able to take from you and don't you ever forget that."

"When I grow up, I'm going to play in the NBA so why do I need to go to school?" I questioned.

"I believe that you can do anything that you put your mind to," she encouraged. "But how do you expect to play professional basketball if you don't go to school?"

"With my jump shot!" I shot an imaginary ball, displaying my form.

"Well when you get to the NBA, you won't have to go to school," she snickered. "But until then, I'm going to need you to get an education. Okay?"

"Okay, but when I get rich and buy you a house; you're going to see that I didn't need what they taught me at school."

Ma Dukes gave me a hug. "Now hurry up and get to class before you be late; I'll see you when I get home from work."

As soon as I walked into class, I was approached by a kid name Danny. Even though we were from different neighborhoods, we were thick as thieves. Danny kept me up to date with the latest fashion and slang. Besides me, he was the only kid in our class that wore the black and white shell toe Adidas with the fat laces. Danny was from a neighborhood known as the Fruit Belt. His family was knee deep into the streets, so he knew all of the hustlers and prostitutes that dwelled on his block. He had come up rough. He never knew his father and at the age of six, he watched his mother overdose on heroin, leaving him and his sister to live with their grandmother. His aunts and uncles were constantly in out of jail, so it was difficult for an elderly woman to keep up with his whereabouts; especially with seven other grandchildren running around the house. Danny was into all type of trouble and he always had a story to tell about who had gotten locked up or knocked out on his block. He had even witnessed someone get shot at a $5 dice game and when the police came to question him, he told them that snitches are like bitches and bitches get stitches. Danny was off the hook; even the teachers feared him.

"What's up homeboy? I've been waiting on you all morning" he claimed, overly excited.

"What's up player?" I gave him dap. "Why were you looking for me?"

"Guess who like you?"

"Who?"

"Rena!"

"Rena?"

"Yeah nigga, Rena," Danny smiled mischievously. "Rena Johnson. I overheard her and my sister Nikki, talking about you on the phone last night."

"What did they say?" I questioned.

Danny took a seat on top of my desk and continued in a low voice.

"Rena said that she thought that you were cute, but you be acting funny when you're around your friends, and you already know that Nikki was kickin salt."

"What she have to say?"

"She told Rena that you were sweatin, Eboni Brown in gym class last week and how you be going extra hard whenever she's watching you play basketball."

"Your sister is always talking shit," I scowled. "I don't be sweating that girl, she be on my dick."

"Don't get mad at me, I'm just telling you what was said," Danny defended. "But you do be going extra hard whenever shorty around."

"Fuck you nigga," I laughed, knowing that he was telling the truth.

"Don't fuck me, you should be trying to fuck Rena, she's the one who likes you."

"I'm going to talk to her after school, now let me do my bell work before Ms. Walker try and give us detention."

♟ ♟ ♟ ♟

Usually I would hang around and chill with my boy's when school ended but I was on a mission this particular day. Exiting the building, I spotted Rena across the street talking to Nikki and Amanda, staring in my direction. Nonchalantly, I smiled and threw up the peace sign as I ditty bop past them.

"C'mere King!" Nikki called out to me.

"What's up?" I stopped in my tracks.

"C'mere!" she repeated with an attitude.

I swung my book bag over my shoulder and walked across the street to where they were standing.

"What's up?"

"You so corny, I know Danny told you."

"Told me what?"

"He didn't tell you that my girl wanted to talk to you?"

"Your girl who?"

"Stop playing stupid," Nikki shoved me. "I know that he told you that my girl Rena like you. He couldn't wait to get to school so he could run his big mouth."

"Well if she's the one that likes me, why are you doing all the talking?" I looked at Rena.

"I don't even know why she likes your black butt? You ain't all that!"

"Whatever!" I waved her off and turned to Rena. "Can I walk you home?"

"I don't care," she blushed.

Rena was one of the prettiest girls in the 6th grade due to her brown skin and almond shaped eyes. Her silky black hair was pulled into a shoulder length ponytail. Many of the other females envied her because they thought that she was conceited but she wasn't. Rena was actually one of the coolest girls at the school. As we walked hand in hand towards her apartment, we talked about everything from music to our favorite television shows. I was surprised to learn that she liked to watch sports and was extremely fond of basketball. Rena was down to earth, and I found it easy to talk to her.

"I didn't know that you were this cool," I told her.

"Well maybe if you would have paid more attention to me, you would've noticed" she smiled.

"I noticed you," I admitted. "But every time I see you, you're with Nikki and them."

"So! You act like that's my mother or something."

"She might as well be. Y'all act like y'all can't live without each other."

"I know that you're not talking," Rena rolled her neck. "You be acting funny whenever you're around your friends, especially when you're with Danny. Y'all think that y'all all that or something."

"No, we don't!" I laughed. "We just be chillin!"

Once we reached Rena's apartment building, she took a seat on her front stoop.

"You know that you be acting funny. And I'm not even talking about when you're around your girl Ebony. That's another story."

"What are you talking about?" I sat down next to her.

"I've seen you all in her face, showing off whenever we're in the gym so don't try and front!"

"No, I don't!"

"Whatever!"

Suddenly a cab pulled to the curb and started blowing its horn. Moments later, a lady appeared from the building, carrying a baby and a diaper bag over her shoulder.

"Rena, you better get your little fast ass upstairs and wash those dishes," she yelled.

"But...

"But nothing!" she cut her short. "Every time I turn around, you got some little nappy headed little boy in your face. Now get your ass up there and wash those dishes and stay in the house until I get back.

Embarrassed, Rena stormed up the steps without saying goodbye as the woman pushed past me and got into the back of the cab, pulling off.

"Bitch!" I mumbled under my breath.

With a feeling of disappointment, I grabbed my book bag and began walking down the street.

"King!" Rena called out.

I looked up and saw her hanging out of the third floor window.

"Was that ya moms?" I asked her.

"No, that was my aunt Tami. She be tripping sometimes but for the most part, she's cool."

"Oh okay, can I call you sometimes."

She scribbled onto a piece of paper then tossed it down.

"That's my phone number but make sure that you call me before eight o'clock."

"What if your people answer the phone?"

"I'm allowed to have boy phone calls as long as you call me before eight!"

"Alright, if I don't talk to you tonight, I'll see you in school tomorrow."

"Don't be acting funny either."

"I'm not," I declared as I turned to walk away.

With a little more pep in my step, I opened the torn piece of paper and read the short note beneath the number.

(Can I be your girlfriend circle yes or no?)

♟ ♟ ♟ ♟

When I arrived at my grandparents' house, Pops was sitting in his Bronco, watching me as I walked up.

"Hey Pop," I hopped in the truck. "What's going on?"

"What's happening man?" he responded. "Where have you been? I've been sitting here, waiting on you for over twenty minutes."

"My fault Pop. I forgot that you were picking me up today."

"Where were you? I rode by the school, but I didn't see you."

"I walked my friend Rena to her house."

"Why didn't you have her walk you home son?" he laughed. "You have to learn to get them girls to bend in your direction King. Did you at least get a dollar or a kiss for your generosity?"

"Nah Pop, It's not even like that," I defended.

"I'm just messing with you son. Are you hungry?"

"I'm starving!"

"Well sit back and buckle up."

I enjoyed riding with Pops. He always took me places and told me things that a normal kid wasn't aware of. We went to African Art galleries and science museums to learn the history of the original man. Pops taught me to be proud of who I am and to never to be ashamed of the color of my skin. He showed me the worst sections of the city and exposed me to how black people were subdued by poverty. Even though he had money, Pop's treated those that were less fortunate with respect and infused those same values inside of me. He always expressed to never forget where you come from because the past can often predict the future. Wherever he went, he was acknowledged and revered by everyone from the junkies to the gangsters; and there were all shades of women at his beck and call. You could consider Pops a generous man but there was also a diabolical side that was displayed whenever he felt disrespected.

Out of all the places that he took me to, the pool hall was my favorite spot. I liked to watch slick hustlers like Bank Shot Slim trick sucka's out of their money. He would give me a dollar every time that he would win a bet and he even taught me how to shoot nine ball.

As we drove up Jefferson Ave, I wondered where Pops was taking me to eat today, GIGIs or Mattie's. My question was answered once we pulled up in front of Fosters, a local bar where Pops often conducted business.

Fosters wasn't crowded when we walked in. There were two women occupying the first couple stools while a well-dressed gentleman sat at the end of the bar, conversing with Sam the bartender.

"Go and order two haddock dinners," Pops handed me a twenty dollar bill before joining the women at the bar.

I grabbed the money and hurried towards the back past the pool table and dart machine.

"Hey George, let me get two haddock fish dinners," I told the man behind the counter.

"Aye, my main man King," George expressed. "I haven't seen you in a while. You still playing ball?"

"Of course! I've been playing for a church league in my neighborhood."

"Don't forget about an old man once you make it to the big leagues," he handed me a free slice of cake. "What are your side orders?"

"Let me get some french fries and coleslaw."

"Alright, I'll call you when it's ready!"

"Okay!" I headed towards the arcade machine.

As I attempted to take down the high score in Space Invaders, I noticed a man exit the restroom. Surprisingly, it was the same guy that was counting money at the kitchen table with Pops the night before. He was immaculately dressed in a cream silk shirt, brown slacks and matching alligator shoes. The gold Rolex decorating his wrist would've caught a blinds man attention the way the diamonds danced around the bezel.

"Do you remember me?" he propped against the pool table.

"I don't know your name but you're my father's friend," I told him.

He extended his hand. "They call me Silk."

"Why do they call you that?" I shook his hand.

"It's just a nickname that I picked up when I was younger," Silk smiled. "Why do they call you King?"

"Pops gave me that name because he said that I'm royalty; and if I think like a King people will treat me like one."

"You're sharp little dude. How old are you?"

"I'm ten but I will be eleven in a few months."

"You'll be ready to run with the big dogs in a minute" he lit up a cigarette. "Caesar told me that you know how to handle the ball on the court."

"A little bit. I still need to work on my left though."

"Keep practicing and it'll come to you," Silk's pager began beeping.

He unclipped it from his waist, viewed the screen and clipped it back on his belt."

"Do you have a girlfriend?"

"Yeah, I got a girlfriend," I handed him the note with Rena's number."

"Oh, you're a young player huh?" he read the paper.

"Yep!"

"That's cool but being a player can get expensive at times."

I distorted my face into a frown and looked at Silk as if he was crazy. "I'm not giving a girl my money; they buy me snacks during lunch."

Silk laughed as he removed a large wad of bills from his pocket.

"You keep thinking like that and you'll be rich someday," he slid me a twenty. "But sometimes you have to give before you can receive. Always remember that!"

I put the money in my pocket and thanked him as he walked to the front to join Pops and the two women at the bar. He moved with the confidence of a man of leisure. Pops always told me to never judge a book by its cover or a man by his appearance because people were never who they appeared to be, but it was something about Silk that symbolized power. It wouldn't be until many years later that I discovered how much power, money, and respect he truly had in the town.

"King your food is ready!" George said.

I paid him for the dinners then wandered to the front where Pops was chastising Jackie, a beautiful red bone that stood five feet nine inches. She reminded me of Apollonia from Purple Rain with her Indian features.

"You see son, this is the perfect example of a trifling bitch!" Pops remarked.

"Don't do that Caesar," Jackie pleaded.

Pops swallowed a shot of Hennessey and continued.

"It's bitches like you that got man all fucked up now!" he slammed the shot glass onto the counter. "Since the beginning of time, men have been falling victim to serpents like you."

"Why are you doing this?" she questioned. "I told you that I would bring you your money tonight."

"Bitch, you better stop playing with me before I get up from here and ram this glass down your mutha fuckin throat. I'm not on your time and I shouldn't have to go through this with you. I feel like you're trying me!"

With tears welling up in her eyes, Jackie got up from the stool and went into the lady's room.

"That's right hoe, get out of my sight, you disgust me!" Pops downed another drink. "If a bitch isn't good for some money then what is she good for? We don't need them around us son. They will try to trick you with that hole in their mouth or the slit between their legs every time!"

"Caesar!" the other woman shouted. "Don't teach him to think like that! King is still a child."

Pops slipped back into a calm demeanor as he turned to face her. Silk sat there quietly, sipping his drink while enjoying the spectacle.

"First of all bitch, ain't nobody talking to you so mind your business. Second of all this is my son so don't tell me what I should or shouldn't be teaching him. I'm teaching King to keep his eyes open for bitches like you two funky hoes."

This wasn't the first time that I'd witnessed my Pop's perform like that. He constantly degraded women and I felt bad when he talked down to a female, especially if it was Ma Dukes. I would often get upset and express that my mother wasn't a female dog; and he'd laugh and tell me to quit being so emotional and to toughen up. This only frustrated me more because I assumed that he was calling me soft. Pops explained that the love that we shared for Ma Dukes was different. In my eyes, she couldn't do any wrong. Ma Dukes carried me in the womb and he enforced for me to respect and honor her more than any other woman in the world. But in his eyes, she was a woman and women were manipulating creatures, trying to deceive man every chance they got. I remember him saying that he loved her, but he didn't trust her. He didn't trust anyone. Pops advised me not to trust anyone or anything but GOD. GOD was the only one that would never let me down. He trained me to look deep inside of a person instead of the façade that they displayed on the surface. The lessons that Pops drilled into my mind when I was a child robbed me of my innocence, but I held on to every word that he spoke.

♟ ♟ ♟ ♟

Back at the house, my brother Damon was nursing his hand in a bowl of ice. As of lately, he had been getting into all types of trouble and the police had picked him up for questioning. After grilling Damon at the precinct, they eventually released him for lack of evidence, promising to catch him at a later date. When I entered the house, I detected that something wasn't right from the look on his face. I tossed my bag on the floor and made my way over to where he was seated.

"What's the matter brah?" I plopped down next to him.

"I'm chilling baby boy! What's going on with you?" he replied.

"What happened to your hand?"

"I had to put in some work."

"Were you fighting again?"

Damon removed his hand from the bowl of ice. "Why do you ask so many questions?

"Because I be wanting to know. Mom said knowing is power."

"Knowledge is power smart ass," he grabbed me with his good hand and began tickling me. "Get it right before you start quoting what mom said."

"Okay... Okay... Okay..." I laughed, attempting to escape his grasp.

"Let me explain something to you King" he released me. "You got two types of niggas out here in the streets; the weak and the strong. The weak will never get any respect out here in the concrete jungle because they don't have what it takes to survive amongst the Wolves. Then you got the strong. The strong is built to endure any situation that they may encounter but along the way, they may bump heads with other predators in the jungle. Do you understand?"

I nodded my head and allowed him to continue.

"The lion is the only king of the Jungle." Damon lit a cigarette. "You have to be a lion out here or else the jungle that we call the ghetto will swallow you alive. I'm trying to prepare you for what's going on out here and that's one of the reasons that I rough you up and put you through training. I don't want you to grow up to be a sucka, but I also don't want you to follow in my footsteps. You have to be smarter than me because the pen is mightier than the sword, you feel me?"

"I feel you!"

"I love you little brah," he gave me some dap. "Now go ahead and do your homework so Ma Dukes don't come in here trippin when she come home."

CHAPTER 3

THE POINT WHEN EVERYTHING CHANGED

Around nine o'clock that night, Pops dropped me off at my aunt Nita's house for the weekend and instructed me to be on my best behavior. Once we arrived, I gathered my belongings, hopped out of the truck and darted up the stairs in a hurry. No one answered when I rang the doorbell, so I began pounding on the door.

"Who is that, knocking like they the police?" Nino yelled from behind the door.

"It's me, King!" I shouted back.

After fumbling with the locks momentarily, Nino opened up and acknowledged Pops with a hand gesture as he drove off.

"What up Nino?" I walked past him and into the house.

"I'm just coolin lil cousin."

"I see you dressed all fly; where you going?"

"I'm about to go to Arena and get up on some of these hoes" he did a little dance.

Nino was dressed in a green Adidas sweat suit with the matching fury Kangol and a pair of matching Stan Smiths. Around his neck hung a solid gold rope with a medallion the size of my fist. Arena was a popular skating rink where the city's teenagers went to party on a Friday night.

"Can I go?" I asked innocently.

"Nah lil cuz, you got a couple more years before you can run with the big dogs," he told me. "But we can chill out tomorrow when I wake up."

"Alright, that's cool," I claimed. "Where's Aunty Nita?"

"She's back there in her room, watching T.V. go ahead and knock on the door."

Before I could knock, the door swung open and Aunt Nita appeared, wearing a Supima cotton nightgown.

"Oh shit boy, you scared me!" She jumped back, holding her chest. "Don't be sneaking up on me like that. What you trying to do give me a heart attack?"

"I'm sorry aunty; I didn't mean to scare you."

"Get over here and give me a kiss with your chocolate self," Aunt Nita squeezed me. "What is your mother feeding you?"

"Everything!"

She stepped back to get a good look at me. "I see. Go and put your things away and tell Nessa to bring me my damn phone. She's been on it all day."

"Okay!"

As I tiptoed up the hallway towards Vanessa's room, I could hear her on the phone, gossiping with a friend. Without knocking, I burst up in the room and stumbled over a basket of folded towels.

"Damn girl, you need to clean this shit up!" I kicked the basket over.

"You need to knock before you come up in somebody's room," Vanessa hissed, removing the phone from her ear. "And you better watch your mouth too; with your disrespectful self. And put those towels back in the basket."

"And if I don't?"

"You wait to I get off the phone, I'm going to jack you up.'

"Oh yeah, Aunty said to bring her the damn phone now, you been on it all day.'

"King, you better watch your mouth, I'm not playing with you."

"I'm just telling you what she said" I defended.

"Girl let me call you back. My little cousin hasn't been over here five minutes and he is already getting on my nerves," Vanessa's spoke into the receiver.

When she ended the call, her focus was on me.

"You a trip, do you know that? Now take my mother the phone before I strangle you."

Over the next couple days, I hadn't spoken to my parents and that was unusual. Ma Dukes always called to check up on me whenever I stayed away from home and as the days past, everyone began acting strange. Aunt Nita was constantly crying; and when I asked her what was wrong, she would instruct me to go somewhere and play. Then I was struck with a devastating reality once Damon showed up at Aunt Nita's and told me that Ma Duke was in the hospital. She had been shot!

CHAPTER 4

LET'S GET IT OVER WITH
(Present)

"Jones, pack it up, you're shipping," the deputy flashed a bright light in my face.

He handed me a plastic bag, instructing me to place all of my personal belongings inside. Quickly snatching it from his hand, I dropped it to the floor and sat up in my bunk. As I attempted to gather my thoughts, I began setting my toiletries and legal mail onto a steel desk attached to the wall. Ready to get this ride over with, I flicked on the light then shook my cellmate awake. He immediately popped his head from underneath the blanket.

"What the matter Ock," he squinted, trying to adjust his eyes to the light.

"I'm about to bounce Ahki," I replied.

"Where you going?" he rubbed his eyes.

"They about to ship me to prison."

Now fully awake, Dawud was taking in everything that I was saying.

"Here," I handed him a piece of paper with my private information. "I need you to call wifey and tell her that I've been transferred to prison, and I need her to send me a money order ASAP."

Dawud was a 19 year old kid from the Pine Harbors. Raised in a family of Muslims, he learned to speak Arabic fluently by the age of thirteen but strayed away from the Deen once his parents separated.

He was facing 30 years for a murder that was committed outside a night club downtown. Many nights he explained how the situation had occurred. Once he became the man of the house, Dawud began hustling to keep food on the table. He started out on the corner slinging packs of crack to the fiends then extended his hustle to pimping when he met two strippers that he named Peaches and Cream.

Cream was a sexy Spanish mami from Brooklyn. Her five feet six inches, 155 pound body was well defined, and her angelic features were picture perfect. She had gotten turned out when she was fifteen by selling her body to the neighborhood dope boys for sneakers and clothes. By the time she was 18, Cream was stripping and turning tricks at most of the popular spots in the city. Peaches on the other hand was a thick thoroughbred that was strait out of the hood with an ass that would give Nicki Minaj a run for her money. She had a silver tongue and exercised it by playing men as well as women out of their money with a little conversation. They were a mack's dream and a sucka's nightmare. Together, Dawud would have them, hustling out of the strip clubs. They would play up under hustlers, corporate businessmen and professional athletes alike, providing them with sexual favors at five hundred dollars a pop. On other occasions, they would blackmail their victims, depending on the circumstances.

One morning, Dawud came to pick the girls up from the club and witnessed a man handling Cream aggressively in the shadows of the parking lot. Without thinking, he jumped out of his Cadillac Escalade with a desert eagle in hand and began squeezing the trigger. He emptied four rounds into the perpetrator, accidently hitting Cream in the course of action. In a state of fear, Dawud put her in the vehicle and rushed Cream to Erie County Medical Center. When he got to the hospital, he was apprehended by detectives and placed under arrest and charged with aggravated assault on Stanly Berks and the murder of Carla Diaz A.K.A. Cream. Carla had died from a shot to the abdomen, but Stanly had survived and told authorities what happened, giving them the description of the SUV, labeling Dawud the shooter.

For the last six months Dawud and I had been cellmates. We stayed up many nights, discussing our cases and exchanging war stories, but most of the time, we we're studying Islam. I learned a lot from the young brother and I was truly going to miss him.

"Let's go Jones; I don't have all night to be screwing around with you!" The officer shouted.

"Alright, give me another minute," I shot back as I gathered the last of my things.

"Hold your head Ahki," Dawud embraced me.

"You do the same my brother," I told him. "Allah won't place a burden on us that we can't handle."

"That's true; but sometimes, we place a burden on ourselves that makes it difficult to bare," he shot back.

"Until we meet again take care of yourself and stay grounded. As salaam alakium!"

"Walakium as salaam wa rahmatullah!" he responded.

CHAPTER 5

EXPOSED TO THE STREETS

The summer of 89 was off the hook. Every Bronco, Blazer and Cadillac had a hustler behind the steering wheel, rocking Gucci links and Cazel shades with Eric B and Rakim blasting through the speakers. Every corner from uptown to downtown, eastside to the westside, there were a gang of juveniles representing their neighborhood. Hood rats walked the avenues all day in the scorching heat just to get a glimpse of a player, driving a fresh whip. I was a 12 year old kid who fantasized about being a part of the underworld. Attracted to the jewelry, cars and the pretty girls that came along with it, I began hanging at the park at School #68. Everything went down at Six Eight. Gamblers shot dice, hustlers sold drugs and some of the best ball players in the city came to display their skills on the court. Then there was those that came to the park just to smoke weed, drink forty's, and tell lies. I quietly sat back, paying attention to every move being made and every word being spoke, soaking up as much game that my young mind could absorb. This was around the same time that I met a kid by the name of TK who lived in my neighborhood. We were close to the same age, but TK was more advanced than me. He was involved in everything from stealing cars to burglaries. I'd heard about him and his crew of young bandits because they were known for jumping other kids for their Air Jordan's and starter jackets. One hot summer day, I had gotten into a confrontation with someone during a basketball game. A particular kid kept fouling me on purpose every time that I drove to the basket. After several warnings, I punched him in the jaw and we began fighting in the middle of the court. In the midst of the scuffle, TK came out of nowhere and knocked the kid to the ground. We both started stomping him as he curled into a fetal position, pleading for us to stop. The older guys at the park laughed and encouraged us from the sideline. Once the boy was laid out unconscious, TK removed the sneakers from his feet and made moves through a hole in the fence. I followed suit and trailed him through a yard. We hit a short cut that led to an alleyway which directed us to an abandoned building. The vacant tenement was dark and humid. The only light in the building was the sun beaming through the cracks and crud on the window. A worn out chair sat in the far right corner alongside a piss stained mattress. With every step that I took, there was cigar tobacco, broken glass, and crack bags beneath our feet on the floor.

Short of breath, I took a seat on the milk crate against the wall. TK took a seat in the chair, examining his new sneakers.

"Damn King, I see that you're nice with your hands," he placed the Jordan's on his feet.

"How do you know my name?" I curiously asked.

"I know everyone that comes through 'Six Eight'."

"But how did you find out who I was?"

"You're Damon's little brother, right?" TK laced his shoestrings.

"Yeah, you know Dame?"

"Yeah, I know Dame. Him and my cousin Bo run with the same crew."

"Word up!" a moment of nostalgia hit me. "I remember Bo saying that he had a cousin name TK."

"That's me!" he smiled. "One day when you were playing ball at the park, Bo told me that you were family and that's the reason why I held you down."

"Good looking out but I had it under control."

"No doubt but our people is like family and I'm always going to look out for family."

From that day forward, TK and I were inseparable. We did everything together. You couldn't mention TK without mentioning King and vice versa. He taught me how to steal a car by breaking down the steering column with a screw driver in less than a minute. In return, I showed him how to crack open the video arcade at the corner stores and remove all the quarters without alarming the Arabs. We always had some type of scheme up our sleeve that kept a few dollars in our pocket. I remember a situation when we went to visit a female that had a

crush on him. When we got to the house, I pretended like I had
to use the bathroom while TK kept her occupied. I crept into
her parents' bedroom and found some jewelry and a 38 snub
nose. After positioning everything back the way I found it, I
joined them in the living room as if it was normal. We always
did things like that!

Junior and I were still thick as thieves, so I introduced
him, Shakim and Shawn to TK and his friends and we formed a
crew called the Young Wolves. Byrd was a natural hustler. He
sold any and everything that he got his hands on. If he had it, he
sold it and when it came to shooting dice, he was the slickest out
the crew. He would lay the dice down and win every time if he
didn't shake them up and hit the wall. Trouble was exactly that.
TROUBLE! Due to his smart ass mouth, we stayed into
something unnecessary. He'll start fights purposely, knowing
that we had his back. Whenever he wasn't stirring up drama
amongst our peers, he was talking shit to the police, causing
them to chase us. Polo was the pretty boy out of the clique who
always kept a crew of young broads around. He was a smooth
young player that always wore Ralph Lauren, earning him the
name Polo. These were my friends, my comrades, my family and
we all had love for one another. The Wolves were like brothers
and there was nothing that I wouldn't do for them. I had their
backs and they had mines. People were terrified to walk up our
block because it was a strong possibility that they would get beat
down. After a while, we began focusing our energy on hustling
and getting money. One day we were all shooting C-lo at Six
Eight when TK approached us smiling.

"What's poppin?" he asked.

Bent down on one knee, I threw the dice against the
wall. "Tryna get this paper."

As I picked up the dice and rolled again, I noticed that
TK had on the new Bo Jackson's.

"I'm tryna be like you. Get em girls!" I snapped my
fingers as the dice bounced off the wall.

"Watch his face when he ace," Byrd hollered.

I rolled a four and stood up, feeling confident in my
point. TK slid up beside me as Trouble grabbed the dice and
shook them up.

"I got something up!" TK whispered in my ear.

"What's up?" I questioned. "Pull me in!"

"You already know."

I collected five singles from Trouble after he rolled a two. Shakim picked up the dice only to fall victim to my point on the first shot.

"Bet another five that beat the four," Byrd snatched the dice. "Pushers break even."

"That's a bet," I tossed an Abraham Lincoln next to his foot. "Money on the wood makes the bet go good. And shake those muthafuckas because I'm not going for any of that slick shit."

After a couple attempts, Byrd spun the dice and rolled 4,5,6, crushing my point.

"My bank!" he scooped up the dice along with the money."

"I'm not fucking with yo slick ass," I put my winning in my pocket.

"You can't quit with my money," Shakim stated.

"Chill Sha, I'll be back in a minute. I gotta make a move real quick."

"Nah, that's some sucka shit," Trouble barked as I prepared to leave. "At least give us a chance to win our money back."

We exited the park and walked towards Bailey Avenue as TK explained how we could get money consistently. I listened to every detail as he described the elements of his plan. As we approached the neighborhood pizzeria, I stopped to talk to Shane while TK went inside to use the payphone. Shane was one of the wildest dudes in the hood. He had caught his first body by the age of fourteen and by the time he was seventeen he'd added two more under his belt. A lot of people thought that Shane was crazy, but he was just a misguided kid with a quick temper.

"Aye King, you got a blunt on you?" he asked me. I attempted to hand him a White Owl but he refused by tossing me a bag of sticky green, indicating for me to roll up. Opening the nickel sack of marijuana, I placed it to my nose to get a whiff of the natural herb. Next, I split the cigar down the center and placed the buds inside then twisted it up to perfection.

"Let me get a light," I required.

Shane supplied me with a lighter and I dried the blunt, admiring my rolling skills. After adding fire to the tip, I inhaled deeply, permitting the smoke to fill my lungs.

"This is some killer!" I exhaled. "Where did you get this from?"

"TK sold these to me earlier," Shane displayed two more bags in his hand.

I dumped the ashes to the concrete then took another pull before handing it off to him.

"Yeah, that shit is fire!" I exclaimed, blowing out another ring of smoke.

Suddenly the restaurant door swung open and TK stepped outside, eating a slice of cheese pizza smothered in blue cheese.

"Walk to the crib with me," he passed me a small box with an extra slice in it.

"Alright bra, I'll get with you in a minute," I turned and gave Shane some dap.

"No doubt!" he reciprocated. "Y'all boys be careful out here because five O been stretching boys all day."

♟ ♟ ♟ ♟

TK lived in a two bedroom apartment with his father about five minutes from the park. His father wasn't there when we entered his house, so I sat on the sofa and began flicking through the television.

"How much money do you have on you?" TK questioned.

"I got about ninety dollars," I confirmed. "Why, what's up?"

"Wait right here!" he disappeared into the back.

When he returned, TK was holding a sneaker box under his arm.

"Check this out!" he opened it up.

Inside held a small amount of marijuana bagged up in the same bags that Shane had showed me.

"I can get this for fifty dollars an ounce," he declared.

"How much can we make?" I quizzed.

"We're going to at least double our money."

"And how long do you think it's going to take us to sell this shit."

"It depends on how hard you hustle and how long you're willing to stay down on the block to get it! Everybody smoke weed so it's going to sell itself."

Knock... Knock... Knock...

"Who dat!" TK yelled.

"It's Mike!" The person confirmed from the other side of the door.

"That's the connect" TK told me. "Give me seventy-five dollars."

I counted out the money and handed it to him. TK signaled me to be cool as he answered the door and I was astonished to see a white boy walk into the apartment holding a back pack over his shoulder. He looked more like a college student versus a drug dealer. We shook hands and exchanged greetings as TK introduced us. Mike retrieved a digital scale from out of his bag and set it on the counter. He then pulled out a zip lock bag filled with dark green buds and placed it on the number machine which read eighty grams. Mike glanced at TK for his approval. A satisfied TK removed the plastic bag from the scale and gave Mike a small roll of bills. After Mike was gone, TK and I went into his room and began stuffing the weed into ten by ten plastic bags. Once we finished, there were sixty-six fat nickel bags sitting on the dresser in front of us. Estimated at five dollars a bag, we would make three hundred and thirty dollars, profiting one hundred and sixty-five dollars if we didn't take any shorts.

The next day we hit the block on a mission, determined to move the product as quickly as possible. Everybody copped their weed from us. The students at school, the people in the hood and even a few of my friend's parents brought a nickel bag or two. TK was right when he said that it would sell itself. There was a glare of hunger lingering in our eyes that was rare in the kids our age and as long as we kept good quality, the money kept coming in. Over the next couple of months our clientele grew and so did our money. We worked our way up to a pound a piece and had more money in our pockets then some adults had in their bank account, but we still weren't satisfied. It seemed like the more we got, the more we wanted.

CHAPTER 6

THE FIRST REAL LICK

I pushed the snooze button on the alarm clock sitting on the night stand then rolled back under the covers, attempting to get ten more minutes of sleep. As I struggled to rest my eyes, I heard a light tapping sound outside my bedroom window.

"Who the hell is this knocking on my window this early?" I grumbled to myself as I got out of the bed.

I walked over to peek through the blinds and saw Trouble standing next to TK dressed in a black hoody and army fatigue pants. Opening the door, I told them to wait for me in the basement while I got ready.

"Who did you just let into my house?" Ma Dukes appeared from the kitchen.

"That's Tim and Jermaine," I referred to them by their government names. "They came to pick me up for school."

"Then why are they dressed in all black?"

"I don't know, I guess that's the color that they decided to wear this morning."

"Don't get smart little boy," she stood there with her hand on her hip. "I will still whoop your behind."

"I'm not trying to get smart Ma, but I don't know why they have on all black. Do you want me to ask them?"

"Are you in some type of gang with them King?" Ma Dukes inquired.

I snickered. "Nah Ma, we're not a gang. They're just my boys."

"Mmm hmm, alright boy, I don't want you out in those streets getting into trouble."

"I'm not doing anything wrong," I assured her. "My friends just came to get me so we can walk to school together. That's all!"

"I've been through this with your father and Damon, I'm not about to go through this with you too so if you're doing something that you don't have any business doing, stop!"

It had been five years since Ma Dukes had gotten shot and she was very cautious about the company that I had begun to associate with. The scar on her neck was a physical reminder of how strong she was and the emotional pain that she had endured.

Taking a shower, I quickly got dressed and returned to where my comrades patiently awaited. We made our way around the corner to a stolen La Sabre that TK had parked. Once we were in, he cranked it up with a screwdriver and pulled off. For the duration of the morning, we rode around the neighborhood, looking for something to get into. Suddenly, TK pulled up to an apartment building and killed the engine.

"Why did we stop here?" Trouble asked.

I knew the answer to that question once I noticed that we were at Mike's apartment building. He attended summer classes at The University of Buffalo Monday thru Friday, so I figured that he wasn't home.

"We're about to break into the white boy spot!" I stated.

TK confirmed it with a nod and smiled.

"I don't know what took y'all boys so long," Trouble got excited. "We supposed to been got at this dude."

Me and TK had discussed robbing Mike on a number of occasions but always dismissed the thought because we needed him to continue to supply us. We agreed to wait until we could figure out a way to get him without any suspicion. We continued to do business as usual and gained Mike's trust quickly. He respected the way that we conducted ourselves to be so young. We were consistent on a weekly basis and never short with money. For the longest Mike wouldn't allow us to know where he lived. He always met us at TK's or my aunt Nita's house until one day he called and told us to meet him on Hertel Ave and Shoshone Street. He had gotten some hydroponic from California and wanted us to get first dibs. Afterwards, we monitored the apartment for over a month and discovered that Mike not only lived there but also conducted business with his college buddies from time to time. There was a good amount of traffic coming in and out of his building, so if we were to break in there was a chance that he wouldn't suspect us.

"Trouble, go and wait for someone to come outside then hold the door open for us," TK instructed him. "It'll look too suspicious if all three of us rushed up in there at the same time."

Trouble exited the vehicle, lit a cigarette and began walking towards the apartment building. As he posted up against the wall, smoking his square, a Caucasian lady who looked to be in her early twenties rushed out and hopped in a red sports car without noticing Trouble slip inside. Me and TK leaped from the La Sabre and scurried towards the door as Trouble held it open. Once we reached the third floor, we stopped at apartment 3-C and knocked, listening for any movement inside. Quickly removing the tire iron from beneath my sweatshirt, I wedged it between the door and the frame, applying pressure until it popped open. We all entered into the domain and split up, searching separate rooms. We rambled through everything; flipping over every mattress and emptying out every drawer. In the process, I discovered an AK-47 assault rifle and a 9mm Beretta.

"Bingo!" Trouble shouted from the back room.

He walked out, carrying a garbage bag full of weed. As TK grappled through all of pants pockets in the closet, he came across a few bankrolls wrapped in multi colored rubber bands. After gathering all of the drugs and merchandise, we left the building just as easily as we had entered it.

Back at TK's crib, we counted out the money and separated the weed from our first real lick. Splitting up seventeen pounds and eighty-seven hundred between the three of us was like a crack head winning the lottery. Mike never mentioned anything about his house getting burglarized and he continued supplying us until we were introduced to a new hustle.

CHAPTER 7

TIME TO SWITCH HUSTLES

It was four o'clock in the evening and it seemed as if everyone was out on the block hustling. Although it was mid-November, it was remarkably warm in the city of Buffalo and the Ave was congested with all types of traffic. School buses and motor vehicles were gridlocked bumper to bumper due to the afternoon rush hour. In front of the corner store, Shawn and Trouble were slap boxing while Byrd, Shakim and Polo instigated from the sideline. Across the street, I was sitting up on a mailbox, bragging to Junior and TK about how many points that I had scored against McKinley High School the night before. Our discussion was interrupted by a loud thump escaping the trunk of a grey 5.0 Mustang trimmed in chrome. It circled the block a few times then stopped where we were posted, blaring the system to the max. The limo tints covering the windows made it difficult to see inside, causing us to become suspicious. Without taking my eyes off of the car, I slid my hand inside the pocket of my jacket.

"Who the fuck is this?" I asked TK while gripping the 38 snub nose I had concealed.

"I don't know!" he responded with an ice grill.

With my attention still on the Mustang, I hopped off the mailbox as the passenger window slowly rolled down.

"You're not going to bust!" a voice stated from inside.

"What?"

Before I could pull my weapon out, I found myself staring down the barrel of a sawed off shotgun.

"Tighten up baby boy!" Damon smiled. "I thought that I taught you better than that."

"Keep playing," I told him a bit relieved. "I was about to start dumping on y'all niggas."

"How are you going to dump on somebody with your face spread over the sidewalk?"

"I would've gotten a couple shots off."

"Yeah okay," he said sarcastically.

Damon turned towards TK and Junior and nodded. They returned with peace signs.

"What's good baby boy?" he focused back on me. "What you about to do?"

"I'm just out here tryna get a couple of dollars," I said.

"Get in and take a ride right quick."

I handed Junior the 38 Special and told him to hold it down. As I climbed into the back seat of the Mustang, Gee sped away from the curb, causing the 5.0 to fishtail.

"Let me get five for the dub," Gee handed me a twenty.

Reaching inside of my underpants, I pulled out a sandwich bag filled with marijuana and gave him a quarter ounce. He examined it in the palm of his hand then passed it to my brother. Damon smelled the fragrance of the weed before rolling up a blunt. For the next two hours, we drove through the town, smoking and listening to music as Gee distributed crack to various young hustlers. I observed from the backseat, estimating the amount of money that he had made in the short amount of time that we were together.

"Damn Gee, your pager is bleeding," I stated.

"This ain't shit!" he boasted. "I got a spot out in Lackawanna doing numbers."

"Word?"

"Hell yeah! You need to come out there and fuck with me. I'll show you how to get some real paper."

"Nah, King need to stay in school and keep balling," Damon interjected. "Lil bra is nice as hell with the rock."

"I heard that he could handle the pill a little bit," Gee said.

"A lil bit? I'm the fucking truth!" I bragged. "My game is exclusive."

"I'm going to have to come and check you out and see what you're working with."

"I got a game tomorrow night at the Gloria J"

"What time?"

"Game starts at seven."

"I'm going to come and check you out," he pulled over at the corner store.

Damon hopped out to use the pay phone. Once he was out of earshot, I leaned up and asked Gee how much he wanted for an eight ball.

"One twenty-five," he said.

Quickly removing a wad of bills from out of my pocket, I counted out $250.00. "Let me get two of them."

Gee wrote his pager number onto a napkin and handed it to me along with two chunks of crack wrapped in plastic.

"Call me and I'm going to make sure you get rich out here," he told me.

"Oh, don't worry; I'm going to get at you," I assured him.

♟ ♟ ♟ ♟

Back in the hood the atmosphere was dreary when Gee and Damon dropped me off on the block. When I emerged from the back seat, I spotted Rena walking out of the store, eating a bag of chips.

"C'mere girl!" I screamed to get her attention.

"What do you want?" she responded with an attitude.

"Girl get your ass over her before I smack the shit out of you," I barked.

"Who do you think you're talking to?" she stood there with her hand on her hip. "Don't be trying to show off in front of your peoples."

"Rena, would you please come here."

With her face scrunched up into a scowl, she sashayed over to where I was brushing the ashes off of my clothes.

"What King! I don't have time for your games right now."

"Why do you be treating me like that?"

"Because you play a lot of games."

"What type of games?"

"I'm not about to go there with you right now King; now tell me what you want."

"Where is everybody at?" I questioned.

"The police ran everyone from up here about an hour ago," Rena replied. "I think that they took a couple people to jail."

"Who did they take to jail?"

"I don't know but Trouble and Polo is at my house with some broads from downtown. I'm pretty sure that they can tell you what happened."

About a year prior, Rena had moved into an apartment upstairs from her cousin Polo. Everyone in the hood thought that we were intimate because of our childhood fling; but she was more like a sister to me versus anything else. Rena was cool as hell. Whenever I was on the block hustling, she would hold my bundle and watch out for the cops, knowing her chances of getting searched was slim to none. Although we weren't in a relationship, I could tell that she still had feelings for me and deep down inside, I still had a thing for her.

Polo and Trouble were sitting in the living room with Precious and Keya, drinking gin and juice when we entered the apartment. Precious was a slim freak from the Jefferson Projects. Word through the pipeline was that she had some of the best pussy downtown and the head was off the chain. Keya on the other hand was thick to death. At fourteen, she had the ass of a grown woman with the breast to match. They both had been ran through by all of the crews from down the way, so they decided to come uptown to share the love.

"What y'all got going on in here?" I smiled, trailing Rena into the living room.

Keya rolled her eyes and sucked her teeth once she noticed that it was me.

"You still mad at me boo?" I smirked.

"Fuck you King!" she spat with venom. "You ain't shit!"

One night, the young Wolves were taking picture at the I.P.E. when Precious and her crew hopped in the flicks and began posing. Later that night once the party was over, she approached me and said that her girl Keya wanted to spend the night with me. Ten minutes later, we were cruising down Main St on our way to the Red Roof Inn Motel. Stopping for the traffic light on Utica, a police car swarmed behind me, flashing its lights. Without giving it any thought, I hit the gas and mashed out through the intersection. I led the cops on a high-speed chase throughout the streets as Keya screamed to let her out. Her plea went on deaf ears as I bent a few more corners and jumped out, leaving her to deal with the heat as I ran off into the night. She didn't tell who was driving the car, so the officers took her to the precinct and called her mother. That was over a month ago and I hadn't seen or talked to her since.

"My bad Key," I said apologetically. "I know that I shouldn't've left you for dead but I had a pistol on me and I couldn't afford to get caught up."

"You're a dirty muthafucka!" Keya said. "You don't care about nobody but yourself."

"Damn shorty, why it got to be like that."

"Because I could've been dead or anything and you didn't even call to see was I alright."

"Yeah, that was messed up!" Precious added.

I dug into my pocket and pulled out fifty-dollar bill and gave it to Keya.

"Can you find it in your heart to forgive me?" I asked her.

She cracked a smile. "I'm just glad that you're okay with your crazy ass."

I didn't want to disrupt the sexual episode that I felt was about to take place so I poured myself a drink and carried it into the back towards Rena's room.

"Where do you think you're going?" Polo questioned.

"Back here with Rena."

"Don't be tryna have sex with my cousin King, I know how you rock."

"C'mon Lo don't come at me like that; you know that Rena is like my sister," I defended.

"More like kissing cousins," he broke out laughing. "Ya'll not fooling nobody."

"Polo, why do you always have to think negative?" Rena barked. "Didn't nobody say anything to you when you brought these bitches into my mother's house. You and Trouble can take these hoes downstairs to your apartment."

"Who are you calling a hoe, bitch?" Precious exploded.

I sensed that it was about to get physical, so I restrained Rena as she exchanged verbal threats with Precious and Keya. Forcing her into the room, I thrusted her down onto the bed and kicked the door shut behind me.

"And you fucked that nasty bitch," she broke loose from my grasp.

"Now you buggin!" I told her. "I never fucked that girl."

"I'm not bugging; you're the one that's bugging."

"Go ahead with that bullshit girl," I picked up the phone and dialed TK's pager number.

I placed triple 2's behind the number so he'd know that it was me as Rena playfully punched me in the chest, continuing her inquires.

"Why did you give her that money then; you aint never gave me any money."

"Oh okay, that's what this is about. You're jealous!"

"Don't flatter yourself," she spat. "All I'm saying is that I'm the one that be holding you down on the block, so why are you tricking off on these raggedy project hoes who don't give a damn about you?"

For the next twenty minutes, I listened to Rena rant and rave. She complained about how she thought that I misused her, taking her kindness for weakness. Although neither one of us would admit it, there was still a physical attraction between us. I was amused as she strutted around the room with an attitude, ranting all types of begrudging slurs towards me.

Suddenly there was a knock on the door as TK eased it open and entered the room.

"What up kid?" I greeted him. "I just paged you a little while ago."

"I know," he responded. "I was right up the street, so I just came through to see what was up."

"What happen on the block? I heard the beast came through bagging niggas up."

TK turned towards Rena. "Can I get something to drink?"

"Y'all are a trip," she said. "If you want me to leave TK just ask me to leave, I'm not trying to listen to what you're talking about."

"Well can you leave so I can scream at my man real quick, damn?" I interjected.

"You know what?" she walked towards the door. "Fuck the both of you. Y'all niggas got some nerve, coming up in my house, acting like y'all run shit. I'm about to make all y'all get the hell out in a minute."

TK watched her as she continued up the hallway cussing us out.

"What's up with her?"

"It might be PMS because she's been buggin today," I told him.

"She probably just needs some dick," TK laughed. "Go ahead and give her what she wants."

"I'm not fucking with Rena, she's already crazy as it is."

"I hear you, but on another note, shit popped off at the park today."

"What happened?"

TK took a deep breath and explained how Shane had bust shots at some niggas from across the bridge, during a dice game at the park. It had been tension between our team and the crew over there, extending from a confrontation at the skating rink that supposedly had gotten squashed. From TK's explanation, everything had started out cool until Smoke; a kid from the other side grabbed the dice and ran the bank up to twenty-three hundred. Caught up in the moment, he began talking reckless; calling the Wolves broke and saying that they were soft as kittens (pussy). Shane never said a word. He just stood at distance, reading between the lines of Smoke's slick comments. Without warning, he drew the 44 Magnum from beneath his hooded sweatshirt and smacked the nigga across the face, causing the pistol to discharge. The thunder from the cannon ceased all movements as Shakim and Junior made everyone that wasn't from the neighborhood empty their pockets and vacate the premises. Moments later, police swarmed the park, searching everyone for weapons. They discovered the

44 in the nearby trash can and arrested Shane and Shakim being that they were the closest to the weapon.

"Did Shane clap the nigga?" I questioned.

"Nah, he just split dude shit open with the hammer."

"That's crazy!"

"That shit was bananas!" TK commented.

After he was finished with the story, I reached down into my underpants and pulled out the quarter ounce that I had purchased from Gee.

"Where did you get that from?" he observed the drugs in my palm.

"I copped it from Gee."

"Who?"

"The nigga who was with my brother in the Mustang earlier."

TK reflected back to the stunt that Damon had pulled a few hours ago and nodded in remembrance.

"While I was riding around with him and Damon, I watched Gee make about five thousand, selling that shit."

After emphasizing how much money could be made if we invested into the crack game, TK was convinced that it was time to switch hustles.

CHAPTER 8

JUNGLE

Within the next couple of weeks, we began hustling out of Disco's apartment. Disco was a dope fiend who had been a boss player back in the day. His addiction to drugs and women had conquered him once the crack epidemic spread throughout the ghettos of America. With his glory days behind him, Disco re-lived his moments of a hustler through us. He knew the ins and outs of the game, so he helped us make the transition from weed sellers to crack distributors. It was difficult in the beginning but with Disco's assistance, we built up our clientele and began flipping money quickly. It was enough for everyone, so we recruited Byrd, Shakim and the rest of the Wolves who were serious about getting their paper up. My man, Danny had just come home from serving 18 months in Lincoln Hall, so I knew that he would be down for whatever. Known for wilding out up in the juvenile detention centers throughout New York State, he earned the nickname Jungle and his reputation proceeded itself. If he wasn't extorting someone for their commissary, he was splitting them open with a razor on the rec-yard over some marijuana. We stayed in contact through letters while he was incarcerated so I knew that he would be hungry when he came home. When I introduced Jungle to the Wolves, they immediately accepted him but once they saw how thorough he was, they didn't have any other choice but to respect him. Jungle could care less about hustling; he was obsessed with guns and wouldn't hesitate to use one. Out of all of the Wolves, he was the deadliest. He was a soldier with a heart of gold, but you never knew what to expect when he was around.

The week before New Year's, I was posted on the block, sipping on a cup of hot chocolate when Jungle drove up in a red Jeep Cherokee that he had stolen; bopping his head to Souljah Story by Tupac.

"Take a ride with me," he screamed over the music.

"Nah kid, I'm cool!" I shot back. "I'm tryna get some of this holiday money."

Jungle smiled from ear to ear as he turned the volume a level higher. "C'mon dawg, you can't get all of the money. Let somebody else eat."

Going against my better judgement, I got into the car. As soon as I shut the door, he sped off into traffic without looking. The gangster lyrics of Pac had Jungle hypnotized. He got excited the more he listened and the more he listened the faster he went. Reaching the intersection of Kensington and Suffolk, we stopped for the red light.

"Check that out!" he pointed to two teenagers walking up the street.

One of the boys was wearing a black shearling coat while his partner sported a butter soft leather Timberland jacket with the tree stitched in the back. They both had on matching boots, stomping through the snow.

"I gotta get em!" he eyed his target.

Jungle circled the block, trying his best to be indiscreet. He parked a couple yards up from where the targets were walking.

"Are you strapped?" he asked cocking the 380 that he had concealed.

I flashed the 38 Special that I had become so fond of. We quickly exited the Jeep and moved towards the guys who looked to be about eighteen years of age. Once they were in arms reach, Jungle struck the taller of the two with the pistol, knocking him to the ground. Caught off guard, the one wearing the shearling stood there frozen with fear as I aimed the snub in his face, instructing him to take the coat off. Jungle stood over the one on the ground, pistol whipping him as he removed his jacket. With the mission complete, we started to move towards the Cherokee as the unthinkable happened. Jungle spun around and let off seven shots, pap...pap...pap...pap...pap... pap...pap...emptying his clip into both teenagers. I looked to where the shots where just fired then hopped into the vehicle, tossing the jacket on to the backseat. Quickly gearing the Jeep into reverse, I backed up to where Jungle was going through the pockets of the motionless body, lying on the sidewalk. My heart was racing a mile a minute as he hurried towards the vehicle.

"Why did you shoot them?" I shouted, speeding up the street.

Jungle ignored me as he counted the money covered in blood.

"Why did you shoot them?" I repeated, checking the rearview.

"Slow down before we get pulled over," he replied in a calm voice.

I drove through the back streets until we were close to the block. In a panic to stash the Jeep, I parked behind the beauty salon on Berkshire. With the coats in our possession, we jumped fence after fence until we found ourselves at Disco's spot. Out of breath, I stumbled into the building and began pacing the floor. Byrd and Trouble were playing a video game, studying our behavior. I was shook up, peeking through the blinds as Jungle tried on the Timberland jacket, examining himself in the mirror as if everything was normal.

"The hoes are going to be on my dick at the I.P.E. this week." he admired the leather.

"This nigga is really crazy," I thought to myself. *"He just shot two people and he's thinking about some broads?"*

I stared in disbelief. Byrd kept quiet but he could feel the tension in the air as Jungle wrapped his arm around my neck and led me to the back room to talk in private.

"You got to chill out brah," he closed the door. "What's done is done!"

"What the fuck do you mean chill?" I was heated. "You didn't have to shoot them boys, we already had they shit."

"Lower your voice before somebody hears you."

I exhaled and took a seat. Jungle pulled up a chair and sat beside me.

"My bad brah, I know that I didn't have to blast them niggas but there's nothing that we can do about it now so be easy. I got to know that I can trust you when shit gets real."

"You already know that I am going to hold you down regardless but you can't just dumb out. You have to think!"

Jungle nodded in agreement as he handed me half of the money that he had taken. I stared at the currency saturated in blood then up into his eyes. At that moment, I knew that he was dangerous but I also knew that his love for me was genuine.

"I just wanted to know what it felt like!" he said.

"What?" I was confused.

"To catch body!" he admitted.

CHAPTER 9

WHEN THE CLUB IS OVER THE PARTY BEGINS

The I.P.E. was the place to be every Saturday night. Majority of the teenagers in the city came to the spot to represent their schools and neighborhoods. Even a few of the old heads drove through in their whips, longing for attention. Earlier that day, I had rented a Seville from a crack head so I was definitely feeling myself. As I turned onto Main Street, I could tell that the night was going to be live from the crowd outside. A number of young tenders stood in a line that stretched around the corner, waiting to get inside the party. Young hustlers rode up and down the strip, playing loud music and showing off their rims. It sounded like a miniature earthquake as they cruised past, hanging out the window and hollering at the females. I parked the car then adjusted the Cazells onto my face. Byrd cocked the Berretta and placed it under the passenger seat. Making our way to the club, we bullied our way to the front of the line. I noticed Junior and Shakim talking to security, attempting to con their way inside once we made it to the door. Once Byrd slipped him a twenty, the bouncer allowed us to skip the line and enter the party. The building was energized when we stepped up in the spot. Music from the Notorious B.I.G. occupied the air as we swaggered through the crowd. Freak broads bounced against the dudes that were drenched in sweat from pop locking all night on the dance floor. On the wall stood a bunch of thugs mean mugging, waiting for something to jump off. As we eased to the back, I acknowledged the DJ with a nod. In return, he gave the young Wolves a shout out over the microphone. Everyone from the hustlers to the stick up kids paid homage. The broads admired; but the jealousy coming from the haters was obvious as we passed by. When we reached the concession area, I spotted Jungle, Shane, and Polo, conversing with some guys from the flipside of the Bailey block.

"What's poppin?" I approached.

We all exchanged pounds and hugs with one another.

"I'm tryna get at these hoes," Jungle replied.

I snickered when I noticed that he had on the jacket from the robbery.

"Yeah, I see that it's mad dime pieces in here tonight," I commented.

"Word up!" Polo said. "Even ya little broad up in here."

"Which one?"

The Neka broad!"

"Oh, okay!" I scanned the crowd.

For the next forty-five minutes, people continued piling up in the club. With all of the Wolves present, the atmosphere became disruptive. We stood twenty deep in the center of the dance floor, representing the hood.

"Big bank take little bank," we screamed over the music in unison. "Money over here and ain't shit over there."

With money in our hands, we bounced around, taunting other crews. In the midst of the excitement, I gazed over the party and spotted Neka standing amongst her girls, staring at me with a gigantic smile. She paraded through a bunch of energetic teenagers until she was standing in my presence. Although she was cool, Neka wasn't nothing more than a piece of ass. We attended the same school and would have sex occasionally but in her mind we were a couple.

"I see you and your boys are in here showing out for these groupies," she gave me a hug.

I placed my arms around her as I palmed her ass.

"We don't have to show off; they already know what time it is," I stated arrogantly.

"Mmm hmm, I bet they do," she grabbed me by the balls. "Don't get one of these bitches fucked up!"

"Don't start that shit in here."

Neka was definitely a dime piece. Her hazel brown eyes accentuated her mocha complexion. Her long legs complimented her small waist, but she was a drama queen and I didn't have the time or patience for her nonsense. As we stood there conversing, a fight broke out across the room. The crew from the flipside began brawling with some guys from Fillmore Ave. During the commotion, two people had been left unconscious. Security shut the spot down and rushed everyone toward the exit before anyone else could get hurt. Although the club had ended, the night had just begun. Outside, in front of the I.P.E. Polo was trying to get Precious and her crew to leave with us.

"Are y'all going back to the spot with us or not?" he questioned her.

"Let me see what my girls are going to do!" Precious told him.

"Okay, hurry up!"

"And tell Keya that I'm trying to see what that's hitting like," I added.

"Don't even try it King," she rolled her neck. "We saw you up in there with your boo Neka."

"That's not my boo," I defended.

"That's not what I heard."

"Believe me when I tell you that it's not like that. Me and shorty just got an understanding."

"A understanding with benefits, huh?"

"Don't get it twisted, shorty is mad cool but she is not my girl."

"Well here she comes now and it doesn't look like she understands," Precious teased. "I hope I didn't get you in trouble?"

I turned around and saw Neka and her girls headed in our direction.

"Excuse me; can I talk to you for a minute?" she asked me, eyeing Precious suspiciously.

Precious excused herself by telling me that she would see me at school on Monday. Before walking off, she complimented Neka on the outfit that she was wearing. Neka responded with an artificial smile then turned her attention to me.

"What were you and that bitch over here talking about?" she questioned.

"We weren't talking about nothing."

"It look like y'all were talking about something, the way she was over here all in your face, smiling and shit."

"Hold up Neak; you starting to get besides yourself," I checked her. "Don't worry about who I'm talking to or who's in my face. What you need to worry about is the position that you should be playing."

"So what are you saying?"

"I think that I'm saying it!"

"So I'm just a fuck?"

"It is what it is. Let's not make it into something that it's not."

Suddenly, Jungle pulled up with a carload of females. Polo and Trouble trailed behind him with Precious and her friends, honking the horn at me.

"Go ahead and play with your little friends," Neka expressed angrily.

"I'll call you later."

"Nah, go and have fun with them bitches," she stormed away.

"C'mon Dawg, let's go and get something to eat, I'm hungry as hell," Polo shouted.

We followed one another in a row until we reached Pete Sakes restaurant on Fillmore Avenue. Pete Sakes was the home of the Hungry Man cheeseburger and everybody who was anybody knew that this was the spot to eat after hours. It was like a car show when we turned on to the strip. There were Benzes, Lexus's and BMW's aligned on both sides of the street and the restaurant was jammed packed. We entered the diner and ducked into a corner, sending Tasha to go and place our order. Tasha was one of the females that Jungle had on the team. She put him up on game and volunteered plenty of information about a variety of hustlers around the city. She would offer every detail from the blocks they hustled on to the places they laid their head. Tasha was thorough when it came to doing her homework. She was willing to do whatever it took to get in a hustler's business. Jungle had been on a robbing spree since he'd been home and Tasha was a valuable asset. Suddenly, a gorgeous red bone, wearing a white full length mink stepped inside of Pete Sakes. All eyes were on her as she strutted towards the counter like she was God's gift to the earth. Tasha greeted her with a hug as she approached. They laughed and engaged in small talk until their food was ready. Once Tasha made it over to our table, Jungle didn't waste any time.

"Who is that?" he asked.

"That's my cousin Omni," she replied.

"Omni... Omni... Omni..." Jungle searched his memory.

"She has the beauty salon on Allen Street," Tasha confirmed.

"Okay, she's the one that be with that boy Ricardo from the Westside?"

"Yeah, Rick is her daughter's father."

"Are y'all talking about the nigga Rick that just came home from the Feds?" I interjected.

"Yeah, that's him," she assured me.

Abruptly, a fight broke out outside and everyone rushed to the window to catch a glimpse of the scuffle. To my surprise, Shane was getting jumped by the crew from across the bridge. Smoke and another thug by the name of Gutter were leading the pack of goons, swarming on my comrade. I quickly raced outside and let off a couple shots in the air, causing the crowd to disperse. Jungle gave chase to someone from their squad and began squeezing his clip until it was empty. The body collapsed to the concrete. In an attempt to get to my vehicle, I identified someone in a dark blue ford pull up on Jungle with a pistol extended from the window. Before I could react, a burst of gunfire rang out in his direction. Jungle ducked behind a parked car only to emerge seconds later with another gun in his hand. He and I both began shooting at the sedan with malicious intent. Slugs ripped through the metal doors as the ford screeched down the block.

"Let's get the hell out of here before the police come," Jungle shouted.

We all hurried to our vehicles and smashed out into the night.

CHAPTER 10

ANOTHER DAY ON THE BLOCK

"Let me get something for these eight dollars King," Snake asked as soon as he spotted me the next morning.

"C'mon Snake, it's too early for your bullshit," I replied. "You still owe me a dub from last week."

"I know that you're not about to trip about that short money?" he followed me into the bodega. "As much money as I spend with you?"

"I can't go and see my plug if my money ain't right so why are you always coming up here with this short shit?

"Come on King, I'll give you your money as soon as I hit a couple of stores. I just need an eye opener to get me started!"

"Snake, I'm not playing with you," I pulled out my stash. "You better have my all of my money the next time that I see you."

As we exited the store, I noticed a 5 series BMW drive by out of my peripheral. It came to a stop as I took Snakes eight dollars. TK hopped out, wearing a multicolored Coogie sweater under a chocolate leather jacket and matching boots.

"You're getting sloppy kid," he approached with a grin. "I saw that transaction a mile away."

Since switching hustles, TK devoted his life to the grind and nothing else. He treated the streets as if it was a real job. He kept track of the entire police departments work schedule by memorizing which officers worked what shift. Eventually, he dropped out of school and ventured off into various neighborhoods, expanding his hustle into the world of heroin. The dope game had taken him to another level that the Wolves weren't prepared for.

"You must be bored or something?" I joked as we embraced. "I thought that you forgot about your people on this side of town?"

"I know that you're not talking?" he shot back. "Since you've been living your hoop dreams, I haven't heard from you."

"I've been going hard too! I dropped thirty-seven on South Park last week and had seven assists."

"I see that you did you're thing. I've been keeping up with your stats in the paper."

"And I'm only a junior," I told him. "I still have another year to do my thing."

"What happened last night?" he changed the subject.

Re-enacting the events from the previous night, I explained in detail what had taken place.

"It got ugly last night huh?" TK asked.

"Yeah, the shit got real funky out there!" I confirmed.

Suddenly, the store owner rushed out of the door, holding a cordless telephone in his hand.

"Get from in front of me store or me call police" he shouted with a strong Arabian accent.

"Go head with that bullshit Abdul" TK shouted back. "We spend our money like everybody else."

"No bullshit. Move from here or me call police" he threatened again.

"C'mon brah, let's go to the park," TK walked towards the Beamer. "It's too early to be going to jail."

"That's some bullshit Abdul," I screamed over my shoulder.

Once inside of the car, I admired the leather upholstery as I adjusted the seat.

"Is this you?" I reclined back.

"A little something to play in for a minute," TK responded nonchalantly.

"This joint is hot! How much did you drop for it?"

"A little over forty!"

"Damn!" I mumbled to myself.

I knew that TK was getting money but I didn't have any idea that he was getting it like that. I was working with four and a half ounces and a little over two thousand and five hundred in the stash but compared to TK, I wasn't doing shit. Spending forty grand on a car at sixteen was unheard of. TK didn't know it at the time but he was my motivation. We pulled up at #68 and parked. I fired up a blunt while he compared the differences between hustling crack vs heroin. Crack was a mental high and the majority of the fiends that used it, were still chasing the initial feeling. Whereas heroin was more physical and a junky would literally get sick if they didn't get their fix. They were willing to do whatever they had to do (rob, kill or steal) not to experience that excruciating pain. TK admitted to earning more in a day selling dope than the average drug dealer made hustling crack all week. I inhaled the weed smoke, allowing him to describe the profit margin when Ice appeared from the rear of us.

"Double me up for this money young world," he extended a crumbled up fifty dollar bill.

"Nah, I can't do it," I replied. "I'll give you seven for the fifty."

"Come now baby boy, do this for ya man Ice," he pleaded. "I got the white boy around the corner. He got a check for twenty-eight hundred and gon spend all day, I just have to keep him going."

"Seven for fifty," I repeated adamantly.

"Damn, young world, you're hard on a player," Ice handed over the money.

I placed the packages in his palm and watched his eyes grow wide with excitement as he examined them.

"Oh yeah, I can work with these. I'll be back in a minute."

Ice tossed the packages into his mouth and raced off around the corner.

"I don't trust that nigga!" TK declared.

"Ice is alright," I defended him. "You just have to know how to deal with him."

TK pulled his face into a scowl and looked at me as if I was crazy.

"That nigga ain't alright, he's a crab. He'll play that cool role and as soon as you let your guard down, he'll get you."

"I'm not worried about that," I replied. "I got something for all of that slick shit."

"I'm not telling you to be worried about it. All I'm saying is that you need to keep an eye on his shiesty ass. He hasn't always been a fiend and he's known to bust a move."

"Yeah, I heard that he got little Moe for an ounce a couple of weeks ago."

"See that's what I'm talking about. You better watch him."

"Ice isn't stupid. He knows who to try that with."

"Alright, you keep thinking that it can't happen and you're going to find yourself in a dumpster somewhere," TK warned. "These fiends don't give a damn about you. The only thing that they care about is getting high and they don't care who they have to cross to get it either."

As the sun struggled to peek through the clouds, the fiends scurried through the park in spurts to cop anything from a dime to a gram. The Wolves emerged from their slumber and hit the block in an attempt to catch the last of the early morning flow. It was only 11:00 a.m. and I had already earned close to six hundred dollars, so I was sure to surpass my daily quota of a grand if I stayed down.

"Yo, Doo Wop!" I yelled across the park to a group of young boys that were rapping in a circle.

They walked across the basketball court to where TK and I were sitting on the bench. With his pants falling below his waist, Doo Wop approached us, accompanied by his two home boys, Melo, and Justice. They reminded me of myself and the Wolves a few years back.

"What's the deal King?" Doo Wop asked.

"I need you to go to the store for me."

"Alright, what do you want?"

"Get me an iced tea and a bag of Doritos," I passed him the money.

"And snatch up some dice too," TK handed him a five dollar bill.

"Do you need anything else?"

"Nah, but make sure that you break bread with ya mans," TK added, referring to Melo and Justice.

Doo Wop pocketed the money as they continued up the block, rapping and beat boxing.

MIND OF A KING

"Yo ain't that ya mom's?" TK pointed to the white Lincoln Town car, moving slowly past the park.

"Yooo Ma!" I shouted with my hands in the air.

Gaining her attention, I jumped up from the benches as she backed up towards the fence and parked.

"What are you doing, sitting out here in the cold?" she questioned.

"I'm out here chilling with TK," I responded.

"You're out here chilling huh?" Ma Dukes reacted with a raised brow. "If I didn't know any better, I would think that you were out here up to no good."

"Up to no good? Nah Ma, I'm chilling."

"Boy, I wasn't born yesterday. I know that you're out here doing something that you don't have any business doing. Don't nobody in their right mind sit outside in the cold all day without a reason."

"C'mon Ma, I'm not…"

"Don't lie to me King," she cut me short.

Staring me in the face, Ma Dukes continued. "I don't want you out here selling drugs then expect me to come and bail you out once you're in trouble."

"I'm not out here selling nothing," I defended unable to look her in the eyes.

"Okay! I didn't come around here to lecture you this morning; I just wanted to see if I could catch you before I went to church."

"What's the matter?"

"Your father called this morning," Ma Dukes paused for my response.

"What did he want?" I reacted with an attitude.

"He wants you to come and see him."

"For what? As far as I'm concerned, I don't have a father."

"Don't you ever let that come out of your mouth again," she snapped. "I know that you're angry and you have every right to be, but regardless of the mistakes that Caesar has made, he is still your dad."

I sighed and turned my head uninterested in what Ma Dukes was saying.

"King, I know what your father did wasn't right and I still can't understand why Caesar would want to hurt me but I have learned to forgive him; and you should to. It's not healthy to harbor hatred inside of your heart."

"I don't hate dude, I just don't have anything to say to him." I said.

"Well at least think about it," she suggested. "And we'll talk when I get home from church."

"Okay."

"And make sure that you be careful out here."

"I will," I promised, backing away from the car.

Ma Duke waved at TK as she shifted the car into gear. *"Lord please protect my boy!"* she whispered in prayer.

Fifteen minutes later, Ice pulled up and hopped out of a car sweating profusely.

"I told you that I was coming back young world," he shouted. "Give me something for this deuce."

I glanced over at the vehicle that he had just gotten out of and noticed a Caucasian male, occupying the driver seat.

"First of all quit all that yelling and broadcasting my business out here," I commanded. "And then you can tell your man to meet you around the corner."

Once the car was out of sight, I retrieved an empty juice carton from out of the trash can and walked over to where Ice was waiting impatiently. Digging inside of the container, I handed him an eight ball.

"I told you that I was coming back," he repeated, fidgeting with the currency.

Quickly making the transaction, Ice hurried off around the corner to catch up with the white dude. When Doo Wop, Justice and Melo returned from the store, we all headed around the corner to Disco's spot. Trouble and Shane were on the porch laughing as Byrd argued with his baby mother Michelle.

"Stop playing Byron!" Michelle screamed his real name. "Jawan needs some diapers.

She attempted to go inside of his pockets while tugging at Byrd's arm. He snatched away then backed up to keep his distance.

"Quit running and come here!" she chased behind him. "If you don't have any money then let me check your pockets."

Byrd flipped his pockets inside out and laughed as he held his keys in the palm of his hand. "Look girl, I don't have any money."

"That doesn't mean shit. You probably stuffed it down your pants when you saw me coming."

"Come back in an hour and I'll have something for you."

Michelle stormed off towards the awaiting vehicle with an attitude.

"You better be here when I get back," she sped off.

"I see that I'm not the only one with problems," I walked up on my circle of friends.

"That bitch is crazy!" Byrd stated, "She thinks that I'm supposed to give her some money whenever she asks for it."

"I told you that she was crazy before you even smashed it."

"I wish that I would've listened to you."

"Fuck what y'all taking about!" TK interjected, shaking the dice. "What is it hitting for?"

Byrd reached into his inside coat pocket and revealed a bankroll.

"You ain't said nothing but a word player!"

He led the way into the backyard with TK and Trouble on his heels, leaving me on the porch with Shane and the young boys. Immediately, Shane began filling in the blanks from last night. He explained that one of the dudes from across the bridge had been shot but wasn't in critical condition. Authorities didn't have any suspects, but they knew that it was tension between the two neighborhoods. Shane advised me to stay on point because their crew had some goons on their team who would be gunning for us every chance that they got. In the midst of the conversation, I observed a gold Nissan circle the block for the second time. My heart skipped a beat, realizing that I had left out the house without my pistol. As the Nissan slowly crept up the street, I prayed that Shane had his gun on him. As the car rode past, I exhaled, identifying the driver as the Caucasian that Ice had with him earlier. A couple minutes past before Ice appeared, jogging up the block, peering over his shoulder. He eased up the driveway and handed me another two hundred dollars.

"Give me another eight ball," he said nervously.

"Hold up Ice!" I was a little uneasy. "What's the matter with you?"

"I just bust the move on the white boy," he admitted.

"He just drove through here a minute ago," I informed him.

"Who, the white boy?"

"Yeah, he drove by right before you showed up."

"Come on young world hurry up before he comes back around here looking for me."

Before I could serve Ice with an eight ball, shots rang out from a couple streets over. Thinking the worst, I looked in the direction that they were fired then back at Ice. Moments later, Jungle and Shakim came running through the yard, carrying a nylon bag.

CHAPTER 11

THE BLOCK IS HOT

Police cruisers combed the neighborhood for the majority of the night in search of evidence. They checked every alleyway, backyard, and shortcut hoping to discover anything suspicious that would give them a lead in their case. The crime scene was barricaded. Homicide detectives took notes as they questioned everyone who they thought may have witnessed anything irregular before or after the shooting. Bailey Avenue was a business district aligned with a number of department stores and restaurants. There were also a chain of liquor stores, barbershops and beauty salons that laced the strip as a front for local gangsters. The neighborhood wasn't exactly poverty stricken but it was gradually declining due to the rising crime rate in the area. When I stepped onto the block there was a mob of spectators congregated behind a blockade of yellow tape, surrounding the jewelry store. They were piled up on one another, attempting to catch a glimpse of the heinous act that had occurred. When I approached the barriers, my eyes grew wide as they locked in on the silhouette of the body stretched out in the doorway. The gossip amongst the bystanders informed me that a Jewish man had been robbed and murdered while opening his shop. The Asian lady who worked at the supply building next door had witnessed the shooting and was still hysterical. Detectives tried their best to help her gain her composure so she could explain what she had seen.

Bzz...bzz...bzz... I checked my pager and noticed the 007 code that Jungle always used. I headed back to the spot to inform him about the report that I had obtained. There was a funny feeling in a pit of my stomach as I made my way back to the hood. A feeling that told me that shit was about to hit the fan.

♟ ♟ ♟ ♟

Over the next couple of weeks, the block was on fire. The police harassed everyone from the fiends to the hustlers, probing for information. Anyone with a criminal history was picked up and hauled downtown for questioning. It didn't take long before the streets began whispering. The news spread quickly about who the streets thought the culprits were behind the slaying once Crime Stoppers offered a thousand dollar reward. Without any real evidence, authorities couldn't charge Jungle or Shakim with the shooting but they were wanted for questioning, concerning their whereabouts the day of the murder. It was obvious that someone was snitching. Something that started out as the neighborhood gossip evolved to be the talk of the town. It was only a matter of time before the police put a solid case together. A Caucasian had been shot and left for dead; and that didn't sit well with law enforcement. They were determined to get to the bottom of the situation even if it was the last thing that they did. If it were a black man or someone from Spanish descent stretched out with their brains splattered across the sidewalk, they would've probably labeled it drug related; but since it was one of their own, they were highly upset. Feeling the pressure, Shakim flew out to California with his cousin Rich until he figured out his next move. Jungle on the other hand was willing to let the chips fall where they lay and hold court in the streets. Back on the block, we were in the trenches, scrambling hard. Although it was hot, it was still money to be made. We began calling the block Crack Alley, due to the enormous amount of drug traffic, flowing through on a daily basis. The entire crew was eating. Every day, we cleared at least ten thousand in dimes, not including the ones that sold weight. Crack had taken the city by storm. Everyone that I knew had some type of association to the drug. I witnessed my own family members do a 360 in connection with their addiction. People that had promising careers allowed themselves to fall victim to the poison. Hustlers, who I had once admired, were now strung out, asking me for a hit. Young ladies who thought that they were too good to speak, were now willing to suck and fuck anyone that could provide them with a rock. For our amusement, we would occasionally have the smokers entertain us for a package or two. I remember one incident where two fiends by the name of Snake and Max were arguing over a stereo system that they had stolen. In the midst of their confrontation, I pulled out a twenty sack and told them to box it out for the prize. Before I could finish my sentence, those fools were in the middle of the street throwing blows like Ali and Frazier. After damn near killing one another, I bought the stereo then gave Max the pack for knocking Snake on his ass. On another occasion, Trouble had Lester and Speedy race down the block butt naked in the rain for a dime while we stood on the porch laughing and taking bets on who would win. Then there was the time when Gloria, the mother of a girl that I went to school with agreed to perform oral sex on a dog for some crack. The compassionate side of me wouldn't allow a black woman to disgrace herself to that extent, so I gave her a package for free.

"I wouldn't have given that crack head bitch shit." Trouble stated. "By the end of the night, she'll be around the corner, giving another dog some head."

"That's Stacy's moms!" I informed him.

"Light skinned Stacy that use to be with the twins?"

"Exactly!"

The pit bull began to bark as Trouble chained it to the pole.

"Fuck that bitch!" he said. "For the right price, she'll probably suck a dog's dick too."

"You can't treat everyone like shit," I reasoned. "You never know when you might need those same people that you shitted on."

"I don't need a crack head to do nothing for me!"

"That's not true brah! Those same crack heads that you're disrespecting are the reason that you have those Timberlands on your feet."

Trouble glanced down at his feet and shrugged.

"So, what are you saying?"

"What I'm saying is that the people that you are belittling are your bread and butter; and if you keep on humiliating them, they're liable to flip on you."

I paused, allowing my words to digest before I continued. "If you show them some love, they'll remain loyal to you and keep spending their bread."

"I never thought about it like that," Trouble admitted.

Suddenly, an unmarked police car vamped down on us quickly.

"Freeze, don't move!" A detective screamed with his weapon drawn.

Caught by surprise, I surrendered my hands in the air while Trouble took off running through the yard. The first nark gave chase while his partner held me at gunpoint.

"Get against the car," he demanded.

Detective Kirkpatrick rambled through my pockets and scattered my belonging on the hood of the vehicle.

"What are you doing with all of this money on you?" he questioned.

"My uncle is supposed to take me to the auction and buy me a car today," I quickly answered.

"Stop lying!" Kirkpatrick scolded. "I know that you're out here slinging that shit."

I remained silent with my hands on top of the cruiser. Kirkpatrick removed his cuffs from his belt and placed them on my wrist before sitting me in the back seat of the Lumina. Out of breath, Detective Williams re-appeared disgusted that he had allowed Trouble to escape. At six feet four inches, Detective William's was an Uncle Tom type of cop, towering over the five foot nine inch frame of his Irish partner. He lived for the hunt and always went the extra mile to prove a point.

"What's your friend's name?" William's snatched opened the door.

"I don't know!" I replied in a cool tone.

He snatched me from the back seat and threw me against the car with force.

"Do you think that this is a game?" he breathed heavily. "Now was that Danny or Shakim?"

"What are you talking about?" I stared with a puzzled look.

"Don't play stupid with us. "Kirkpatrick chimed in. Your friends Jungle and Shakim! The assholes who like to shoot people."

"I don't have any idea what you're talking about."

"You know what we're talking about," William's pointed in my face. "Jungle and Shakim robbed the jewelry store and killed the owner and until we find them, we're going to make it hard for all of you little punks."

"Like I said, I don't know what you're talking about," I repeated.

William's struck me with a blow to the face.

"Listen you little bitch. I'm not going to rest until I put all of you bastards behind bars, so tell your friends that they can run but they can't hide."

"Why did you hit me?" I cried out. "I didn't even do anything."

"Shut up before we really kick your ass," Kirkpatrick removed the cuffs. "Now get lost."

"What about my money?"

"What about it?" he stuffed the roll of bills in his pocket.

"That's fucked up! How are you just going to take my money?'

"Shut the fuck up before we take you," William's roared.

"Now get out of here!" Kirkpatrick added. "And you better not be out here when we come back."

CHAPTER 12

THE NEW GIRL

Monday morning, I was asleep during 1st period English class when a dark skinned female, wearing micro braids entered the room. I raised my head from the desk as she approached Ms. Carson with her schedule but was too tired to appreciate her presence. Placing my head back on the desk, I intended to catch a power nap but five minutes into it, I felt someone nudging me awake.

"There won't be any sleeping in my classroom today Mr. Jones," Ms. Carson said. "Unlike you some of us are here to learn, so I suggest that you wake up and pay attention."

The students snickered in unison as I sat up and focused on the clock. There was a half hour left before the class ended. I was tempted to lie back down but decided against it because Ms. Carson and I had been through this a number of times and her patience was wearing thin. Peering three rows over, I locked eyes with the girl that Ms. Carson had addressed as Keisha Mitchell. I examined her from the micros to the 54 11's on her feet and noticed that she was kind of cute. Between watching the clock and Ms. Carson recite Shakespeare; I was beginning to grow impatient. When the bell finally sounded, the entire class gathered their belongings and scurried out of the room. Heading into the atrium, I was engulfed by a multitude of students changing from one room to another. The halls were alive with teenagers, yelling and slamming lockers, releasing an hour worth of stifled energy. My swagger demanded attention as I strutted up the hallway as if I owed them. Once I reached the end of the hall, I positioned myself against the lockers next to Rico, a kid that played on the basketball team with me. We both watched Keisha as she sashayed through the herd of unruly students. She smiled and waved to Rico, displaying a set of deep dimples in both cheeks.

"What up with shorty?" I nudged Rico as she passed by.

"Who, Keisha?"

"Yeah, what's her story?"

"She's cool as hell," Rico confirmed. "She's from around my way. Her and my sister Shae is real cool."

"Does she have a nigga in her life?"

"Nah, I think that she's single; and if I'm not mistaken, she might still be a virgin."

"Good looking out," I thanked him for the information.

Instead of going to my second period Biology class, I decided to head to the gymnasium. A Cuban link swung around my neck as I entered with confidence. The Olympic Jordan's that were on my feet complimented the Pelle Pelle jean suit that I was wearing.

"Ugh, what are you doing in here?" Precious distorted her face.

She was standing near the bleachers with a group of females, watching the guys run up and down the court. I picked up a basketball and began dribbling in their direction.

"You know that I do what I want to do around here," I smacked her on the ass.

"You better quit before your girl Neka come in here and start wilding on you," she smirked.

"Watch ya mouth girl; I already told you that's not my girl."

"Mmm hmm, whatever King!"

Precious seduced me with her eyes as I bounced the ball to the other end of the gym. After the game came to an end, I handed her my chain to hold then picked up four people from the losing team to run with me. For the remainder of the period, I displayed my skills by exploiting the opposition one by one. I knew that I had an audience, so I showed out and went hard with my game. At the end of class, I toweled off, wiping the sweat from my brow. One by one, the fellas gave me my props with salutations and high fives. Removing the chain from around her neck, Precious approached me with a grin on her face.

"Am I leaving with you after school?" she gave me my possessions.

I examined my pager and noticed that I had been contacted twice with '$250' behind the number.

"I have to go to practice after school," I told her.

"That's too bad because I had something special for you," Precious licked her lips.

"We can dip out and come back."

"I'm ready if you're ready."

"Meet me at my whip in five minutes," I passed her the car keys. "I have to make a call right quick."

I hurried to the pay phone to return the page.

"Somebody paged King?... Who is this?... oh, what's up kid?... That's cool; I'll meet you at Burger king in fifteen minutes."

It was routine for me to dip out of school with a female and make it back before anyone could notice. Sometimes I wouldn't even come back, but being that I had basketball practice, I decided against the latter. I rushed out of the back door and advanced quickly towards the Maximum which was parked behind the school. As I cut across the football field, I spotted Mr. Smith, the security guard securing the perimeter. Precious was already inside the car listening to All I Need by Method Man featuring Mary J. Blige. As I entered the vehicle, Mr. Smith attempted to approach me before I could pull off. I eased away from the curb and checked the rearview mirror. He removed a small notepad from his pocket and scribbled down the license plate number.

"Damn!" I cursed. "I let this toy cop peep the move."

"Do you think that he's going to report you to the principal?" Precious questioned.

"I hope not because I'm not tryna hear Coach Pete's mouth."

♟ ♟ ♟ ♟

I turned into the Burger King parking lot and scanned the area, looking for Short, a hustler from the flipside of Bailey Ave. Backing into an empty parking space; I grabbed 'the nine' from out of the glove box and cocked it before placing it on my lap.

"What are you about to do?" Precious questioned suspiciously, eyeing the pistol.

"Chill out!" I smirked. "I got my peoples about to meet me up here."

"It's always some extra shit with you!"

We sat in the lot for another five minutes before Short appeared from out of the restaurant smiling. He noticed that the front seat was occupied so he hopped in the back.

"What's poppin? he slammed the door shut.

"You tell me?" I replied. "You're the one bouncing around here all happy and shit."

"I've been trying to get at this lil broad that work up in there for a minute and she finally took the bait."

"I hope the pussy piss gold the way you came out here skinning and grinning."

Precious cut her eyes at me and sneered.

"What's up though, what do you need?" I attended to the business at hand.

"Let me get a quarter," he passed me a small roll of bills. After counting the money, I handed Short two eight

balls.

"Do this weigh up to seven grams?" he examined the product.

"C'mon dawg, don't even come at me like that. Each one is three and a half."

"I'm just making sure because one of these is for my man and I'm not trying to hear anything about it being short."

"I'm always on point player but this paper a little light." I held the money out in front of him.

"Oh yeah, let me owe you twenty-five dollars and I'll straighten it out next time that I see you."

"Nigga, you got a lot of nerve getting in here, asking me about how much something weighs and your paper not even right!"

"C'mon King, you know that I got you," Short pleaded.

"Alright man, I'll holler at you later."

As Short exited the vehicle, I placed the Ruger underneath the seat before pulling into traffic. As I merged into the left lane to get on the expressway, Precious began tugging at my belt buckle. She unzipped my pants and grabbed my dick, caressing it before placing it into her mouth. Precious bobbed her head up and down, adding a slight twist in the motion. It was difficult to concentrate on the road as she did her thing. The vehicle swerved as I released a load of semen down her throat. Tasting the fluids that exploded into her mouth, Precious sped up the pace until I went limp and every drop was in her stomach.

"You good?" she looked up at me.

"Yeah, I'm good," I chuckled.

Minutes later, we turned on to my street. Quickly, I reduced the volume on the music before pulling up to the house. Although Ma Dukes had already left for work, I didn't want to draw any unwarranted attention from the neighbors due to the 12 inch speakers inside of the trunk. After backing into the driveway, we exited the car. Precious was directly behind me as we entered the house and headed towards the bedroom to finish what we had started in the car. Without any hesitation, she kicked off her shoes and stripped, revealing a firm petite frame. I followed suit and snatched my shirt over my head. Pushing me onto the bed, Precious began kissing all over my chest. She worked her way down to my manhood until it was stiff as a board.

"Hold up!" I reached for my pants.

I handed her the condom from out of my pocket and watched her roll the latex onto my love muscle. Mounting me like a horse jockey, she eased on to me slowly.

"Ooh!" she cooed softly.

Precious bit down on her bottom lip as she gyrated her hips, staring me in the face. Savoring the moment, I returned the glare that was in her eyes.

"Turn around!" I instructed.

She propped her knees onto the edge of the bed and bent over, leaving her ass in the air. I slid into her from behind and gripped her around her waist, stroking her long and slow.

"Damn!" she whined. "Damn King!"

I continued in and out of her repeatedly. She found her rhythm and threw herself back at me with every stroke.

"Do you like that?" I smacked her on the ass. "Do you like that?"

"Mmm hmm... Give it to me daddy... Give it to me!"

I pulled on her hair and drove harder.

"Please don't stop... I'm about to cum," Precious moaned. "Ooh yes... Ooh... Ooh. Oooooh..."

"Arrrggghhh!" I grunted.

We both came at the same time then collapsed onto the bed.

♟ ♟ ♟ ♟

Before going back to school, I detoured through the hood. There were a few old heads posted up on the block, exchanging war stories and drinking beer as if they were still in the eighties. I hit the horn as I passed by and they returned with the deuces then continued conversing.

"Yo King!" someone yelled.

As I looked up into my rearview, I saw Max weaving through traffic in an attempt to flag me down. I pulled over on Stockbridge giving him the opportunity to catch up.

"Let me get 3 for twenty-five," he huffed through the window.

"Get in," I replied.

Max jumped into the back seat and passed me the crumbled up bills inside of his hand. I popped out the vent from the dashboard panel and reached down into the empty space. Once I came up with a sandwich bag filled with crack, I handed him what he'd asked for.

"Good looking out nephew," he tossed the packages into his mouth.

I put the work into the stash and popped the vent back into its place as Max got out of the vehicle. The entire time, Precious sat patiently in her seat, admiring my hustle. I circled the block and made a couple more plays then headed back to school. As I crept passed the building, I surveyed the area for any sign of Mr. Smith. I dropped Precious off on the opposite side of the building and advised her to go in before me. Proceeding with caution, I eased out of the Seville and just as I was about to enter into the school, Mr. Smith appeared from out of nowhere.

"Mr. Jones!" he called out with authority. "Come with me!"

He escorted me to the assistant Principals office and radioed the security, informing them that he had the student that had left the school earlier that morning.

"Wait here for Mr. Washington," Mr. Smith instructed.

The assistant principal, Mr. Washington was an overweight, balding Caucasian known for his leniency. He treated everyone with the same respect no matter the ethnicity or gender. Holding the telephone between his shoulder and ear, he motioned for me to have a seat while he finished his conversation.

"What seems to be the problem?" he questioned as he placed the phone in its cradle.

"I don't have a problem sir," I responded.

"Apparently, you do because you seem to think that the rules don't apply to you. Do you think that you can just come and go as you please?"

"No sir!"

"Good, because I don't care how good you are on the basketball court, if you're not here to get an education then there's no need for you to be here. Do I make myself clear?"

I slouched down into the chair and cut my eyes in Mr. Washington's direction. He held my stare for a moment and continued.

"This school is responsible for you as long as you walk through those doors and I'm not about to allow you to keep me from doing my job."

"How am I keeping you from doing your job?" I gave him a puzzled look.

"By leaving this building without getting authorization" he replied.

"The only reason that I left the school this morning was because I had my brother's car keys and he had to be to work by ten o'clock."

Mr. Washington leaned back into his chair and shook his head in disagreement "Come on now Mr. Jones, this isn't the first time that you've snuck out of this building and came back. I've received plenty of complaints concerning students missing class and I don't think that it's a coincidence that your name continues to pop up at the top of the list."

"I had to take my brother his keys," I defended.

"Even if that was the case, there is a procedure that needs to be followed."

"Okay, it won't happen again."

"It better not happen again because if it does, I'm going to suspend you and you won't be eligible to play ball," he assured me. "Now get to class before I decide not to let you play in the game this Friday."

♟ ♟ ♟ ♟

Rico and Daquan Price were at the lunch table laughing when I stepped into the cafeteria. As I made my way over to where they were seated, I spotted Neka eyeing me with an evil expression. She rolled her eyes when I acknowledged her with a nod.

"What's the matter with your girl?" Rico asked as I took a seat.

"I don't know what that girl problem is," I replied. "What are y'all over here laughing about?"

Daquan began telling a story about a fiend that lived in his building who claimed to see aliens whenever he got high. In the middle of explaining how the police found buddy on top of the roof, smoking the pipe with nothing but a pair of cleats and a football helmet on, Daquan paused. The expression on his brow caused me to turn around. Neka was walking our way and by the look on her face, I knew that it was about to be some drama.

"So you're sleeping with Precious now?" she questioned with an attitude.

'What are you talking about?" I responded nonchalantly.

"You know what the hell I'm talking about!" she raised her voice. "Don't play stupid with me. My peoples seen her getting into your car this morning and I know that you took her somewhere and had sex with her by the way that she was smiling at me in the hallway."

"Get the hell out of my face with all of that noise. And why is someone reporting back to you about who they seen in my car?"

"Because they wanted to, that's why. Now keep it real and tell me the truth. Are you and the bitch fucking or not?"

Rico and Daquan sat there quietly as Neka and I ranted back and forth. Before I could spit out another sentence, Precious strolled into the cafeteria with a grin on her face as if she had the answer to the million dollar question.

"Bitch, what are you smiling at?" Neka approached her.

Precious looked over at me. "King you better get your hoe before she gets what she's looking for."

That's the last thing that she said before Neka caught her with a solid right to the mouth, knocking her off balance. Once Precious gained her composure, she rushed Neka and began swinging uncontrollably. Neka grabbed a fist full of hair and pulled Precious to the floor on top of her. I snatched them apart, restraining Neka as Rico held Precious at bay. In the midst of the confusion, teachers stormed the lunchroom and demanded everyone to quiet down. Once everything had settled, the girls were reprimanded and escorted to the office.

CHAPTER 13

IF IT'S NOT ONE THING IT'S ANOTHER

For the first 30 minutes of practice, Coach Pete had the team warm up with cardiovascular exercises and calisthenics. We ran a series of suicide drills and wind spirits, preparing for Friday night's game. We had gone undefeated during the regular season and were the favorite to win the state championship.

"Push it out... Push it out..." Coach Pete yelled, looking down at the stop watch in his palm. "Don't get lazy on me now... Down the stretch is where it counts... Come on boys, three more minutes... Plrr..."

He blew the whistle and allowed us to take a two minute break.

"Coach is trying to kill us," I breathed heavily.

Daquan squirted some water into his mouth.

"I know but it's going to pay off when we play against Bennett on Friday night, he bumped fist with Rico.

"This is going to be the last game that we all ball together as a team, so you know that we got to go out with a bang," Rico stated.

"It's only right that we go out in style," Daquan passed me the water bottle. "We've put too much work in to let the championship slip away from us."

"I feel you kid!" I exclaimed. "As long as we stop that boy Tariq Childs, we'll be straight. If we let him heat up, he can become a problem."

Daquan and Rico were both seniors who had been playing for Kensington High school since their freshman year. Rico stood at an even six feet and was built like a tank. He was actually the star running back for the football team, but his athletic agility allowed him to play point guard gracefully. Daquan on the other hand was born to play the game of basketball. Determined to take his skills to the next level, he hit the gym religiously and perfected his already pure jump shot. Over the off season he had added an additional ten pounds of muscle to his six foot three physical frame due to the tremendous hours of training. Daquan thought, slept and breathed basketball. He was set on using his athletic capabilities as a ticket to get his family out of the Langfield Projects. Unlike Rico and me, Daquan was academically inclined. His grades complemented his abilities on the court, giving him the opportunity to attend the college of his choice on a full scholarship.

"Plrr…" Coach Pete blew the whistle. "Come on fellas get back to work."

I grabbed the ball and inbounded it to Rico. He dribbled down the court, displaying his dexterous ball handle as he wiggled his way to the rim for the easy layup. On the next possession, Daquan came down and hit a jump shot from outside the perimeter with two defenders facing him. At full speed, a sophomore named Jamal came right back up the court and shook me off balance with a crossover then ditched it off to a kid named Tone. Tone laid it off of the glass for two points. Set on redeeming myself, I dribbled down the court with Jamal in front of me, playing tight defense. I was a step quicker than the sophomore, so I switched the ball from my right to the left hand and blew past him. I noticed Daquan out of the corner of my eye and bounced the ball off of the backboard as he elevated towards the rim. He snatched the ball in midair and slammed it through the hoop. Four possessions later, I stole the ball from Tone and raced up the floor. Stopping at the top of the key, I pulled up for the three point shot and missed. Coach Pete became vexed, being that it wasn't anyone under the basket.

"King what the hell are you doing?" he screamed at the top of his lungs. "Get aggressive and follow your shot to the rack. I've told you guys about all of that fancy stuff. Let's stick to the basics. The fundamentals are going to win us the ball game."

Over the next hour, we practiced the rudiments of basketball. Coach Pete continuously drilled the principles of the game into our mind until he was convinced that we were done screwing around and ready to take the Championship seriously. As we went through our playbook, we concentrated on running a high tempo offense. The strategy was simple. Coach wanted us to run the floor until the other team was tired. Once they were fatigued, we would play a zone defense to protect the inside, forcing the opponent to shoot from the outside.

"Plrr…. Bring it in and take a knee," Coach Pete instructed.

As everyone crowded around and knelt down, three Gatorade bottles circulated throughout the team. I took a long swig as Coach Pete began his speech.

"As you all know, our brother Daquan Price has had many offers from various college institutions across the country, providing him the opportunity that most players only dream about."

We all cheered and applauded in unison as Daquan remained calm, wiping the sweat from his brow. When the noise simmered down, Coach Pete continued.

"This moment isn't only special for Daquan but it should be a special moment for each and every one of you. You all have made a contribution in helping this young man shine; and when one of us shines, we all shine. These last four years, I've watched him bust his ass on as well as off the court and his work ethic has paid off. His presence is appreciated and it will definitely be missed but right now, we have one more mission to accomplish and that's to win the State Championship Friday night."

The team exploded with excitement as we high fived, pumping ourselves up.

"Alright… Alright… Alright, save some of that energy for the game," Coach Pete advised. "Let's meet back here tomorrow at the same time. Now go home and get some rest."

Making my way over to the bench, I sat down and retrieved a white T-shirt from a black duffle bag. I toweled off and changed clothes, swapping out my Jordan's for a pair of Timberlands. As I placed the soiled garments into the bag, someone called my name. I looked up and saw Coach Pete standing in the doorway.

"I need to speak with you before you leave," he said seriously.

I followed him into the office and sat down in a chair across from his desk. The wall was decorated with a number of plaques, degrees and other achievements that Coach had acquired over the years. He studied me suspiciously as I prepared myself for the lecture that I knew he was getting ready to deliver.

"Over the last twenty years, I've come across so many gifted young men that have sat in the same seat that you're in right now that I have lost count" he began. "You're a raw talent kid. You have the intelligence and the athletic ability to take it to the next level but your about to blow it."

"What do you mean, I'm about to blow it?" I asked puzzled.

Coach Pete wasn't green to the streets. He had grown up on the city's eastside, during a period when violence was rampant in the urban community. In the 70s, the Mad Dogs, Manhattan Lovers and the Pythons was some of the most feared gangs throughout the City of Buffalo and Coach Pete managed to avoid getting caught up in those circles. He had lost two of his older brothers to the evils of that era; one to the penitentiary and the other to the graveyard. Adamant not to follow in their footsteps, Coach Pete used sports as an outlet to escape the ghetto and into a college classroom. He earned a bachelor's degree in physical therapy and a Masters in Biology. His passion for sports and the love that he shared for the African American youth was sincere and he would bend over backwards in order to help a kid succeed.

"The most gifted kids are either in prison, cemetery or strung out on drugs, hanging out at the liquor store with a bottle in their hand, talking about what they used to do," he said. "Then there are kids like you! The one who thinks that he's slick, got all of the game and all of the answers but doesn't know a damn thing about the real world; headed in the same direction as the other three."

"Where is all of this coming from coach?" I broke my silence. "All I did was skipped a few classes. You're acting like I killed someone."

"This isn't about you leaving the school building or about that fight in the lunchroom this afternoon," he emphasized. "This is about you trying to con a conman. Believe me son, I've been where you're at, so I am familiar with the places that you're headed, and it hurts me to see you travel down that road."

"Coach, I still don't understand where all this is coming from?"

Coach Pete leaned back into his chair and slightly rubbed his chin. "What do you know about that robbery that happened at the jewelry store on Bailey a few weeks ago? he suddenly asked.

"Huh?" I responded nervously, shifting in my seat.

"I know that you hang out with a group of guys from that area and when I saw the incident on the news, you popped up in my head for some reason."

He continued to study my body language, choosing his words precisely. "I'm worried about you King because over the last year, I've witnessed a change in your behavior and I don't want to see you get caught up."

"I'm alright Coach," I said. "You don't have to worry about me. I don't know anything about what happened at that jewelry store except what I've seen on the news."

Unexpectedly, Coach Pete handed me an envelope and smiled at me for the first time since we had entered the office. I stared at the piece of mail and noticed that it was from the University of Syracuse. Eagerly ripping it open, I read that their program was interested in me playing for the Orangemen upon graduating. I looked up from the letter and into the face of Coach Pete. He was still smiling.

"The clock is ticking kid and the ball is in your hand; don't blow it!"

♟ ♟ ♟ ♟

The 36 Chambers by The Wu Tang Clan pumped softly through the speakers as I drove up East Delevan, thinking about the direction that my life was heading. Analyzing the situation, I entertained the thought of leaving the streets alone and focusing on my studies. If I planned to attend Syracuse and play ball on a collegiate level, I would have to tighten up academically because my grades were slipping. To be eligible for any kind of scholarship, I would have to score at least a 750 on the S.A.T. Coach Pete and Ma Dukes were two out of the few people who truly believed that I could do something extraordinary with my life. Although I didn't want to disappoint them, my pride wouldn't allow me to see five years down the line. I didn't want to be one of those athletes that went away to school only to return home broke with a degree; and I definitely wasn't about to work at some factory for minimum wage. I refused to struggle and the people that I knew who were so called fortunate enough to receive a college education were struggling, living check to check. Ma Duke had a number of years of higher learning to compliment her resume and she still found it difficult to get ahead. Ever since Pops had been incarcerated, she had been caught up in the rat race, fighting for a piece of cheese. When I looked outside of my window, I didn't see any lawyers and doctors in my neighborhood, I saw hustlers scrambling to get a dollar. The life of the Huxtables wasn't reality to me. The only people that seemed to be successful where I lived were the individuals that went hard in the streets and were for real about their hustle. What were the odds of a kid from the ghetto, making it to the NBA, earning millions? I figured that I had a better chance of getting rich, selling crack.

"Cash rules everything around me… CREAM, get the money dollar… dollar bill y'all," I rapped along with the song, coming from the stereo.

As I turned onto Bailey Ave., I noticed a car trailing behind me. It flashed its high beams repeatedly, signaling for me to pull to the side. Thinking that it was one of my comrades, attempting to get my attention, I permitted them to pull alongside of me. To my surprise, the occupant in the passenger seat extended a semiautomatic weapon out of the window and opened fire.

Rata… tat… tat … tat… tat… tat… tat… tat..

I ducked down and accelerated on the gas as pieces of shattered glass struck me in the face. I felt around on the floor, searching for my firearm unsure if I was shot.

Tat… tat… tat… tat… tat… tat… tat… tat… The rounds rang out as they gave chase. Tat…tat…tat…tat…

In fear of my life, I ran through every stop sign, desperately trying to escape. I swerved and sideswiped a parked car almost losing control of the steering wheel.

Tat...tat...tat...tat... They let off of a couple more shots before turning off, allowing me to slip away unharmed.

Nervous as hell, I drove to Snakes house and stashed the vehicle in the garage and then walked over to Disco's spot. Jungle had been M.I.A. for about two weeks so I paged TK. As I waited for him to return my call, I began putting pieces of the puzzle together. I paced the floor, smoking a blunt to calm my nerves. Thankful to be alive, I took a long pull, contemplating my next move.

"King, TK is on the phone," Disco handed me the cordless.

"Hello!" I spoke sharply into the receiver. "Come to the spot and bring some understanding with you!" I added, referring to the pistol.

I hung up and played the situation back inside of my head, labeling the crew from across the bridge the culprits behind the shooting. Disco observed my behavior from the kitchen.

"Is everything cool?" he asked in a sincere tone.

"I'm cool!" I returned in a distant manner.

"I've known you long enough to know when something is wrong so if you need me, I'm here for you nephew."

"Good looking out Unk but I'm cool. I got everything under control."

Ten minutes later there was a knock at the door. I jumped up and peeked through the blinds only to see Gloria standing in the rain, looking pitiful.

"Yo Unk open the door for Glo," I instructed Disco.

"Let me get a twenty until I get my check," Gloria walked in whining.

"There's nothing shaking right now aunty, you're going to have to come back later.

"Come on sweetie, you know that I'm good for it."

"I don't have shit right now Gloria, damn!" I snapped
Honk... honk.. honk...

The sound of the horn grabbed my attention, causing me to leap from the couch and peek through the blinds again. TK was incognito inside of a black Ford Taurus. I stepped into the rain and moved quickly towards the vehicle as he popped the locks. Seeing the silhouette of a passenger behind the tinted windows, I hopped into the back seat.

"Yo, they tried to assassinate me today," I stated vexed.

"Who tried to assassinate you?" TK asked perplexed.

"The niggas from across the bridge!"

"Calm down and tell me what happened."

I played the incident back in my head and explained how a burgundy Buick pulled beside me and began shooting. TK listened closely as he drove up the block. Royal sat next to him silently, nursing a pint of Hennessy.

"What are you trying to do?" Royal handed me the bottle.

"What's understood doesn't need to be talked about," I took a swig. "You already know what I'm trying to do."

We drove the town, keeping our eyes open for the burgundy Buick or anyone that looked like they may be affiliated with the crew from across the bridge. The kid Gutter had the most heart out of their clique, so I was pretty sure that he was the one behind the shooting. Due to the rain, the city was desolate. The only ones roaming the streets were the drug addicts who were ready to blast off.

"Where these bitch ass niggas at?" Royal inquired. "I'm ready to put this work in."

Royal was a thoroughbred who was a few years older than us. He was well established in the town for his knuckle game however his gun was known to go off as well. He was originally from uptown but he had family all throughout the city. For the last couple of months, he'd been getting money in Cold Springs with TK, distributing heroin.

We rode around until the early hours of the morning. Finally, TK pulled in front of my crib and parked, leaving the engine running.

"It doesn't look like we are going to find these niggas tonight brah!" he said. "Go ahead and get your mind right and I'll holla at you tomorrow."

"Yeah, go ahead and fall back, we'll catch them in traffic," Royal reassured me.

"No doubt!" I got out of the car. "I'll politic with y'all boys on the A.M."

♟ ♟ ♟ ♟

The following morning, I went to show the neighborhood mechanic, one eye Willie the damage that was done to the car. He roughly estimated the impairments and assured me that he would be able to replace the windows and repair the bullet holes, but a body shop would have to do the paint job. As he examined the holes in the frame, Willie stated that it was only by the grace of GOD that I was still breathing. I watched every vehicle that drove past as we stood in the driveway, negotiating a price for the maintenance. Suddenly a silver Sterling turned the corner and sped recklessly up the streets. I quickly snatched the Ruger off of my hip and stepped into the cut. Willie observed my movements and followed suit behind me. I raised the pistol and was about to start squeezing when the car came to a halt, but I noticed that it was Jungle behind the wheel smiling. He rocked his head to the Notorious B.I.G. Ready to Die album.

"What's good brah?" he rolled the window down. "Why are you acting all shook?"

"Keep playing!" I slid the toast back on the hip. "I was about to air that shit out!"

"Old school looked like he was about to hit the gate." Jungle nodded towards Willie.

"Hell yeah, I was about to jump over that muthafucka." Willie admitted. "I don't know what's going on with y'all young boys out here."

"Where you been?" I asked. "You've been missing in action for about two weeks."

'Yeah, I've been trying to move under the radar," he replied.

"I feel you! What are you about to do?"

"I'm about to go and get me something to eat; what's up?"

"I'm about to hop in with you."

"Come on and get in."

I provided Willie with a gram of crack and the money to purchase the parts he needed from the junkyard.

"Page me if you need anything else," I told him.
I hopped in with Jungle and he pulled off.

"What's been going on around here?" he inquired.

"It's been hot as fish grease around here. The beast has been sweating niggas every day, asking questions about you and Shakim."

"Word?"

"Word is my bond!" I replied. "Y'all got to chill until this shit die down."

Jungle didn't respond.

"What are you going to do?" I asked.

"I'ma do what I do," he answered. "The beast dont have anything to prove that I did that shit. The only thing that they got is these bitch ass niggas running their mouths."

In the parking lot of GG's, there was a panhandler begging for change. I donated two dollars to his struggle as we exited the car and into the restaurant. GG's served some of the best soul food and breakfast in town. It was one of the places that my Pops brought me to eat so I often thought about him whenever I dined there. We took a seat in the far right corner, underneath a photo of Dr. Martin Luther King Jr. Although I examined the menu, I already knew what I had the taste for. A waitress approached us politely and placed two glasses of water down on the table.

"Are you guys ready to order?" she asked.

"I would like three cheese eggs and grits with a double order of turkey sausage," I replied. Toast comes with that right?"

She nodded, scribbling down the order on an invoice. "And what would you like to drink?"

"A half and half," I added.

"And you?" she turned her attention to Jungle.

"Let me get the pancakes with the sausage and a large glass of milk."

The waitress wrote down the remainder of the order then gathered the menus and disappeared into the kitchen area.

"Remember those boys that we were banging at outside of Pete Sakes?" I whispered.

"Yeah, what about them?"

"They got at me on some Vietnam shit yesterday. I thought that I was a body the way that they were gunning at me."

Jungle began laughing.

"Oh, you think that shit funny huh?" I asked offensively.

"I'm not laughing at you brah," he began to laugh harder. "Tell me what happened."

I explained everything from the shooting to how I rode with TK and Royal looking for the culprits responsible for it. Jungle stared at me from across the table with his signature smile, listening to every word. I could tell that the wheels were spinning inside of his head by the spaced out look that he exposed when he was in deep thought. We changed the subject once the waitress returned with the two hot plates.

"Can I get you guys anything else?" she placed our meals on the table.

"No thank you, we're good," I said.

"Okay, let me know if you guys need anything else."

We both watched her sashay away from our table and back into the kitchen.

"Damn, she got a fat ass," Jungle emphasized what I was thinking.

Once we were finished with our meal, I paid the bill, suggesting that Jungle leave a tip for the waitress.

Bzz... bzz... bzz... My pager vibrated on my hip.

"Take me back to Willie's spot," I scanned the number. "I know that he's not done with my car yet."

Before taking me to see Willie, Jungle stopped on the block to see what was going on with the crew. Junior, Polo and Trouble were seated on the porch when we pulled up while Byrd debated with an unruly fiend across the street.

"What's good with y'all niggas?" Jungle hopped out of the Sterling.

"Oh shit, What poppin?" Junior clapped his hand.

"Ain't shit. What's good with y'all boys?"

"It's the same ol shit," Polo replied. "We're out here trying to get it."

"That's what's up!" Jungle retorted. "Let me holler at you for a minute."

Polo rose up from the steps and followed Jungle into the backyard in order to speak in private. I stepped onto the porch and accepted the half of blunt that Trouble was smoking on.

"I heard that nigga's tried to get at you on some cowboy shit," Junior stated.

"Yeah, they caught your boy slipping," I admitted. "But they can't kill the kid."

"I should've known that something was up when I saw the boy Gutter, riding through here the other day."

"Who was he with?"

"He was on a dolo mission."

"You knew that we had beef with this nigga, so why didn't you say something?" I passed him the blunt.

"I thought that he was over here, visiting his baby's mother," Junior defended.

"Who is his baby's mom?"

"The girl Donna who stays a few blocks over."

"You should've been said something Junior! We could've laid on the broads building until we caught the nigga."

"My bad brah, I wasn't even thinking."

Suddenly, a police cruiser bent the block slowly. My heart skipped a beat as I alarmed Jungle, giving him the heads up. Junior cuffed the blunt inside of his palm, so it wouldn't be detected. To our relief, they kept it moving but took a second look as they drove by.

"C'mon dawg, let's get out of here before these cocksuckers circle back around," I shouted to Jungle.

Slowly jogging from out of the back yard, Jungle's head was on the swivel as he jumped into the Sterling and pulled off.

♟ ♟ ♟ ♟

Lying on top of a creeper underneath a Toyota Camry, one eyed Willie was too busy changing the oil to hear me approaching. I crept alongside the vehicle and knelt down, grabbing him by the ankles.

"What's up now nigga?" I disguised my voice.

"Ahh, help!" Willie screamed, wiggling his legs. "Get off of me, help!"

"Calm your scary ass down," I laughed.

He slid from underneath the car and lit up a cigarette.

"You almost gave me a heart attack. "Willie held his chest. "You know that my nerves are bad."

"My bad! I see that you paged me, what's up?"

"Let me get something for these eight dollars."

"I know that you didn't call me over here for eight dollars?"

"Come on nephew!" Willie pleaded. "You know that I'm going to spend some money with you as soon as I finish changing this oil."

"First of all, why are you working on someone else's car when mine isn't finished yet?"

"I'll have you knocked out in about an hour. I already put in the windows; all that I have to do now is patch up the bullet holes."

"Then get it done," I broke him off a piece of crack. "And I'm subtracting that from what I owe you."

CHAPTER 14

LET'S RIDE

Later on that afternoon, I was hanging out the sunroof of the Sterling in front of Bennett High School. There was a multitude of teenage females pouring out of the front door and I made sure that I was in position to holler at them.

"What up Ma?" I yelled to a red bone strolling with a pack of females.

She ignored me and kept walking with her friends.

"Fuck you then, you bucket head bitch!" Jungle screamed.

"Yo momma a bitch!" she shouted back.

"Jungle, why are you always starting trouble?" A squeaky voice screeched from the crowd.

We turned around and seen Tasha standing there with her hands propped up on her hips.

"What up Tee?" Jungle hopped out and gave her a hug. "What's up with that situation that we talked about?"

"Are you talking about the situation with Rick?' Tasha shot back.

"Yeah, I thought that you were going to let me touch the nigga?"

"I tried calling you but your pager was off," she defended. "I thought that you weren't rocking with a bitch no more."

"Nah, you know better than that," Jungle said. "I got a new number."

Tasha reached in her bag and pulled out a pen, jotting down the number as he pronounced it. "When do you want me to call?" she asked.

"Whenever you're ready."

'Alright, I'll call you later on tonight so you can come and get me and I'll show you where he lives."

"That's a bet! Then afterwards, you can show me what that pussy hitting like."

"Oh, you already know that's not a problem,"
she replied seductively before walking away.

♟ ♟ ♟ ♟

Later on that evening, Jungle received a phone call from
Tasha around eight o'clock, telling him to come over. She and
her friends were bored and suggested for us to stop by and
smoke some weed with them. An hour later me, Byrd, Polo and
Jungle were in Tasha's living room, twisting up, getting
acquainted with her girls Tonya, Rhonda, and Kim.
     "Where's your mom?" Jungle asked, lighting the blunt.
     "She's at work, why?"
     "Because I'm trying to holler at you in the back for a
minute."
     "Uh uh boy, slow your role and run me to the store
right quick," Tasha told him.
     She really didn't want to go to the store; she just needed
an excuse to show Jungle where Rick lived. After they left, the
weed continued to circulate the room. Polo and Byrd didn't
waste any time accommodating the girls with their charming
personalities. I had my eye on Tasha's cousin Kim; nevertheless
I remained cool, inhaling the essence of the smoke. Kim was a
sexy ass Jamaican. Her dreadlocks ran down the center of her
back with a touch of auburn which enhanced her brazen
complexion. At five feet six inches, her body was well defined
but the most alluring attribute that Kim unveiled was her
Caribbean dialect. Rhonda was the average hood rat. She was
always running her mouth and gossiping about things that never
concerned her. She was kind of cute despite the scar that
decorated her cheek from a scuffle that she had over a guy that
lived on her block. Tonya was the prettiest as well as the
freakiest out of the crew. She was down for whatever if it was
related to sex. She was a high yellow red bone with a pair of
long sexy legs and an ass like a donkey. As the marijuana took its
effect, Byrd and Polo didn't hold any punches, convincing
Rhonda, and Tonya into Tasha's bedroom. Kim and I were left
alone to watch television in the living room.

"What choo doin ova dere all by ya self?" Kim spoke in a Jamaican accent. "Me not gon ta bite cha star."

"How do you know that I won't bite you?" I responded. Kim eyed me enticingly as she hit the weed. "Maybe me wan cha to bite," she stated boldly, blowing out a ring of smoke.

"In due time, I might just do that."

Kim walked over and sat down in the seat next to me and began playing with my braids. "So do ya lady let choo get away oftin?"

"Who said that I had a girl?"

"C'mon star me ere dat ya quite the ladies man," Kim declared.

"Do you always believe everything that you hear?"

"Not every ting."

"Well, I don't believe nothing that I hear and only half of what I see."

"And whut ya see rite now star?"

"I see an angel without its wings!" I replied.

Kim smiled, exposing a deep set of dimples. "So ya gon let dis angel take ya ta paradise and show ya some tings?"

"Some tings like whut?" I mocked her vernacular.

"Me like ta be you missing piece ta de puzzle."

"And what piece might that be?"

"Ya eyes and ears ta da streets," Kim confessed. "Meez been eyeing ya fa some time now and me like da way ya move."

I transformed into 'Mack' mode once I realized that Kim was choosing to be on the team.

"Listen baby girl, I don't know what it is that you think that you know about me, but I want you to understand what you're getting yourself into," I spoke in a calm and controlling voice.

She leaned closer to me as I continued.

"I must admit that you're sexy as hell; and I believe that your energy can be an asset to catch one of these suckas slipping."

I placed my hand under her chin and lifted her head, staring directly into her eyes. Without blinking, she returned my gaze. "It's a dirty game out here and if you're going to be on the squad, I need to know that I can trust you," I emphasized.

"And me understand dat trust is some ting earned not givin so tell me whut you need me to do and me will do it."

"Give me a hundred and ten percent without allowing your personal feeling to interfere with the business at hand."

"Me tink me can take care of dat."

Kim listened diligently as I explained everything that I expected from her. Most of the game that I revealed to her was something that I'd remembered Pops telling a woman with a little of my own flavor. As I picked at her brain, I learned that Kim was two years older than me. She was currently residing in the Langfield Projects, facing the struggles of everyday life with her three year old son. Her child's father was serving a five year sentence in Attica for an attempted murder. Kim was still in love with him, but she still entertained male friends without any strings attached. I respected the game so I agreed to put her in position to earn some money if she played her cards right. By the time Jungle returned from scoping out the target with Tasha, Kim had basically told me her life story.

"What's going on in here?" Tasha questioned as she came through the door. "Where is Rhonda and Tonya?"

"Dere in the back with Byrd and Polo," Kim informed her.

"Oh, hell nah!" Tasha snapped. "I know them bitches are not back there fucking in my room?"

Kim shrugged her shoulders.

"Me not kno whut dere back dere doin but dey been back dere for a minut."

Seconds later, the bedroom door opened and Byrd appeared without his shirt on, sweating.

"You back there getting it in, aint you?" Jungle laughed.

"Something like that!" Byrd smiled.

"Uh... uh... y'all go have to come from back there." Tasha said. "I don't know where y'all negro's been!"

"Shut up and quit cock blocking," Jungle grabbed her and led her into the back.

"You shut up!" she returned. "Ain't nobody cock blocking."

They vanished into the opposite room and closed the door. Byrd walked over and sat in the lazy boy that was placed in the corner. He pulled the wooden handle on the side of the chair and reclined back. Suddenly, Tasha's bedroom door re-opened and Polo headed directly for the bathroom. Shortly afterwards, Rhonda appeared in the doorway, adjusting her clothing followed by Tonya.

"Yo Tonya, grab my kicks and shirt for me," Byrd instructed.

Polo exited the bathroom and brushed past her as Tonya went to collect Byrd's belongings.

"Jungle hasn't gotten back yet?" Polo joined Rhonda on the couch. "I'm ready to bounce."

"Now that you got some pussy, you're ready to leave?" Rhonda nudged him playfully.

"Yeah that's just like a nigga!" Tonya tossed Byrd his shirt. "He's ready to bounce on a bitch after he done got his little dick wet."

Polo pulled Tonya onto his lap and squeezed her closely.

"Don't act like that," he pleaded. "We got some business to handle."

"Whatever Polo!" Tonya remarked. "I already know that you're full of shit but it's cool. I'm not trippin!"

♟ ♟ ♟ ♟

In the back room, Jungle was laid back in the bed in a state of rapturous delight as Tasha rode him backwards. She bounced up and down, causing her ass to slap against his pelvis. The juices from her vaginal canal seeped down Jungle's thighs onto the sheets. He quickly flipped her onto her stomach and began pounding it from behind.

"Mmm! Take this pussy nigga!" Tasha groaned. With every pump, her head slammed against the wall as he stroked her forcefully.

"Who's my bitch?" Jungle questioned through clenched teeth.

"I'm your bitch… I'm your bitch…," she replied, feeling him inside her stomach.

Once he felt himself about to explode, Jungle pulled out. Tasha quickly spun around and wrapped her mouth around his shaft until it reached the back of her throat.

"I'm about to bust!" Jungle huffed.

After the volcano erupted, Tasha jerked the creamy lava all over her face and lips.

Before collapsing onto the bed, Jungle watched his unborn seeds discharge onto her face. For the next couple of moments, he laid there lost in his thoughts.

"My mother will be here in about an hour, so you and your boy's need to get ready and go," Tasha slid her panties on.

Jungle didn't respond, he continued to stare up at the ceiling fan as Tasha began cleaning up the room.

"Jungle…. Jungle…. I know you hear me!" she said.

"Life is crazy!" he broke his silence. "Sometimes, I feel like I'm moving in the same direction as that fan. Round and round but still not going anywhere."

"What are you talking about?"

"I'm just thinking out loud," Jungle brushed her off.

"So when do you think that we'll be able to hit ol boy spot?"

"We can probably do it this weekend, but I'll let you know what's up!"

"Don't be bullshitting when it's time to put this work in."

"Nigga, aint nobody bullshitting," Tasha said. "I got my part taken care of; you just make sure that you're not bullshitting when it's time to cut that check; because I know how you and them shady ass niggas in there gets down."

"Don't worry about that baby girl, I got you!"

Tasha moved around the room gracefully as she cleaned up. Jungle admired her firm body as she changed the linen on the mattress. Feeling his penis hardening, he slid up behind her and grabbed her by the hips.

"Let me bust that thing open one more time before I leave."

"Uh… uh boy, stop playing," she escaped his grasp. "Y'all have to go before my mother get here. I'll call you tomorrow and let you know what's up."

♟ ♟ ♟ ♟

It was a quarter past twelve o'clock when we left Tasha's apartment. The streets were damped due to the light drizzle of rain. Once we were inside of the car, Jungle didn't waste any time filling in the blanks. He explained how we were going to break up in Rick's house as soon as he got word from Tasha. I was already daydreaming about spending my share of the lick before any of the money was even in my possession. Caught by the traffic light, I snapped back to the moment as we came to a halt. Waiting for the light to turn green, Polo bragged about the sexual episode that he and Byrd had experienced with Rhonda and Tonya.

Those two bitches are some freaks!" Polo declared. Jungle rummaged through the shoebox of cassettes, searching for some music to listen to.

"Tasha keeps some young broads around her that's ready to shake something," Jungle told him.

"They were down for whatever! Me and Byrd switched up on them and everything,"

The light turned green and Jungle popped in a tape by Onyx. As he accelerated on the gas pedal, the last days began screaming through the six by nine speakers.

"After I bust'd off, I laid there for a minute, watching Rhonda play with herself while Byrd smashed Tonya from behind," Polo continued. "Next thing that I know, Tonya grabbed my wood and threw it in her mouth."

"Get the fuck out of here," I shouted. "I'm not going for that!"

"Brah aint lying," Byrd confirmed. "Those broads freaked out."

"Y'all boys went raw too didn't you?"

"Hell nah, I aint go raw!" Polo blurted out with an expression of guilt.

"Stop fronting!" I told him. "I know that your ass went raw."

Aye yo Jungle let me run in the store right quick," Byrd pointed to the corner deli.

Jungle pulled over at the 24-hour delicatessen and handed Byrd a dollar for some loose cigarettes. When Byrd got out of the car, I continued.

"Y'all some dirty dick ass nigga's," I laughed.

"Go ahead with that shit," Polo replied. "Don't hate me because that nonchalant shit didn't get you laid."

"I'm not hating on you because you got your rocks off. I'm a player. I wasn't stunting those hoes or their juice box. It's bigger than that for the kid!"

"That's what your mouth say!"

"Alright, I'm not going to say nothing when you got all type of green shit shooting out of your dick," I said. "I'm just going to escort your hot ass down to the Rath Building and make sure that you get that shot."

"Nigga, you act like you aint never…"

"Chill out, here comes five O," Jungle interjected.

We quickly straightened our posture and faced forward, trying our best to look inconspicuous. The unmarked vehicle crept by slowly. I peered out of my peripheral, releasing a deep breath once the Lumina had past.

"Fuck!" Jungle huffed, eyes glued to the review mirror. "Here they come."

They shifted their vehicle into reverse and jumped out with their weapons drawn.

"Let's see your hands!" the officers yelled.

I looked up and saw officer Williams and Kirkpatrick. They were aiming their weapons at head level, ready to pull the trigger if there were any sudden movements. Quickly snatching us from out of the vehicle, they placed us in the back seat of the police car, neglecting to put us in handcuffs. Kirkpatrick holstered his weapon and sat up front smiling while Officer William's ransacked the Sterling. They were ecstatic that they had actually captured Jungle. Kirkpatrick peeked through the hole in the glass to get a good look at us.

"Where have you been Bishop?" he referred to Jungle by his last name. "We've been looking all over for you."

"Found it!" William's announced, holding the 357 that was stashed next to the engine.

Kirkpatrick got out of the vehicle and joined his partner. William's placed the revolver onto the hood of the car and dispatched the station, informing them that Danny Bishop along with two others was in custody for a loaded weapon. Moments later it seemed as if every officer and detective from Precinct 16 were on the scene, smiling and shaking hands. They were delighted that their murder suspect had been detained.

Our hands weren't cuffed so I began to contemplate an escape route, seeing that Kirkpatrick had forgotten to close the sliding glass window, separating me from freedom.

"I'm about to climb through the window and jet," I said skeptically.

"Do you think that we can fit through it?" Jungle asked.

"I know that we can."

I turned around to see what the police were doing before I made my move. Jungle didn't hesitate. He maneuvered through the hole in the glass and pulled off in the squad car before I could react.

"Hey... hey... hey... stop!" The police screamed as they scattered to their vehicles in an attempt to stop us. In a hurry, I slid through the same hole that Jungle had slithered through seconds earlier. I was in a state of disbelief as I sat in the passenger seat of the unmarked police car. Jungle switched on the sirens, signaling for vehicles on the road to pull over out of the way.

"Let me out!" Polo began to panic. "Let me out!"

Jungle bent a few more corners, leading the police on a high speed chase through the neighborhood side streets. I began to laugh although the situation wasn't funny. It was serious, and I knew that we had crossed the line.

"I'm out!" Jungle announced.

He slowed down right before jumping out of the car. I tried to grab the wheel to gain control of the moving vehicle but was too late. We collided head on into a tree. Barely coherent, I stumbled out of the car and ran away into the depths of the night unable to let Polo out of the back seat.

CHAPTER 15

THE RIDE TO PRISON
(Present)

The ride to prison was long and depressing. I stared out of the window in silence, wishing I could turn back the hands of time as I watched the world move without me. As the county van veered onto Interstate I-290, I took one last glimpse at the city that I was leaving behind. There were nine men along with myself occupying the caged vehicle. Our hands were cuffed in front attached to a chain that wrapped around our waist, extending to the shackles on our ankles. I shook my head in disbelief, disgusted that I had allowed myself to be tricked into the prison system. My past flashed before my eyes as we passed through a number of rural areas with cornfields and cows dwelling on farmland. I thought about everything that had led me up to this point. When we finally reached the prison, the officers pulled behind a long line of county and state vehicles, containing a number of prisoners. Some of the men had been sentenced to prison for a matter of months or even years but many of them were destined to spend the rest of their days breathing behind the walls of confinement. After surrendering their weapons at the gate, the officers proceeded through the high fence surrounded with razor wire. Elmira wasn't only a reception area, it was also used as a focal point to import and export inmates across the state of New York. As we stepped out of the van, the officers began unlocking the shackles of each individual one by one. Once I was unchained, I rubbed my wrist and took a look around. All types of criminals had begun to pour out of the buses in packs; each one carrying their life inside of a plastic garbage bag. They scampered around the large parking lot to their assigned area. Some paused for a smoke break while others stopped to converse briefly with other convicts who they had served time with somewhere during their bid. I scanned the area for a familiar face when a guard instructed all of the new prisoners to follow him inside. As I stepped through the crowd of convicted felons towards the castle like fortress, I spotted my man Gemini in the cut, smoking a square.

"What's good fam?" I shouted in his direction.

He looked up and was shocked to see me.

"What happened family?" Gemini questioned with confusion. "What did you get locked up for?"

"The street is wicked fam. One of my man's snitched on me!" I stated as the officer rushed me into the building.

Inside of the intake area stood seventy men listening to Officer Moore explain the rules and regulations of the institution. Sergeant Moore had been working for the Department of Corrections for twenty years, but he didn't relish at the opportunity to keep the black man confined in modern day slavery.

"As of this moment, you are all property of the state," Moore announced. "I'm not here to baby sit you or hold your hand. You're all grown men and as long as you act like men, we're going to treat you as men."

Everyone remained quiet.

"For those of you who think that you are Billy Bad Ass, we can play that game too!" he continued. "I'm not here to make time hard but I'm also not here to be your friend. I'm here to do a job and whoever makes it difficult is going to have a horrible time while they're here. I know that many of you have a family to get back to out there so make it easy on yourself and do what needs to be done to get it together. Do I make myself clear?"

Yes sir!" twenty out of the seventy men mumbled.

"That's unacceptable gentlemen so let's try it again," Moore roared. "Do I make myself clear?"

"Sir yes sir!" Sixty out of the seventy shouted in unison.

"That's better! Now place your property on the floor and take off all your clothes, including your underwear and stand on the line in front of you."

We all stripped naked and stood shoulder to shoulder with our toes touching the red line on the floor. As the prison workers pushed a laundry cart past us, we dropped our orange county garments inside. Another worker walked by and handed everyone a small white bottle.

"The bottle that you all have in your hand is for those lice and crabs that some of you picked up in the county," Moore said. "I want you to rub that gel on to the areas where there is hair and make sure there isn't a drop left."

I poured the liquid into my palm and applied it to the pubic area and underneath each armpit. After listening to another short speech, we were allowed to take a cold shower. I quickly washed up and toweled off, then dressed into the issued state greens that were supplied.

For the next few hours, we were taken through a series of events. Visitation rights, job history along with diet and medical ailment forms were filled out and submitted to the institution. I had been awake since 3:30 a.m. that morning so by the time I was finished filling out the paper work and answering questions, I was exhausted and ready to lie down.

Each inmate was given a mattress, pillow, and a pair of sheets along with towels and toiletries before being escorted to the assigned building. The iron gates slammed shut, echoing through the corridors as we walked up the hallway in a single file line. Once we reached B-House, the sergeant handed the C.O. in charge of the cell block our I.D. cards and a roll call sheet. Officer Harper called out the names one at a time and ascribed us to our cells. "Briggs 203, Courtland 177, Green 118, Miles 208, Jones 222."

Once I heard my name, I collected my belongings and stepped inside of the unit. I glanced around the compound, eye boxing with the guys standing in the doorway of their cells. I could see the hunger in their gaze as they watched us closely, trying to see who was weak or not. Prison veterans could smell fear a mile away.

When I made it to the small chamber in which I would be spending the next couple years of my life, I noticed a middle age man lying on his bunk. He was reading the 33 Strategies of War by Robert Greene.

"Peace god!" he greeted. "What's your name?"

"King!" I replied.

"I'm Sincere," he extended his hand.

I looked him directly in the eyes, trying to read his approach. Sincere matched my stare with a look that I recognized all too well. When I finally shook his hand, there was an unspoken understanding between us.

"Don't mind me; go ahead and get settled in," he said. I made up my bunk and folded my towels, then stored them away, according to the diagram displayed on the wall. Meanwhile, Sincere had begun doing pushups and asking me questions between sets. Once he left to go and take a shower, I hopped up on the rack and zoned out, thinking about better days.

CHAPTER 16

GAME TIME
1995

Friday night, the gymnasium was filled to the capacity. Everyone awaited the championship showdown between the Kensington Knights and Bennett High school. Although we were undefeated, Bennett was the returning champs from the previous year and they were determined to uphold the title. Both teams warmed up and shot around while teenagers and young adults continued to pack in the bleachers. I gazed up into the audience and saw Keisha and her girl Shae walking through a host of people. The game was moments from getting underway and we were fired up.

"Are you ready?" Daquan extended a clenched fist.

"I'm about to give them the business!" I replied in confidence, meeting his fist with mines.

"Let's get busy then."

We were center stage and my adrenalin was pumping as I anticipated the opening tip off. Just as the game was about to begin, TK, Jungle and the rest of the Young Wolves made a grand entrance. Dressed in army jackets and fatigues, they looked like they were ready for war. The smell of marijuana lingering in their clothing made their presence felt as they stormed through the building as if they owned it.

The whistle blew and Daquan leaped up over Rick Pearson a junior from Bennett and tipped the ball in my direction. I snatched it and dribbled past my opponent and scored a quick point off of the glass. I hurried and got back on defense as Bennett's point guard; Anthony Carter brought the ball up the court. As Tariq Childs cut towards the basket, I anticipated the pass and intercepted it in midair. Dequan was already in full stride headed in the other direction. I tossed up the alley-oop and he caught it above the rim and dunked it with authority. The crowd exploded as I jogged to the other end of the court and took my position on defense.

"Good pass," Dequan pointed at me from across the court.

Carter kept his poise as he pushed the ball up the floor. Unable to get the ball to Tariq, he slung it to Dorian Jackson for the easy layup.

The first two quarters were close. Both teams held the lead, but neither for more than five points. By the end of the second quarter, we were up 51 to 49. I had 11 points and was leading the team with seven assists and three steals. Tariq Childs wasn't having the game that everyone had expected. Daquan was having his way with him, scoring at will. He was in his zone with 18 points and 6 rebounds but Dorian Jackson wouldn't let up.

Leading his team in points and assist, he had a burning desire to win. The horn sounded, ending the first half. The momentum was in our favor as we headed towards the locker room, but there was still another half to play.

"What's the matter with you guys?" Coach Pete questioned. "You're acting like you don't want to win this thing. Bennett is good but we've beaten teams that were way more aggressive and talented than these guys. How are we allowing them to keep it this close? Their star player isn't the one beating us; it's some kid that I didn't even know existed until today. He's killing us down low!"

"We got it under control coach, calm down," Dequan said courageously.

"Well let's get back out there and finish this team off since you got it under control."

"Bring it in!" I instructed.

"We all gathered around with one hand on top of the other.

"Defense on three, one… two … three…"

"DEFENSE!" we shouted in unison.

When we entered back into the gymnasium, the energy was electrifying. We were determined as we stepped onto the court, ready to tend to our business. The second half began like the first one had ended. Both teams came out gunning at the hoop, playing the game with passion. Jamal and Rico applied pressure to Jackson. They boxed him in with a double team and stayed in his face. The opposing tension forced Jackson to find

Tariq in the corner for the three point shot. A possession or two later, I came down and stuck a shot inside the perimeter and immediately got back on defense. I guarded Tariq as he pushed up the court with the left. After slinging it to Carter, he quickly cut to the basket. Carter shot the ball right back to him as Tariq elevated gracefully. I jumped up to contest the shot but was a step too late. He slammed the ball with force, causing me to tumble on to the floor.

"Ooooohh," the crowd roared.

"Step your game up!" Tariq taunted me.

He jogged to the opposite end of the floor, clapping hands with his teammates. I looked up at the scoreboard and seen Bennett was up by eight points; the largest lead of the game.

"Time out!" I formed my hand into a letter T.

I tossed the referee the ball then stepped over to the bench. There were a number of fans cheering for Bennett. It seemed like every blue and orange pom-pom in the stands was waving emphatically. Coach Pete drew up a demonstration on a clipboard, explaining the mistakes that he saw being made. He pointed out the weaknesses in our defense and other areas where we needed to tighten up. I stood there drenched in sweat, listening to him instruct us on what he expected.

"Don't get frustrated. We're still in this thing as long as we don't lose our head," Coach Pete said.

I took a swig of Gatorade and peered over my shoulder, locking eyes with Gutter. He was standing next to the kid that had gotten shot outside of Pete Sakes alongside some other goons I'd recognized. They were all ice grilling me as I stared them in the face. Without thinking, I raced into the mob of spectators and dropped Gutter with a wild haymaker. His boy Smoke caught me with a hard right to the jaw, knocking me off balance. We were locked up, tussling around when the rest of their squad began to pile up on me. I found myself curled up on the floor in a fetal position, covering my head to avoid injury as they kicked me continuously. The Wolves quickly responded and came to my aid. They swung punches and threw chairs at anyone that was partaking in jumping on their comrade. I hopped to my feet and went into a blinding rage as the two crew's collided head to head, blow for blow. I blacked out once I saw Gutter standing there mean mugging me like I was something sweet. I had forgotten about the Championship and all of the hard work that my team had sacrificed to make it to this point until I heard shots.

Pap... pap...pap...pap ...pap...

The entire place exploded into an uproar. All the students stormed from the bleachers in a panic as the shots echoed throughout the gym. Teachers and parents screamed, ducking, and running to get out of harm's way. It was pure pandemonium throughout the building.

I took flight amongst the chaos, racing towards the exit as a million and one thoughts flashed through my mind. Once outside the building, I ran in the same direction that I noticed Royal and TK scampering in. It was just as much confusion outside as it was in. People were pointing fingers and staring as I passed by.

"King!" someone called out.

I turned around and was face to face with the disappointment and pain inside of Coach Pete's eyes. Without another word, he just shook his head with grief. Hearing the police sirens in a distant, I got in the car and drove away; knowing that my chances of playing ball for Syracuse was slim to none.

CHAPTER 17

NO TURNING BACK

Shane was sitting on the milk crate in front of the corner store on Stockbridge and Bailey, reading the newspaper when I stepped up. He was dressed in the same clothes from the previous day so I assumed that he had pulled an all-nighter.

"What were you thinking?" he questioned.

"What are you talking about?" I replied, rhetorically.

"This is what I'm talking about," he handed me the paper.

[STAR BASKETBALL PLAYER STARTS FIGHT DURING CHAMPIONSHIP GAME, ENDING IN GUNSHOTS] Is what the headlines read in bold letters?

I read the article and became a bit nervous when I saw that the police suspected King Jones, a junior at Kensington High School to be involved with a group of young teenagers, selling drugs on the city's Eastside. Jones is a tremendous talent and has made a name for himself throughout Buffalo for the raw gift that he displays on the basketball court but is believed to be engaged in criminal activity, taking place in the University District. Friday night, during the championship game between the Kensington Knights and Bennett High School, Jones got into a physical altercation with a group of males that were spectating from the stands. The conflict ended in gunshots after a number of punches were thrown. No one was hurt, but authorities believe that the person who fired the weapon happens to be a friend of Jones and is also wanted for questioning, concerning an unrelated shooting earlier this month.

What were you thinking?" Shane repeated.

"I don't know!" I replied. "When I saw them boy's, I just spazzed out."

"It's a time and place for everything. You have to be smart and lay on them boy's, then strike when they least expect it."

"I didn't know that brah was going to start dumping like that."

"What else did you expect?" Shane started laughing. "Jungle is a loose cannon and he don't give a fuck about nothing or nobody except for the people in his circle."

"You're absolutely right."

"This isn't about me being right or wrong. This is about you being smart. That basketball is your ticket up out of here and you might've ruined that opportunity."

Confused and frustrated, I rubbed my head. Shane stood up from the milk crate and embraced me.

"You'll be alright, but you're going to have fall back until this blows over," he said.

"No doubt," I returned with some dap.

"I'm about to go and get something to eat; are you hungry?"

"Nah, I'm cool. I ate before I left the house."

"Alright, I'll holler at you in a minute."

"In a minute."

I took Shane's spot on the milk crate and scanned through my pager, checking all the calls that I hadn't retuned.

"I wonder who this is," I mumbled to myself, eyeing a number that I didn't recognize.

I eased over to the payphone and placed the call.

"Did somebody call King?" I questioned, hearing a female on the other end.

"Dis ya lady friend," she replied.

"Oh, what's up with you?" I recognized the voice. "I was just thinking about you?"

"Den why ya not reach out ta see me?" Kim asked.

"Because I've been mad busy but I have been thinking about you."

"And whut were ya tinking bout?"

"I was wondering when I was going to see you again?"

"Wheneva ya want."

"I'm tryna see you today."

"What ya doin bout three o'clock?"

I looked down at the watch on my wrist and said. "I got a couple of moves to make but I'll call you when I'm done."

"Don't keep me waiting all day."

Meep… meep… meep.. Across the street, Jungle was blowing the horn to gain my attention. I nodded as I held up my index finger, signaling for him to give me a minute to end the call.

"I'll be over there after I get through handling my business," I assured Kim.

"Dat's cool star," she replied. "Call me wen ya on de way."

"Peace," I cradled the receiver.

As I crossed the street, I noticed Trouble reclined in the passenger seat, smoking some trees.

"What's the deal with ya'll boy's?" I leaned into the window.

"What's the deal with you?" Jungle shot back. "It's a war going on out here and you're on the phone with your back turned, making love and shit."

"Yeah, you slippin King," Trouble added.

"That's the least of our problems," I said seriously. "That shooting that happened last night is all in the paper and they talking greasy too.

"Word?" Jungle turned the music down.

I gave him the paper as I accepted the blunt from Trouble. I filled my lungs with smoke while Jungle read the article.

"You're a wild boy!" Trouble stated.

"Why you say that? I questioned.

"One minute you were on the court balling and the next thing I know, you were in the stands wilding out. That shit happened fast as hell."

"They buggin!" Jungle looked up from the paper.

"I told you!" I replied.

"Forget what they're about; we're about to go and bust this move right quick. What are you about to do?"

"What move?"

"Tasha gave me the green light on that situation."

"It's on?" I looked him in the eyes.

"It's on," Jungle confirmed. What you gon do?"

"Make it happen," I slid into the back seat.

Moments later, we were circling the block of a residential area downtown. Trouble got out of the vehicle in order to canvass the premises while we parked around the corner. I cocked the nine, placing one in the chamber as Jungle and I exited the car.

Already inside, Trouble opened the door once he saw us easing up the driveway. We ransacked the place immediately. After about ten minutes of searching the house, we heard the sound of some keys entering the lock.

"Shh," Jungle gestured for us to be quiet.

We all drew our guns and stepped off to the side behind the door. When the door opened, a big black dude entered the house followed by another guy that I instantly recognized as Gee.

"Oh shit!" They were startled, starring down the barrel of our weapons.

"Shut up and lay down fat boy," Jungle put the gun to the back of Rick's head. "You know what it is."

They both cooperated, lying face down on the floor. I quickly bound both of their hands behind their back. We weren't wearing mask to cover our identity so I knew that Gee was aware of whom I was but he remained silent.

"Where that paper at?" Jungle questioned with authority.

"I don't keep anything here," Rick responded. "It's at my other spot.

I struck him across the face with the butt of my gun and watched as blood gushed from his mouth.

"Don't make me shoot you in here playboy," I threatened.

"Alright... alright... alright," he pleaded. "I'll give y'all boys whatever you want just don't kill me."

"Tell us where it's at?" Jungle pressed.

"It's in the back room across from the bathroom.

Jungle snatched Rick to his feet and walked him to the back room with the gun to his ribs. Trouble followed suit, leaving me alone with Gee.

"If that nigga move, shoot him in the face," he said. "Don't do nothing stupid King," Gee whispered.

"Chill brah, I'm not going to do anything to you," I told him.

"What are you doing? This aint you, you're a hustler. Why are you out here robbing?"

"Chill out before my mans and em come out here and hear you."

Suddenly there was a loud shot in the back followed by two more. Surprised from the deafening sound, I jumped slightly, perplexed at the thought of what had just taken place. Gee looked up at me with fear in his eyes as Trouble and Jungle hurried back with a knap sack. Without being told, I already knew what had to be done as I pointed my pistol at Gee's head.

"Don't do it King. I promise that I won't say anything" he pleaded for his life. "I'll do whatever y'all say. Please don't kill me."

Those were the last words that Gee said before I squeezed four bullets into his face, leaving him lifeless. As I watched the blood seep into the carpet, I knew that I couldn't turn back and that my life would never be the same.

CHAPTER 18

KIM

Kim greeted me with a hug and a kiss on the cheek as she opened the door to her apartment. Her perfume was alluring and the only thing covering her nakedness was a long white t-shirt which made her all the more tempting. She twisted her ass with every step as she made her way back into the two bedroom apartment. I could tell that Kim was well put together as I admired her walk.

"Make ya self comfortable," Kim handed me the remote control.

I kicked back as she went into the kitchen to attend to the steaming pots that were on the stove. The midnight blue living room set brought life to the project walls. I flicked through the channels and noticed a picture of a guy in prison, sitting on the coffee table. I automatically assumed that it was the father of Kim's three year old child. As I stared at the television screen, I replayed the murder back in my mind. Gee's last words were burning inside of my head as I pictured him sprawled out across the floor, absorbing in his own blood. Was his life worth thirty-three thousand and a kilo of cocaine?

"Ya want something to eat?" Kim snapped me out of my trace.

"Yeah, I can eat a little something," I told her. "What are you putting together?"

"Oxtails, rice and cabbage."

"Don't be trying to put that West Indian root on me," I joked. "Have me all fucked up in the head and shit not wanting to leave."

Me not need any root fa dat. Me got something else dat make ya wanna stay," she said seductively.

"I gotta watch you," I laughed.

She walked over to the entertainment center and pressed play on the stereo system. The room came to life with the vocals of Bob Marley, singing Is This Love as Kim removed her t-shirt, revealing a pair of perky breasts. We looked at one another with lust in our eyes as she climbed on top of me. Our lips intertwined, causing my tongue to explore her mouth. She moaned when I slid my hand between her legs, slipping two fingers inside of her. For several minutes, I caressed her clitoris with the touch of my hand. Kim yearned for more as she removed my hand and placed it into her mouth, licking the juices off of my fingers one at a time. In a matter of seconds, I stiffened up as she worked her way down to my manhood. I grabbed the back of her head and watched her bop up and down. Her tongue felt like a warm piece of silk as she licked the shaft of my penis. Once, I was nice and hard, Kim mounted me, easing down slowly. The pussy was hot and wet as she rode me in every direction. The sex was impeccable, and it seemed like the more wood that I gave her, the more she wanted. We freaked off all over the apartment for at least an hour. We went from the living room to the kitchen, from the kitchen to the living room floor. Finally, we found our way to the bedroom thrusting into one another. She held her ankles as I plunged her from behind.

"Hit dis poon poon like ya wanna," Kim cooed.

I pushed deeper inside of her with every stroke.

"Me bout ta cum….," she cried out in pleasure. "Don't stop, me bout to cum."

We both climaxed with excitement and fell to the carpet. I wrapped my arms around Kim's naked body and kissed her on the nap of her neck. She smiled and snuggled up under me. As I drifted off to sleep, I thought back to Gee's last words, trying to remove any feeling of guilt that was lingering inside of my mind.

CHAPTER 19

CONTEMPLATING THE NEXT MOVE

The next day, TK and Royal were counting their daily earnings when I arrived at their spot. The heroine game had put them on another level. The money that I was earning from selling crack was peanuts compared to the numbers that they were doing. I stepped into the room and took a look at the set up. The walls were freshly painted white with the typical poster of Scarface above the black leather sofa. A recliner sat directly across from the 60 inch television set that gave the apartment a bachelors touch. Yeah, TK was definitely eating well! Royal separated the money into G-stacks then wrapped them into rubber bands before placing it into the duffle bag. As they counted out the cash by hand, I estimated it to be around fifty thousand. Royal placed a cancer stick in his mouth and added fire to the tip as he blew out a stream of smoke.

"What's good with you King?" he asked. "What brings a player like you to this part of town?"

"I just wanted to see what was going on with y'all boys," I told him. "The hood is on fire."

"I don't know why you ain't been coming over here to rock with ya boy," TK said. "I been told you to come and get you some money."

"This is your thing bra. I don't know anything about the heroin game."

"This could be our thing," he urged. "Anything that you want to know, I could show you."

"Word up brah, you need to come and eat with us," Royal chimed in. "It's enough paper for everybody."

"What do I need to do?" I questioned.

TK cracked opened a cigar, dumping the tobacco into the trash can. "Don't worry about nothing, I got you. All you need to do is be around and I'm going to give you the game."

"Say no more."

As the blunt circulated, TK and Royal took turns explaining how they ran their operation. Suddenly there was a knock on the door."

"Who is it?" TK hollered.

There was no response.

"Who is it?" TK repeated.

Still no one responded but whoever was outside was now banging on the window. With the trey pound in hand, Royal hopped up from his chair and peeped through the blinds.

"Who is that?" TK looked at him irritated.

"It's your man Vontae," Royal answered.

"Let him in."

Vontae was a young boy that TK had recruited when he first began hustling in the Cold Springs. He knew everyone from the hustlers to the junkies which made it easy for TK to get money without any problems. Vontae was the quiet type but quick to pop his pistol under any circumstances.

"What's up with y'all boy's?" he asked coming through the door.

"Ain't shit up!" TK barked. "Why are you banging on my door like you're the muthafuckin police?"

"It's cold as hell out there," Vontae defended. "And y'all niggas are up in here high as hell, acting like y'all don't hear me knocking."

"I screamed who is it but you didn't say shit," TK countered.

"My bad, I didn't hear you," Vontae joined us at the table.

He pulled out a brown paper bag from his hoody pocket and handed it to TK.

"That's the last of the money from that last package that you gave me."

"I'm about to bounce," I stood up from the table. "I'll get with y'all tomorrow."

"Make sure that you come through early so you can see how we operate around here," TK said.

"Yeah don't be frontin," Royal added. "I already know how you do when you get around one of your slut buckets."

"Nigga, I know that you're not talking," I responded jokingly. "You'll probably still have your face between some broad legs by the time that I get over here."

"I might!" he admitted.

♟ ♟ ♟ ♟

Before calling it a night, I rode through the block and spotted Byrd and Polo at the park surrounded by a few hood rats. They began to make their way towards the vehicle as I pulled up to the gate and rolled the window down. I could tell that something wasn't right by the disturbed look that Byrd wore on his face as they approached.

"What the matter with you?" I prepared myself for the worst.

"You haven't heard what happened?" Byrd shot back.

"Nah, what happened?"

"Cousin got knocked."

"Who?"

"Jungle!" he established.

"Damn!" I punched the dash board. "When did this happen?"

"It happened about an hour ago," Polo chimed in. "He was supposed to come back through here after he got dressed but never made it."

"That doesn't mean that he got knocked," I replied.

"Rena and them said that the beast swarmed up on him at the gas station up on Bailey," he nodded towards the girls, sitting on the park bench.

"Let me hit that," I referred to the cup of liquor in his hand.

Polo passed me the Styrofoam cup and continued. "And she said that he got bagged with the toast on him."

"C'mere Rena," I waved her over to the car.

She got up from her seat and eased over to the window.

"What's up King?"

"What happened to Jungle?" I asked her.

"He was in the back seat of the police car, trying to tell me something about a gun but, I couldn't hear exactly what he was saying," she replied. "And when I tried to get closer, the police made us leave."

I sipped the Hennessey from the cup and passed it back to Polo.

"Go ahead and kill it," he suggested. "We got some more over there."

"Alright, let me get out of here before the jakes pull up on some shit," I dapped them up.

"No doubt!" Byrd responded. "Hit me up if you hear anything else."

As I drove through the night, I thought about the events that had taken place over the last three months. I felt as if I was at my limit and needed to put things back into its right perspective. Jungle was a warrior and implicating me or any of the Wolves was the least of my worries, but his arrest did have me stressed out. I was more concerned about the snakes that were still slithering around, smiling, and laughing in my face. Without a destination, I rode around the city, trying to contemplate my next move. I felt like the police capturing Jungle was just the beginning of our problems. Something that started out as fun and games had evolved into something serious. We'd got into this game as a group of kid's searching for a quick come up and now we were considered amongst the city's most dangerous criminals.

CHAPTER 20

KEISHA

Jungle had been incarcerated for a little over two months and things weren't looking good for him. We corresponded through letters and he advised me to remain on the low until the heat died down. He was more than positive that someone from the crew was supplying the authorities with information that only the Wolves knew about. Ma Dukes had heard about all of the drama that had been happening in the neighborhood which only confirmed her suspicions. She was really concerned about my well-being and questioned me daily about my whereabouts.

"King, you need to get up before you're late for school," she announced.

The time on my pager read a quarter past eight as I glanced at the electronic device on the night stand. Slowly peeling myself from the bed, I dragged to the bathroom to take a shower. After getting dressed, I quickly left the house before Ma Dukes could interrogate me any further. Ever since the incident had occurred during the Championship game, I rarely attended school. Whenever I did decide to show up, I only stayed long enough for the homeroom teacher to mark me off of the attendance sheet. The moment that I stepped into the classroom, I could feel the stares from my classmates. I acknowledged a few people with a nod of the head before taking my seat. At the desk next to me, Shae was completing the morning assignment. She flashed me a pleasant smile as I cracked opened my notebook.

"What's up Shae?" I spoke first.

"Hey King, you're a sight for sore eyes," she replied. "How have you been?"

"I'm good! But what's up with your girl Keisha? I'm jive feeling shorty!"

"Keisha is good people. She minds her business and she is not around for the bullshit."

"Pull ya boy in."

"Write your number down and I'll give it to her when I see her" she assured me.

"I tore off a page in my notebook and jotted my number down. Make sure that she gets it."

"I got you!"

Ms. Thomas peeked over the rim of her glasses and checked off the attendance sheet as Mr. Washington gave the morning announcements. The moment the principal was finished speaking over the loud speaker, the bell sounded, causing everyone to rush out of the door. As I headed up the hallway, I spotted Keisha walking towards me.

"You're not going to speak?" I asked as she passed by.

She stopped and placed her hand on her hip.

"Why didn't you speak?" Keisha remarked. "You see me just like I see you."

"I've been asking myself that same question for a minute now. As fine as you are, I should've been said something to you."

"Oh really?"

"True indeed!" I smiled. "I've been checking you out since the first day that I saw you and I'm feeling your resume."

"What do you mean that you're feeling my resume? she smiled back.

Fucking with a dude like me is a full time job so I had to do a background check before I submitted your application."

"I didn't know that I was applying for a position."

"Well if you knew better, you would do better."

"Why are you so conceited?"

"I'm not conceited, I'm confident. It's a difference!" I told her.

"A little too confident if you ask me."

"Nah, it aint like that boo, but I did give your girl Shae my number to give to you so make sure that you use it."

"And what makes you think that I want to call you?"

"C'mon ma, every queen needs a King in their life," I walked off, leaving her with something to think about.

♟ ♟ ♟ ♟

Three days had gone by without a call from Keisha but I expected that she would eventually get around to it. The following Saturday, my assumption became a reality when I received a page while watching the N.B.A. playoffs.

"Ro, let me see your cellphone."

Royal took a bite into a hot wing as he tossed me the phone.

"Pass the damn ball," he yelled at the television.

"Hello Johnson residence," Keisha answered the phone.

"Did someone call King from this number?" I asked.

"This is Keisha," she replied. "What are you doing?"

"I'm at my man spot, watching the game."

"Do you want me to call you back?"

"Nah, you're good! What took you so long to get at me?"

"Excuse me if I didn't break my neck to call you, but I do have a job."

"Where do you work at?"

"I work at the McDonald's on East Delavan."

"Oh that's what's up," I told her. "I like a girl that's not afraid to work."

"What else do you like in a girl since you have so many to choose from?" she shot back.

"That phone is for business not for making love player," Royal shouted from the couch.

I stood up and walked towards the back room to talk in private, muffling Royal out once I shut the door.

"What do you mean by that?" I referred to Keisha's last statement.

"I see how the chicken heads be sweating you at school so don't act like you don't know what I'm talking about."

"Why do they have to be chicken heads?"

"I just call it how I see it."

"What about you?"

"What about me? she questioned.

"What types of niggas do you fuck with?"

"First of all, I don't mess with niggas," Keisha corrected. "I don't know why y'all call one another that?

"Excuse me Miss Thang!" I didn't know that you were so sensitive."

"Yo King, let me get that phone; I'm about to go and bust a move," Royal screamed from the other side of the door.

"Who is that?" Keisha asked.

"That's my man Royal," I told her. "He wants his phone so I'll call you when I get to the crib."

"I'll call you tomorrow because I'm about to lie down and go to sleep I had a long day."

"Well when can I see you?"

"You can see me every day if you start coming to school like you're supposed to."

"I'm talking about…"

"I know what you're talking about," she interjected. "And if you really want to see me then you'll start coming to school."

"I might just do that!"

"We'll see."

After ending the call, I went back up front where the crew was observing the game. I noticed that Trouble had joined TK at the table when I entered back into the room.

"What's good Trouble? How did you get over here?"

"I jumped in a cab," he retorted, swinging a Dutch Master my way.

"What's been going on around the way?"

Trouble exhaled and said, "The beast has been snatching niggas up left and right. The other day, they bagged Byrd with a hammer, coming out of the barbershop. Then they beat the shit out of him before they took him to jail."

Casually peeping out of the blinded windows, I focused on the construction workers across the street. For some reason or another, they seemed suspicious to me.

"I heard that five O has been taking pictures of everything coming through the block," I stated.

"Word up!" Trouble confirmed. "They have been on some shit since that shit happened with Jungle."

Royal picked up his car keys and headed towards the door. "When Cocoa pull up, tell her that I said to stay here until I get back."

As we watched the second game of the triple header, TK had dosed off. The number of blunts that had been smoked had taken its effect, leaving him comatose. Trouble was in the kitchen boiling a pack of Ramen noodles to help satisfy his munchies while Vontae remained in silence across the room. Vontae hadn't said more than three words all night and he seemed to be a little uncomfortable.

"Are you watching this?" I broke the stillness in the air.

"Nah, you can turn," Vontae replied in a dry tone.

The Bulls were up over the New York Knicks by seventeen points with only a minute left in the fourth quarter so I changed the channel. For the next few moments, I flicked through the stations but there wasn't anything worth watching, therefore I stood up and gave Vontae a pound.

"Tell TK that'll holler at him tomorrow."

"A'ight."

As I was leaving, I made a mental note to have a conversation with TK about his man Vontae. There was a weird sense of energy, coming from the young boy but I just couldn't wrap my head around it.

CHAPTER 21

CAT AND MOUSE

I played the game of cat and mouse with Keisha for about a month before she finally agreed to let me take her out to the movies. Through conversation, I found her to be interesting. It was something different about her. She wasn't like the other females that I was used to dating. She was from the hood but she wasn't of the hood. Under her rough exterior, there was a touch of innocence that I was attracted to. Keisha was the forbidden fruit and went against everything that I stood for. She thought about marriage, the big house surrounded by a white picket fence with a bunch of children running around. I had my mind set on crack spots with metal bars over the windows with the fiends running back and forth, copping blow. I thought that the fairytale life that she imagined was amusing, but I catered to her ego to get what I wanted. Every night before going to sleep, Keisha would call just to say goodnight and advise me to be careful on the block. Some nights we stayed on the phone until the early hours of the morning, discussing our dreams and aspirations. She even conned me to come to school more frequently once we started spending time together. Being that her parents didnt allow her to have boyfriends, Keisha would have me pick her up from Shae's apartment. One evening when I pulled up, I was impressed with what I saw when she stepped out of the house. Unlike her usual apparel, she was sporting a channel blouse and a pair of leather jeans that were hugging her hips like a glove.

"Hey King," she spoke in the sweetest voice. "How long have you been waiting out here?"

"I haven't been out here that long," I replied.

She adjusted her seat as I shifted the gear into drive.

"The show starts at seven o'clock," she said.

"What theater did you call?"

"The one at the Galleria Mall."

"Well let's get something to eat before we go to the movies because popcorn and candy is not going to be enough for the kid."

She nodded in agreement.

"I'm going to turn you on to a spot around my way where the wings is banging," I told her. "The old head who owns the spot makes a mean BBQ sauce."

"We'll see!" she sneered playfully. "You probably got the munchies, so everything tastes good to you."

"Alright now, I don't want to catch you at my spot with one of those choir boys that you be dealing with."

"Shut up, I don't deal with choir boys!" she nudged me.

"You don't like gangsters or choir boys. What type of guys do you like? Oh, I forgot, you only deal with gentlemen," I remarked sarcastically.

"I don't deal with niggas; I never said that I didn't like gangsters," Keisha corrected.

"Oh, I guess that I am halfway there. All I need you to do is to teach me how to be a gentleman."

Keisha pinched me on the cheek.

"You're not a gangster," she teased in a childlike voice. "You're a big ole cream puff, trying to be tough."

"That's what I want you to think," I flashed a smile.

"These broads really got you thinking that you're all of that? All that stuff that I be hearing about you and your boys doesn't impress me."

"What are you talking about?"

"Wouldn't you like to know?" she smirked. "But I will tell you this. It's not cute."

"I'm not trying to be cute," I defended.

"Well, why are you always fighting and getting into trouble? Like that time at the game; you didn't have to come in the stand and punch that boy in the face."

"It's deeper than you think."

"Is it that deep that you're willing to risk the opportunity of a lifetime? King, you are fortunate enough to have a chance to go away to college and get an education while playing ball. Do you know how many people would love to be in your shoes? Why would you be out there risking your life in the streets?"

"I see that I wasn't the only one out here doing their homework?"

"I noticed you the first day that I walked into class," she admitted. "There's something special about you."

"Well why didn't you say anything?"

"Because you have this arrogant attitude and plus I wasn't trying to be in the middle of anything, concerning those broads that you deal with."

"What's so different about me now that made you change your mind?" I asked.

"People label you a trouble maker but the time that I've spent getting the chance to know you, I see so much more than what you portray to be and I hope that you don't continue to waste the talents that GOD has blessed you with."

The last few sentences fell on deaf ears as an unmarked police car cruised by us, staring into the car. With my eyes glued to the rearview, I removed a quarter ounce of weed from my pocket and stuffed it down into my underpants.

"What's the matter?" Keisha asked, reading my body language.

I remained focused in the mirror, ignoring her question. Once the police bust a U turn, I snatched the 38 Special from underneath the seat. They sped through traffic and pulled directly behind me, flashing its lights.

"Put this in your purse!" I tried handing Keisha the pistol.

"Uh… uh… boy is you crazy?" she responded in a shaky voice. "I'm not touching that thing."

I pulled to the side of the road. "You're a girl so they're not going to search you without a female officer present."

Reluctantly, Keisha grabbed the gun and stuck it at the bottom of the bag as both officers approached the vehicle.

"Well… well… well if it isn't out friend Mr. Jones," Kirkpatrick flashed the light in my face. "Can I see your license and registration?"

"Ah… ah… I don't have a license sir," I stuttered. "The car is registered to my mother but I was just giving my cousin a ride home."

Officer Williams flashed his light into Keisha's face from outside the passenger window.

"Are you related to this thug young lady?" he questioned with authority.

Keisha squinted from the brightness of the light and nodded her head.

"Do either of you have any drugs or weapons inside the vehicle with you?"

"No sir!" I quickly replied.

"For some reason, I don't believe you," Kirkpatrick implied. "Step out of the vehicle."

He searched me thoroughly before cuffing my wrist and placing me the back seat of the squad car.

"I'm going to jail?" I asked sympathetically.

Without answering, Kirkpatrick slammed the door shut in my face and made his way over to where Williams was grilling Keisha. I knew that she was nervous but to my surprise, she held her composure. After plundering through the car for a half hour, they allowed Keisha to take the vehicle, considering they thought of her being my cousin. Somewhat relieved, I exhaled back into the seat, watching her disappear up the block. I was hoping that I would receive an appearance ticket once I got to the precinct but all expectations dissolved once William's turned onto the expressway, headed downtown. Swiftly maneuvering my hands down into the back of my pants, I grabbed the marijuana and stuffed it down the seat of the squad car. At the station, I was placed in a small room, containing a table and two chairs. My heart rapidly raced as I thought about what was next to come. Every minute that ticked off of the clock seemed like an eternity. Suddenly, two men dressed in plain clothes entered the room. They closed the door behind themselves and the smaller of the two took a seat across from me. He placed a folder on the desk and began scribbling on a pad while his partner towered over us drinking coffee.

"Hello, I'm Lieutenant Ford and this is my partner Sergeant Simpson." The one in front of me spoke. "We're homicide detectives. Do you have any idea why you're here?" I gave them a puzzled look, mixed with a bit of fear and shook my head no. "I didn't kill anyone; I got caught driving without a license."

"No one said that you killed anyone," Ford said. "We just want to ask you a few questions."

He removed some pictures from the folder and placed them in front of me. "Do you know him?" Ford pointed to a picture of Shakim.

"Nah, I don't think so," I replied.

"What about him?" he referred to a mug shot of Jungle.

"Nah, I don't know dude either."

"Are you sure?"

"Positive!"

"That's funny because everyone else that we asked about these guys seems to mention your name," Simpson interjected. "As a matter of fact, they say that you all are best friends."

"Do I need a lawyer?" I asked.

"It depends," Ford said. "Where were you on the afternoon of September 27th?"

"I'm not saying another word without a lawyer."

Ford removed his glasses and rubbed the bridge of his nose.

"Just answer the question kid."

"Lawyer!"

Simpson lost his patience and smacked me viciously across the face. "I don't give a damn about your rights!" he said aggressively. "You're going to tell us something."

"I aint telling you shit!" I shot back.

He snatched me out of the chair and tossed me on to the floor like a rag doll.

"Hold on Serge!" Ford held him back. "He's only a kid."

"I'm tired of playing games with this asshole!" Simpson shouted.

"Alright Serge, let me talk to him in private."

Sergeant Simpson stormed out of the room in a rage, slamming the door behind him.

"Are you alright kid?" Ford helped me up.

"Oh, I get it," I rubbed my head. "You must be the good cop."

"This isn't television Mr. Jones; this is reality. Whether you help us or not, we're going to get the facts and when the smoke clears and we find out that you're mixed up in this, you're going to be sorry. I'm giving you this one last chance to help yourself before it's too late; so what's it going to be?"

"I'm not answering anymore questions until I talk to a lawyer."

By the time that the detectives were finished interrogating me, it was three o'clock in the morning. I was given an appearance ticket for a traffic violation and released from central booking. As I stepped into the morning air, I felt drained. Although I didn't allow the police to see me sweat, I was nervous as hell. They had turned the heat up another notch and I couldn't help but wonder how much they actually knew. I was shown pictures and questioned about various people from the neighborhood. Someone was definitely running their mouth and it was only a matter of time before it surfaced because everything in the dark will eventually comes to light.

CHAPTER 22

FRANK

The following day, there was a morning breeze cutting through the intersection of Jefferson and East Utica. Although it was a nippy afternoon, it didn't stop the junkies from the hustle and bustle of keeping that monkey off of their back. There was a number of people congregated on the corner, loitering and soliciting goods. Across the street in an abandon lot, TK was seated on a milk crate, watching everything from the junkies to the vehicles passing by while Royal exchanged verbal assaults with one of his many female companions. With the same attire that I had on the day before, I pulled up to their block in a cab and hopped out, allowing the driver to keep the change.

"Where is the whip at?" TK acknowledged.

"This shorty name Keisha got it," I replied.

"She must got some good twat if you let her push ya V?"

"I haven't even smashed her yet," I admitted. "We got pulled over last night and Kirkpatrick let her take the car."

"He took you to jail?"

"Yeah, they took me downtown and homicide questioned me until three o'clock in the morning."

"Homicide?" TK frowned. "What did they question you about?"

I took a seat next to him on the crate. "They were asking me about that shit that popped off at the jewelry store a couple months back."

"What did you tell them?"

"I wasn't answering any questions without my lawyer being present so one of the detectives snuffed me on some sucka shit."

"I told you that you're going to have to fall back from all of that hot boy shit."

"I feel you!"

"Nah, I'm going to need you to do more than feel me and start listening to what I'm telling you," TK insisted. "You already know that somebody in the hood is snitching and there's no telling what they've told the police. I'm about to get another spot around here and I'm going to let you hold it down, but you have to stay low until we find out who's talking."

"I got you!"

TK switched the subject as an old scruffy looking junkie approached us. He was pushing an old shopping cart filled with a bunch of bottles and cans that he'd collected from the streets.

"What's the business with you pimps?" he approached, scratching his neck.

"We're out here trying to get this paper up," TK replied. "What's up with you Frank?"

"A pimp is down on his luck, hopping on his last leg right now, but I'm cool. A true mack always bounces back like a fat cat, I just need to set a couple of rat traps, ya dig?"

"I can dig it," TK chuckled.

Discreetly peering over his shoulder, Frank dug inside of his pocket and pulled out a pair of gold earrings and a broken herring bone.

"Check this out" he held the jewelry inside of his palm. "Give me a hundred dollars."

"What am I going to do with that?" TK questioned.

"Give it to one of those lovely ladies that be coming around here chasing after you."

"They don't be chasing me, they be after that nigga Royal."

"Who's after me?" Royal walked up on the conversation.

Frank spun around and held the gold pieces in his direction.

"We're talking about that little sweet thang that just pulled off in that jeep; but I know that you're not about to slow down to let her to catch up," Frank said. "What you need to do is cop some of these fly accessories so that she'll ease up off of you and allow a player to attend to his business in these streets."

"I don't want that slum gold that you done snatched off of somebody's neck," Royal pushed his hand away.

"What about you, young player?" Frank turn to me. "I know that you like to keep your lady looking good."

"Nah, I'm good O.G," I responded.

Frank stopped for a short period of time and examined me from head to toe.

"You look familiar young fella. Where do I know you from?"

"You don't know me brah, I'm not from around here."

"I've traveled the world twice and shook the hand of every major player in the nation at least once so if I don't know you then you ain't nobody."

Amused by his vernacular, I began laughing.

"They call me King."

"King... king... king... he searched his memory. "Is your father name Caesar?"

At the mention of my Pops name, I stared at the old man for a moment.

"Yeah that's my Pops," I clarified.

"Boy, I thought that you were playing ball. What are you doing out here hustling?" Frank attempted to wrap his arms around me.

"Whoa, hold up pimp," I shoved him lightly. "You don't know me like that."

"Awe nigga, you got your weight up a little bit and now you too good to give your old cousin Frank a hug. I remember when you were running around with snot in your nose and shit stains in your draws, hustling me out of quarters."

"Cousin Frankie?" I finally recognized his face. "What happened to you?"

"These streets are what happened," he admitted. "I had love for them but they didn't love me back. Between the money, hoes and dope, I lost my way and forgot about what was important."

"Damn cousin, I remember when you was a boss player."

Frank stared into the sky and smiled, revealing a set of rotten teeth, thinking about when the times were much better.

"When your father and I first came to Buffalo, it was wide open," Frank remembered. "We had whores humping from Genesee to Chippewa Street."

"My Pops used to tell me those stories," I said.

"Yeah, your dad was a cold boy. How has he been doing anyway?"

"He's holding it down."

"Well the next time you talk to him tell him that I said to hold his head and to keep it pimpin."

I reached into my pocket and pulled out a crispy hundred dollar bill and handed it to him. In return, Frank attempted to give me the jewelry.

"Nah, I'm good," I refused the items. "That's for all of the quarters that I hustled you out of when I was a kid."

"Good looking out baby boy; I owe you one."

"You don't owe me anything; just get yourself together."

"You sound just like Caesar," Frank said. "He used to always check me whenever I was slipping. Now here you are twenty years later, telling me the exact same thing."

Frank spent the next two hours reminiscing about the good old days. He told us about all of the money and women that he and Pops had ran through. Although Frank knew that the day of trafficking dope and exploiting women were far behind him, there was a light in his eyes that still desired the good life. I recalled seeing photographs of cousin Frankie and Pops at their best. With their three piece suits and alligator shoes, they both fit the description of the classical gangsters. I took a look at what Frank had become versus what he used to be and I made a solemn oath to never do any drugs besides marijuana.

♟ ♟ ♟ ♟

Later on that day, TK was talking on his Motorola flip phone as we rode up E. Ferry Street. Due to a traffic light; he brought the Beamer to a stop at the intersection on Fillmore and blew the horn at a girl that he'd recognized who was admiring his rims. The album Illmatic was blaring through the speakers. Reclined back in the passenger seat, I zoned out to the music, thinking about the conversation that I held earlier with Frank, concerning Pops. It had been seven years since the last time that I had actually laid eyes on him and I was pondering about how he was holding up. Regardless of the fact that it was an accident the night that Ma Dukes had gotten shot, I found it difficult to forgive him. I was angry for all of the days that he was absent when I needed him most but more importantly for all of the nights that Ma Dukes spent crying on my shoulder. Although I resented him for the pain that he had caused our family, there wasn't any denying the love that I held in my heart for him.

"What are you thinking about?" TK flipped the phone shut.

"I'm thinking about my Pops," I replied in a low tone.

"When was the last time that you hollered at him?"

"It's been a minute!"

"You need to go and see what he's talking about," he suggested. "If he's as thorough as Frank says that he is, it'll be worth the trip."

"It's definitely worth thinking about."

TK pulled into the Mobil gas station and handed me a twenty dollar bill. I slammed the door behind me as I exited the car and into the store.

"Can I get twenty on pump three?" I handed the clerk behind the counter the money.

"Is there anything else?" he asked politely.

I grabbed two sodas and placed them on the counter. "Let me get a box of Dutch Masters too."

The clerk began punching the buttons on the cash register.

"That'll be $25.87," he put the items into a bag.

When I returned to the car, TK was pumping the gas while conversing with two females inside of a Ford Escort. They looked to be a year or two older than us.

"Where are y'all about to go?" TK asked the one in the passenger seat.

"We're just riding around," she responded. "What are you about to do?"

"We're trying to see what's up with y'all."

"Okay, write your number down."

I strolled over and glanced inside of the compact vehicle in order to see what we were working with. The passenger was official. She favored a young Vanessa Williams with her flawless complexion and cat like eyes. The driver was cute but a little on the chubby side. I hurried up and slid back into the BMW without saying a word because I already knew which one TK was attempting to push off on me. Once the pump stopped, he cradled the nozzle and gave his number to green eyes. She quickly accepted and promised to call him later on that night. Ten minutes later, we were staked out in front of my crib with the engine shut off. The radio was playing a little above a murmur.

"Do you remember what I told you on the first day that we met?" he lit up a blunt.

"Are you talking about the day that we pounded homeboy out at the park?" I questioned.

"Yeah, when we ran up in the abandon building; do you remember what I said?"

Reflecting back on the memory, I cracked a smile. "You said that the reason that you held me down was because we were family."

"Exactly, and I'm going to always take care of family." TK emphasized. "As long as I got it, you got it. You'll never want for anything as long as I'm in the streets. I'm about a hundred fifty grand to the good and by this time next year, I should have enough money to get out of the game."

I turned face to face with TK as I digested what he had just revealed to me.

"I'm going to need you to have your Timberlands laced up tight once this paper jumps off," he continued. "Because all types of snakes are going to start popping out of the grass."

"So basically what you're telling me is that I need to keep the grass cut?"

TK nodded. "This next move that I'm about to make is going to create enough room for everyone to eat."

"I'm with you," I assured him.

"Well like I told you before, you're going to have to chill with all of that cowboy shit," he countered. "I need you out here with me, not behind the wall."

There was a brief silence before I spoke again.

"Who do you think is snitching?" I finally asked.

TK inhaled the weed before passing it off to me. "I've been asking myself that same question, but I can't figure it out," he released a ring of smoke.

We slapped hands as I got out of the car.

"I'll get with you in a minute," I closed the door.

"King!" TK called me back to the car.

"What's up?"

"You need to think about using that ball to get us up out of these streets.

"I'm trying."

"Nah, don't try, do that shit," he said seriously. "You have a talent that can make all of this street shit legal and if playing ball is what you want to do then do it, I'm going to hold you down regardless."

"Good looking out Brah!" I gave him another pound.

As I made my way into the house, I felt a sense of confidence, knowing that my friend had my back.

CHAPTER 23

WHEN THE GOING GETS TOUGH

The following evening, Keisha came over to the house to bring me the car and braid my hair. We had become better acquainted and besides the fact that we hadn't experienced sex together, I was feeling her, and I believe that she was feeling me. What other reason would she risk her freedom?

"Be still so I can finish," she instructed.

As she parted my hair, Keisha tugged, pulled and twisted it into a braid.

"Ahh girl!" I winced. "You're doing that shit on purpose. I told you that I was tender headed."

"Quit whining, I'm almost done. I got three braids left."

I readjusted between her legs and focused back to the PlayStation.

"I don't understand how you can sit around all day, playing a damn video game?" Keisha stated.

"I don't understand why you always have something smart to say," I returned sarcastically. "Just braid my hair and be quiet."

"You shut up!" she pulled my hair.

"Ah shit!" I yelled.

"That's what you get for running your mouth."

"You got one more time to pull my hair before I hurt you."

"You're not going to do anything but run your mouth."

Bzz... bzz... bzz... I pushed the pause button on the joystick to search for my pager. After reviewing the screen, I put the small clear box in my pocket and resumed to playing the game.

"You're beginning to get real flamboyant with your tongue," I warned her.

"Stop crying and go look in the mirror," Keisha suggested.

I pulled myself from off of the floor and stretched before walking over to the mirror.

"Okay, you put me in the game," I admired her work.

Despite the trash talking, I enjoyed being in the company of Keisha. She held a positive aura that helped me forget about all of the madness that had invited itself into my life. I usually became bored with a female, especially if we weren't having sex, but I became more interested with Keisha by the day. She was my get away from the streets; my retreat from the stress and confusion. Besides playing ball, she was the only thing that seemed to be real. Keisha didn't care about my reputation or the material things that most girls required. She looked beyond the surfaced and accepted me for who I truly was. Staring at this ebony princess, I appreciated her smooth chocolate skin. Her eyes radiated with maturity but the inner beauty that she displayed was the most valuable asset that she possessed.

"Why are you looking at me like that?" she asked.

"How am I looking at you?" I returned.

"It's like you're up to something."

"I just like what I see."

"And what is it that you like so much?"

"I like everything from your hips to your fingertips."

"Yeah, I bet," she snickered.

"Nah, on the real, I just like being around you," I told her. "It feels like I've known you forever."

Keisha smiled, displaying a set of dimples in both cheeks. "Cut it out King. Save some of that game for those broads that don't know any better."

"I'm serious Keish; I'm feeling everything about you," I confessed. "I like the way that you smile, the way that you carry yourself and your conversation. I've never felt this way about a female before."

From the expression on her face, I could tell that she was considering the words that had exited my mouth.

"I'm really not trying to be mixed up in all of the drama that you have going on," she said.

I took her by the hand and looked her in the eyes to let her know that I was being sincere. "I promise you that I'll never put you in harm's way again or ask you to do anything that you're not comfortable with."

Uncertainty flashed across her brow. "What about all those girls that be in your face?"

"Those broads don't mean anything to me," I assured her. "All I'm asking you to do is give me a chance."

Keisha leaned over and positioned herself underneath my arm as she kissed me in the mouth. I closed my eyes and permitted our lips to lock as we engaged in a tongue wrestling match. I proceeded with caution as I unsnapped her bra and removed her shirt. A pair of erect nipples were staring me in the face, screaming for attention. I gently ran my tongue across her breast as my hands explored prohibited places. Keisha didn't resist; she laid back and enjoyed the moment. Her tender spot was moist as I penetrated my fingers deeply inside of her. She panted softly in pleasure.

Bzz.. bzz... bzz... Ignoring the vibration of my pager, I continued to seduce Keisha.

Bzz... bzz... bzzz...

"Go ahead and check your beeper," she removed my hand from inside of her pants. "It's obvious that someone needs to talk to you by the way their blowing you up."

"They can wait!" I replied.

Re-fastening the buckle on her belt, Keisha stood up, leaving me on the couch with a swollen penis.

'What's up?" I asked confused.

"I'm sorry King," she apologized. "I like you a lot but I'm not about to play myself. I'm not ready for this."

I tried disguising my disappointment by grabbing my pager.

"I understand!" I skimmed over the numbers.

"No you don't."

I stood up and wrapped my arm around her waist and said, "We don't have to rush. Good things come to those who wait and I'm willing to wait until you're ready."

"Are you sure that you're not mad at me?"

"Nah boo, how can I be mad at you for protecting your heart?"

"Awe, you're so sweet!" she hugged me.

I picked up the phone and dialed the number. "Did someone call me from this number?"

I was placed on a brief hold as the person who answered the phone went to get the one who had called. Moments later Trouble returned to the phone upset, crying.

"Where you at brah?" he asked hysterically.

"I'm at the crib, what happened."

"Meet me at ECMC."

"Calm down and tell me what happened."

"TK and em got shot and I think he's dead."

"What the hell do you mean that you think he's dead?" my heart dropped.

"Somebody ran up in the spot of Jefferson, trying to rob him and Royal," Trouble said. "It got ugly in there and niggas dumbed out and started blasting. By the time that the paramedics showed up, TK was already gone. Royal got rushed to ECMC and I'm on my way up there now to see what's going on."

"Alright, I'm on my way," I hung up.

♟ ♟ ♟ ♟

I sped through the streets in silence, rushing to get Keisha home as I pondered on the shocking information that Trouble had just revealed. I didn't want to believe that TK was dead. We were just together the day before and death seemed to be so far away. Reflecting back on our last conversation, I thought about the power move that he had spoken of and wondered could that be the motive that lead to his demise. If Keisha was able to read minds, she would've seen the murderous thoughts traveling through my brain because whoever did this was going to die.

"Are you okay?" Keisha broke the silence.

Without taking my eyes off of the road, I nodded as if everything was cool but deep down, I was burning inside. When my comrade needed me to have my boots laced tight, I wasn't anywhere to be found. Instead, I was laid up with a broad, trying to get a nut, and now my friend was dead.

"I'll holler at you later," I pulled in front of her house.

"King, don't go and do something crazy," Keisha advised.

"I have to go; I'll talk to you later," I said, getting agitated.

Keisha looked as if she was trying to find the words to console me before speaking.

"King I'm sorry. I don't know what else to say. I'm just trying to help."

"It ain't shit that you can do or say to help," I snapped. "If I wasn't fucking with yo ass, I would've been there to hold my boy down."

"So now this is my fault?" she questioned with tears in her eyes.

Struggling to keep my composure, I took a deep breath.

"Look shorty, one of my closest friends just got murdered and another one of my friends is lying in the hospital, fighting for his life. I need to get up there and find out what's going on."

Keisha kissed me on the cheek as she reached for the door handle.

"Please be careful," she exited the car.

♟ ♟ ♟ ♟

The waiting area at ECMC emergency room was crowded with the friends and family of both TK and Royal. At the information desk, Royal's mother Ms. Yolanda was cursing out one of the reception workers when I stomped through the door.

"Ma'am please calm down," the nurse pleaded.

"I'm not calming shit down until somebody tells me what's going on with my son," Ms. Yolanda screamed back.

At that moment, a short Asian man, wearing a stethoscope around his neck approached Ms. Yolanda. "Excuse me, are you related to Mr. Royal Hunt?" he read the medical chart.

"Yes, that's my son," Ms. Yolanda replied. 'Is he okay?"

The man extended his hand as he looked up from the clipboard. "Hello Mrs. Hunt, I am Dr. Chuang."

As Ms. Yolanda shook his hand, a somber expression overcame her face.

"Your son is in stable condition, but he has lost a lot of blood," Dr. Chuang explained. "He's suffered multiple gunshot wounds to the upper torso and a bullet has pierced him in the neck."

"Is my son going to be alright Doctor?"

"Well, we were able to stop the bleeding but we weren't able to remove one of the bullets that's lodged in his chest."

"Oh my God!" Ms. Yolanda gasped.

"Mr. Hunt is about to undergo surgery within the next ten minutes," Dr. Chuang glanced at his watch. "I'll be the one performing the procedure and we have the best medical team on staff tonight, so we will do everything possible to pull your son through this."

"Please save him, he's all I got."

Dr. Chuang shook Ms. Yolanda's hand again before he headed back into the ER. I took a seat next to Trouble who was angry with tears. Cocoa, the mother of Royal's child was ducked off next to the vending machine and I could tell that she had been crying as well. Her eyes were swollen and her face was stained from tears. The atmosphere was fraught with distress and my eyes had begun to well up as the seriousness of the whole ordeal began to sink in. We lingered around; mourning TK's death as we impatiently awaited the outcome of Royal's surgery. It felt like a scene out of a movie, but at the end of the day, there wasn't a director yelling cut. This was real life.

"I can't believe that TK's is gone" I wiped away the tears.

"Yeah, that shit is unbelievable," Trouble muttered.

"What the fuck happened?"

Trouble gestured for me to follow him towards the exit. We stepped into the night air and took a deep breath, allowing the fresh oxygen to fill our lungs.

"All I know is that somebody ran up in the spot on some robbery shit," Trouble spoke just above a whisper.

"Do you think it was the boys that we've been beefin with?" I asked.

"I don't know. The only person that can answer that is Royal."

Two hours had passed by without a word on Royal's condition. He was still in surgery and Ms. Yolanda was a nervous wreck. She drank coffee and paced the floor, speaking to GOD in prayer. Meanwhile, the Wolves and I were huddled up off to the side, discussing the possibilities of what could have taken place.

A quarter past midnight, Dr. Chuang walked in with the results.

"The surgery was a success," he announced. "Mr. Hunt is very fortunate to be alive. The bullet that we had to removed missed his heart by a few centimeters."

Ms. Yolanda began crying tears of joy mixed with pain as she hugged him. "Thank you doctor; is it possible for me to go in and see him."

"Although Mr. Hunt is a strong young man, he has been through a great ordeal tonight. I think it's best if we allow him to get some rest."

"Doctor please, I need to see my son."

Dr. Chuang rubbed his chin as he took a moment to decide. "Alright, I'll allow you to go back and sit with him for a while but everyone else will have to wait until tomorrow."

♟ ♟ ♟ ♟

The next morning, I went back to the hospital bright and early to check on Royal. When I reached his room, I tapped on the door lightly before stepping inside. There was a CNA, changing the dressing on his wounds as I entered.

"Oh, excuse me," I backed up into the hallway. "I'll wait out here until you're finished."

At the sound of my voice, Royal peered over the care takers shoulder and mustered up a weak smile.

"You're okay," the CNA assured me. "I'm almost done, switching his bandages."

She advised me to have a seat while she checked Royal's vital signs. With an I.V. in his arm and speculum in his nose, I realized how close to death, he had actually come. Once the nurse exited the room, I moved near his bed side.

"What's going on kid?" Royal spoke in a fragile voice.

"You tell me," I replied. "I'm glad to see you pulled through."

"I guess GOD wasn't ready for your boy to check out yet."

"I guess not, but you had a nigga worried for a minute." Royal placed a pillow behind his back and sat up.

"I can't believe that TK is gone," he stated.

"Yeah, that shit got me fucked up right now. "I told him. "How did they get the drop on y'all?"

"Vontae!"

"What!"

"Vontae!" Royal repeated. "He came up in the spot with some other niggas that meant business."

I propped back in the chair and allowed my mind to race as everything started to make sense. "I always knew that something wasn't right about that nigga."

Royal nodded in agreement as he continued. "They came to murder whoever was in the spot and the only reason I'm alive is because the lights went out."

"What do you mean the light went out?" I asked.

Royal explained how Vontae burst up in the apartment masked up with two other goons, demanding TK to take them to where he stashed his money. TK immediately recognized the voice behind the disguise and called him out by name. Vontae removed the ski-mask and became extremely loud, threatening what would happen if his demands weren't met. TK was unwavering and refused to take him anywhere but was willing to give him everything that he had in his personal possession. The two goons stood at bay with their weapons held at shoulder length, ready for Vontae to give the order. The chances of making it out alive were slim so TK rushed at Vontae, knocking the lamp over in the process. The entire room went dark, causing all hell to break loose.

"When the lights went out, they started dumping." Royal remembered, reliving the moment in his head. "About 30 seconds of non-stop gunfire. The only light that I could see was the fire coming out the tip of the barrels.

"Damn, I know that shit was crazy," I remarked.

"King, I'm not going to front, I thought that it was over," Royal admitted.

"Was TK gone before the ambulance got there?"

"The last thing that I remember before I blacked out was telling him to get up but he wasn't moving." Tears welled up in Royal's eyes. "I couldn't see but I knew that I was shot because I felt the blood running down my back. All of a sudden, it got real hot and I lost consciousness."

"If it's the last thing I do, we're going to see about them niggas," I promised.

Suddenly there was a knock at the door. Cocoa appeared from the other side, holding the hand of a little boy who was the splitting image of Royal. On their way over to Royal's bed side, she greeted me with a simple wave of the hand. I returned the gesture in a similar manner.

"What's up little man?" I stuck my hand out to their son.

He stood their pouting without a response.

"R.J.," Royal called out. "You're not going to speak to King?"

"Hi," R.J. solemnly replied, shaking my hand.

"What's the matter with him?" Royal asked Cocoa.

"He's mad because I wouldn't take him to McDonalds."

"I'm about to be out," I rose from my seat. "Make sure that you get some rest brah."

"I'm going to try," he said.

I went inside my pocket, peeled off a few singles and handed them to R.J.

"Tell mommy to take you to McDonalds."

Uh... uh, King. That's his problem now, he's spoiled." Cocoa declared.

R.J. smiled and put the money in his pocket.

"What do you say?" Royal questioned.

"Thank you," he said, cutting his eyes over at his mother.

CHAPTER 24

IT SEEM REAL

Camped out down the block, watching a particular building from behind tinted windows, I waited patiently to spring into action. After seeing the last light in the house go out, I quickly exited the vehicle and headed in the direction of the side door. The glow from the moon illuminated the pathway as I shuffled past the parked van in the driveway. The dogs in the back yard barked uncontrollably as I turned the doorknob and eased into the hallway. An instant later, the silhouette of a female appeared from the shadows.

"Is that you King?" she pronounced.

"Yeah, it's me," I assured, securing the lock.

My heart thumped with excitement as Keisha and I embraced. Against all odds, she led me by the hand up the steps into her bedroom.

"What took you so long to come inside?" she sat on the edge of the bed.

"I was waiting for your peoples to turn out the lights," I took a seat next to her. "I'm not trying to have your pops catch me in his house."

"I know that you're not scared."

"Nah, I'm not scared, I just don't want to get you in trouble."

"Why haven't you been coming to school?"

"What's up with all of the questions?" I asked. "I didn't come over here to get interrogated."

"We'll why did you come over here?"

"I came over here because I missed you and needed to see you."

"I missed you too," Keisha grinned.

"I might've said some things the other night that was inappropriate and I wanted to apologize."

She placed her finger on my lips, gesturing for me to be quiet. "There's no need for an apology. I understand that you've lost someone that was close to you and I probably would've reacted the same way if one of my friends had died."

"Yeah, it's tough."

"Are you alright?"

"I'm cool."

"Are you sure? The other night, I saw pain, hate and revenge in your eyes and it scared me."

"You saw all of that, huh?"

"Yes I did, and the eyes don't lie."

"And what are they saying now?" I stared her in the face.

Keisha didn't respond. She leaned over and started kissing me, tugging at my belt.

"Hold up!" I pulled away from her.

Perplexed with confusion she stared at me for a moment.

"What's wrong?"

"I don't want you to do something that you're going to regret. You're special and I want your first time making love to be special. Think about what you're about to do because once you make that decision, you can't take it back."

"I have thought about it," she assured me. "And I want to share this experience with you."

Her eyes gleamed off of the moon, making her look vulnerable. I leaned over and swiped the loose hair from out of her face.

"Every King needs a Queen in his life," I said.

Keisha smiled and kissed me until we found ourselves naked, traveling on a journey to ecstasy. I explored places on her body that no man had ever ventured. We had sex until the early hours of the morning. When I finally awoke, Keisha was sitting on the edge of the bed, admiring my nude physic.

"What's up Boo?" I groggily asked.

"You should get ready to leave before my parent wake up," she warned.

"The clock on the wall read 5:53 a.m., causing me to hop up and get dressed.

"Call me when you get home from school," I instructed.

"You need to bring your butt to school."

"I know that I've been fucking up but I have a lot going on in my life right now. When all of this shit blows over, I'll get back on track."

"Do you promise?"

"I promise!"

"I worry about you and I pray that nothing happens to you," Keisha clung to me.

"I'm good!" I said. "Nothing is going to happen to me."

"The other night, I had a dream that someone was trying to kill you."

"That's only a dream."

"I know but it seemed so real."

"I think that it's sweet that you're concerned about me but I'm a big boy and I can handle myself."

Keisha bit down on her bottom lip as she glanced down at the crotch of my pants.

"Yeah, you're definitely a big boy who knows how to handle himself alright," she expressed seductively.

"Let me find out that you're becoming a little a freak."

"What are you talking about?" she laughed.

"You know what I'm talking about," I smacked her on the ass. "If you keep it up, your father is just going have to catch me up in here."

"Well, let me get you out of here before you start something that we can't finish," she led me to the door.

Beyond her beauty, it was something about this girl that had me mesmerized. She seemed much more mature than her age warranted. Once we were outside, we stood in the morning darkness. The stars glittered brightly above us, but there was a slight tint in the sky, warning the coming of dawn. We embraced one last time before I stepped off.

"Hey King!" Keisha called out.

I stopped at the foot of the driveway.

"What's up?"

"Be careful!"

CHAPTER 25

IT'S ABOUT TO GO DOWN

"Yo kid, where you at?" Byrd anxiously questioned from the other end of the phone.

"I'm at the building," I replied. "Why, what's up?"

"Junior just hit me on the hip and said that he seen Vontae and his crew outside on Northland."

"Word?"

"True story. He's on the way to come and snatch me up now. Meet us on crack alley."

It had been twenty-seven days since we buried TK, but I could still hear his laugh. His voice was vividly clear as I re-played our last conversation over in my mind for what seemed to be the thousandth time. In the process of absolving my conscious, I isolated and cut off all communication with everyone in the hood except Byrd, Royal and Trouble. Royal had made a full recovery and was back on his grind. He and Trouble kept my ear to the pavement, updating me with the latest events in the streets. The Wolves had combed the streets daily in the hunt for Vontae and his crew. During my sabbatical, my heart had hardened and the bitterness that I felt made it difficult to trust anyone. The treachery that Vontae had displayed left me questioning the motives of even my most dependable comrades. If I were to continue to play the game, I was going to have to play for keeps. At this point, I was in too deep to turn back. When I reached Crack Alley, Junior gave us the rundown of the set up on Northland. He explained what he thought might be the best approach to catch Vontae and his boys off guard. In order to get them while they were slipping, we would have to be smart. Vontae was a killer and it wasn't any doubt in my mind that he would be strapped and ready to shoot if we ran up on them recklessly. Inconspicuously, we eased passed Northland and peeped down the block to see the schematics of the lay out. Sure enough, Vontae was posted up on the porch with two other guys besides him. Junior parked on the next street over, leaving the car running as Trouble, Byrd and myself got out and crept up the drive way. We climbed the fence and found ourselves in the backyard directly across the street from where they stood. As we laid in the cut, watching them closely, I noticed the person standing to the right side of Vontae to be a guy name Strong. The other dude also looked familiar, but I couldn't put a name with the face. Eagerly pulling the mask over our faces, we stepped into the streets and opened fire, sending an array of bullets towards the target. Strong never saw it coming. The first two shots from the Mac-10 tore through his face. The bullets that followed ripped holes the size of a quarter into the house as Vontae and his partner took cover behind the truck in the driveway.

"Get his ass!" Byrd bust the nine aimlessly.

To my surprise, Vontae rose up from behind the vehicle and sent a couple shots our way before ducking back down. I was stunned at the sight of Trouble falling to the pavement. I quickly rushed to his aid and dragged him out of harm's way behind an old station wagon. Byrd held us down, popping the remainder of his clip at the opposition. He chased them through a yard, striking Vontae in the shoulder as he tumbled over the chained fence.

"Damn!" Byrd yelled, discouraged that he had allowed them to escape.

"C'mon brah, let's get out of here before the cops come," I helped Trouble to his feet.

When we made it back to the car, Junior was waiting impatiently.

"What happened?" he shifted the car into gear.

Trouble had taken a shot to the chest and his clothes were soiled with an excessive amount of blood. I removed my mask and laid his head onto my lap.

"Did y'all get … cmph… cmph…" Trouble attempted to speak but began coughing.

"Hold on brah, we're going to get you to the hospital," I told him.

Junior sped through the streets on the way to the medical center.

"What happened?" he repeated.

"Vontae shot him," Byrd answered.

"Cmph... cmph ... cmph..." Trouble continued coughing.

"Hang in there brah, we're almost there," I declared.

"We can't go to the hospital like this," Byrd alleged. "We're dirty."

"What are we supposed to do, let him die?" I shouted. "We're taking him to the hospital."

"I agree," Junior remarked. "Even if we have to drop him off and keep it moving."

"Let's at least get rid of the guns first," Byrd suggested. "I can't afford another weapon charge."

He wiped the pistols off and placed them into a bag. Junior pulled next to a sewer, allowing Byrd to get rid of the weapons by dropping them down the drain.

"Help, I need help, my friend has been shot."

In a state of hysteria, I screamed for assistance when we pulled up to the emergency entrance of the hospital. There was a nurse that happened to be outside who hurried to aid the paramedics by getting Trouble out of the car. They placed him onto a gurney and began a procedure to stop the bleeding as they rushed him inside.

♟ ♟ ♟ ♟

"Good evening, you're watching the six o'clock news. I'm Chad Kaufman, coming to you live from Northland Avenue on the eastside of Buffalo. What you're looking at behind me is the scene of a shooting that has left one man dead. Witnesses say that three masked men emerged from a backyard across the street from where the victim was standing with two other males and began firing automatic weapons in broad daylight.

Authorities don't have any leads at the moment but believes the shooting to be drug related. There's a possibility that others were wounded, during the exchange of gunshots but the police haven't released any information at this time. The residences of this community are shaken up from the violence that has encroached, which was once a conservative neighborhood. If you have any information that may lead up to any arrest,

*concerning this community, please contact the Buffalo Police Department at
(716) 885-4545. This is Chad Kaufman, reporting live, Eyewitness
news."*

    (Click)

    I turned off the television and sat in the dark,
contemplating what I planned to do next. The news didn't say,
Trouble's name but it did insinuate the fact that someone else
may have gotten wounded, during the exchange of gunfire.
Once homicide checked the local hospitals, looking for anyone
that had been afflicted by gunshots, they were certain to come
across Trouble. I just hoped that he didn't incriminate himself
or say anything that would lead back to us.

    Ma Dukes stepped into the living room and began
fumbling through the dark. She flicked on the light and was
startled at the sight of me sitting there on the couch.

    "Boy, what are you doing, sitting here in the dark?" she
jumped back.

    "I'm thinking!" I replied.

    "What are you thinking about?"

    "I'm thinking about my life."

    Ma Dukes took a seat across from me and studied me
closely before she spoke.

    "What's the matter?" she asked.

    "I'm cool, I'm just trying to get my head right."

    "Don't give me that cool crap. I've been raising you for
seventeen years so I know when something isn't right. Now tell
me what's wrong."

    "I'm good."

    "I see so much of your father in you that it's scary," she
said.

    "Why do you say that?"

    "Because he used to act like he had everything under
control even when he didn't."

    "Trust me ma, I'm alright."

    "King, I know that you're going through something
emotionally behind what happen to TK but you can't continue
to walk around with your feelings all bottled up. You're going to
explode if you're not careful. I'm worried about you and you
need to change the way that you're living."

"Nothing is going to happen to me mom so quit worrying."

"You don't know what tomorrow may bring. I'm pretty sure that TK didn't expect his life to be stolen from him at such an early age."

"I may not know what's going to happened tomorrow but I'm prepared for today. And I refuse to walk around in fear, worrying about what's going to happen next."

"I remember when you were a little boy and you use to run around imitating everything that you saw Caesar doing," Ma Dukes said. "Now you're an adult and you're still imitating him. I know what you're doing out there in those streets and I can't understand why you're out there risking your life for that fast money."

"Ma, what are you…"

She raised her hand to cut me off. "I'm not stupid. Just because I'm not out there, ripping and running the streets, it doesn't mean that I don't know what's going on. I can't force you to do anything that you don't want to do but if you're going to act like you're grown; and continue on with your illegal activities then you can't continue to stay here any longer."

"Are you kicking me out?" I asked puzzled.

"That's your decision," she replied. "I've worked too hard to allow you to jeopardize my career."

"How am I jeopardizing your career?"

"I don't know what you're bringing into this house and if the police decide to kick in my doors and find something in here, who do you think that it's going to affect?"

"I don't have anything in your house."

"Well, I don't want to find out once it's too late. And it's not only the police that I'm worried about. It could be someone that you're close to that will come up in here and kill you if they think that there's some money in here."

"But I don't have anything in here," I repeated.

"My point is that I don't feel comfortable in my own home."

"You trippin!" I huffed.

"Boy, I don't care about you huffing and puffing."

"But Ma, you don't understand…"

"There's nothing to understand," she reprimanded. "As long as you're living under my roof, you're going to have to abide by my rules and if you can't respect that then you're going to have to find somewhere else to stay."

"Alright Ma, I'm going to get it together."

"You better or else you're going to find out the hard way. It's a cold world out there in those streets."

Ma Dukes walked over and wrapped her arms around me. "I just want the best for you King. You have so much potential and I don't want you to waste it and wind up dead or in prison."

"I'm going to start doing the right thing," I promised.

"Well you can start by getting the rest of the groceries out of the car."

I looked at Ma Dukes with compassion in my eyes. She wanted me to do what was right, but I honestly wasn't ready to make that transition. Caught between a rock and a hard spot, the demons that were dwelling inside of my soul had me possessed. Even if I wanted to do what she considered right, it would only be a matter of time before I allowed the devil to creep back in and corrupt my thoughts. I was confused; a ticking time bomb waiting to explode.

CHAPTER 26

POPS

The very next morning, I went to visit Pops at Green Haven Correctional Facility. The prison was structured like a dungeon from the Renaissance era, surrounded with razor wire and a solid concrete wall. As I made my way inside, chills ran through my bones. I glared around and took in the atmosphere as people of all shades and colors signed in for visitation. I hadn't seen Pops in over seven years, so I didn't know what to expect or where to begin. There were many questions that needed to be addressed and before I could forgive him, I needed an explanation.

I stepped to the control booth and handed my identification to the guard behind the security glass.

"Who are you here to see?" he asked in a husky baritone.

"Caesar Jones," I replied.

"What is your relation?"

"He's my father."

"Okay, sign in and empty your pockets."

I did as he instructed then placed my belongings inside of a plastic container as I stepped through the metal detector. After an overweight redneck inspected my property, he directed me through the visitation doors and told me to have a seat at table twelve. As I maneuvered my way through the visitation area, I browsed around at all of the men that had been separated from society. I wondered how many of them had left a family out in the world to fend for themselves. When I reached table twelve, I took a seat and waited. Ten minutes had gone by and Pops still hadn't come out. Suddenly, he walked in wearing a ironed creased state green uniform. His hair had greyed a lot since the last time I'd seen him but for the most part, he still looked the same. He cracked a slight smile once he noticed that it was me who was visiting him. Pops took a seat across from me and stared into my eyes for a moment.

"Hey son, it's been a long time," he said.

"Seven years,' I replied. "How have you been?"

"It's the same fight but a different round. I'm just trying to stay afloat, bobbing and weaving," Pops spoke in a calm voice. "What's happening with you?"

"Nothing."

"So, I see that you finally decided to come and check on your old man."

"Yeah, I thought that it was about time that we set our differences aside and get an understanding."

"Lord knows that it's overdue," he agreed.

"So, what's up, how are you holding up in here?" I asked.

"Believe it or not, I'm at peace with myself. These crackers may have me in physical but I'll never allow them to trap me mentally," Pops pointed to his head.

"I feel you."

"Tell me what's on your mind," he leaned back in his seat. "I see that you're still looking good."

"Ma Dukes said that I get that from you," I told him.

"Let her tell it, I get a lot of things from you."

"Speaking of your mother, how is she doing?"

"She worries about me a little too much but besides that, she's good."

"Your mother worries about you because she loves you. There's nothing like a mother's love, so cherish her."

"Why didn't you cherish her?" I boldly blurted out.

Pops locked eyes with me and rubbed his goatee as he searched his brain for the right words to say.

"What happened to your mother was an accident," he confirmed. "I wasn't in my right state of mind son. I would never do anything to hurt your mother intentionally. I loved Janice and I will always love her. The lifestyle that I was living was detrimental to our marriage and I wish I could change some of the decisions that I made."

I had heard the story on a number of occasions about what happened the night that Ma Dukes had gotten shot. Seemingly after Pops had dropped me off over my aunt Nita's house, he decided to take Ma Dukes out to a club to have a couple of drinks. Two hours and a bottle of Hennessey later, Pops began getting loose. He left Ma Dukes at the bar and accompanied an associate of his to the restroom to snort a few lines of heroin. Once he was nice and high, he became reckless by entertaining various women despite the presence of my mother. Ma Dukes understood the fact that beautiful women came along with the lifestyle that Pops led but this particular night was different. This was supposed to be a night that they enjoyed together and Pops was being blatantly disrespectful. Unable to suppress her emotions, she snapped and demanded for him to take her home. He deliberately ignored her request and continued his conversation with a gorgeous young female. Ma Dukes became loud and obnoxious with her demands and shoved Pops, causing him to spill his drinks. Overwhelmed with embarrassment, he smacked her viciously across the face, sending her to the floor. Security quickly gained control of the domestic dispute but that wasn't the end of it. Later that night, the arguing progressed into another physical conflict once they made it home. When Damon heard all of the commotion that was coming from their room, he raced up the stairs and barged in. seeing that Ma Dukes was being abused, he rushed Pops and knocked him off of his feet. My brother had filled out enormously and being that Pops was intoxicated; Damon was too strong for him to tussle with. Pops pulled out the 38 Special that he had holstered under his suit jacket and threatened to kill him if he didn't back up. Immediately the motherly instinct kicked in as Ma Dukes hopped up to protect her child. Alarmed by the sudden movement in his peripheral vision, pops accidently squeezed the trigger. Ma Dukes fell to the floor. Pops dropped the pistol after realizing what he had done and rushed to her aid. Damon stood there in shock, stunned by what had just occurred. By the time the police had arrived on the scene, Pops was holding my mother in the pit of his arms, apologizing and begging for her to forgive him. He fabricated a fanciful story, telling authorities that there was an intruder inside of the house when they returned home from an evening out. Being that there wasn't a forced entry, the police didn't believe him and decided to search the premises. They found a kilo of heroin inside of the garage and ninety thousand in the closet. Pops was placed under arrest and charged with possession of a controlled substance. He was acquitted for the shooting of Ma Dukes because of her lack of cooperation but sentenced to ten years for the money and drugs.

"Do you know how many nights that I had to hold my mother and dry her tears because of you?" I quizzed.

"What do you want me to do?" Pops snapped. "There isn't a day that goes by that I don't think about what happened. Every day that I sit in my cell, I wish that I could rewind that moment in my life but I can't! I live with the mistakes that I've made and I pray that you don't repeat the errors that have landed me in this hell hole.

"What do you mean by that?" I referred to his last statement.

"These walls talk King. Sometimes I hear what's going on in the streets before the streets hear about it," he expressed. "I hear that you think that you're a gangster, running with a crew that call themselves the Young Wolves. I also hear that you had a chance to go away to school and play ball but instead you're running around like you don't have any damn sense. Yeah, I hear a lot of things."

"Well maybe if you would've been there to show me how to be a man, I wouldn't have chosen to run the streets."

"First of all, you're going to watch how you talk to me." Pops stared me in the eyes. "I know that I fucked up so you don't have to keep reminding me. I'm sorry that I wasn't there to hold your hand when you were a little boy, there's nothing that I can do about that. Now that you're a young man, I'm going to speak to you like one and I expect you to do the same."

"I respect that!" I said.

"Son, I'm not going to sit up here and preach to you like what you're doing isn't wrong because I think that you know the difference between right and wrong. I know that I've been away for some time now and I can only imagine the type of affect that it has had on you, but you can't continue to use that as an excuse for your actions."

"I'm not trying to use your situation as an excuse for me to run wild," I told him. "I was fascinated by the lifestyle ever since a child and I probably would've chosen the streets even if you weren't locked up."

"I've kept up with every game that you ever played from the beginning. Your mother has sent me every news article that has been written about you. You're good and you will only get better with time."

"That's the same speech that every father gives to his son," I said.

"I'm not just saying this because I'm your father, it's the truth. That basketball can take you places that you never imagined. Those streets are only going to get you a trip to Forest Lawn Cemetery or in a cell next to mines. So why would you choose a game that you can't win over something that could make life easier for you and the family?"

"Making it to the league isn't guaranteed."

"And hustling is?" Pops reasoned.

When I didn't respond, he continued. "The game doesn't change only the faces that play it change. Every year that I sit inside of this cage, I see the faces getting younger and younger. Boys are who barely old enough to drive are coming behind these walls with life sentences, thinking that this shit is cute. That shit isn't cute, that shit is stupid and I don't want that to be you. You need to be enjoying your youth not wasting it on the streets."

"So I'm supposed to turn my back on my friends and just walk away from the game?" I questioned.

"Those little niggas don't give a damn about you, they only care about themselves. Those same friends that you're willing to throw your life away for will be the same ones trying to have sex with your girl when you're locked up. Ten years from now, half of them dudes will be dead or in jail and the other half will be strung out on the same drugs that they're selling now. Trust me; I've seen it all too often."

"My crew is different Pop, were like brothers and we'll die before we're disloyal to one another."

"Don't be so naïve son," Pops shook his head. "That's how it starts but it never ends that way."

"I don't mean any disrespect, but I didn't come up here to debate with you," I told him. "I understand that you want what's best for me but I'm going to do what I have to do to survive regardless of what you say."

Pops began laughing as the couple seated next to us glanced over at our table.

"What's so funny?" I asked.

"Your mother told me that you were stubborn," he replied.

"That's something else that she said that I get from you."

"Yeah but I've been trying to be more considerate of people's opinions lately."

"I hear what you're saying but I'm not turning my back on my friends."

"So your mind is made up huh?"

I nodded.

"And there's nothing that I can do to change your mind?"

"Nah, not at this point."

"It's a dangerous game that you're out there playing son and no matter how much love that you got for the streets, they'll never love you back. Trust your instincts and remember that those that are close to you are always the first to betray you, so keep your eyes open and always watch for the signs of a snake because all snakes don't rattle. Be unpredictable and never allow anyone to calculate your moves and if you're a real hustler, spread out, don't limit yourself to the hood."

With that being said, Pops removed a folded piece of paper from his top pocket and handed it to me. When I opened it up and read the name above the number I gazed up at him in confusion.

"Do you remember my partner Silk?" he asked.

"Yeah, I remember him. I replied.

"Well call that number and ask for him. Everything has already been arranged so he'll be expecting your call."

I sat there puzzled, searching Pops face for a clue. Reading my mind, he spoke. "Preparation son. I figured that this day would eventually come sooner or later so I prepared."

CHAPTER 27

MAIL CALL
(Present)

"Mail call…. Mail call…" The C.O. yelled as he walked up the tier. He stopped at my cell and slid four envelopes through the bars. I jumped up off of the floor from doing my daily pushups to retrieve the letters that were addressed to me. Settling down at the desk, I tore open the first envelope and began reading it.

Hey son,

I received your letter and I was extremely happy to hear from you. I'm taking everything one day at a time as I maintain my health. The stress still comes but it's not as bad as it used to be. I'm struggling to keep a peace of mind because things are still crazy out here. In your last letter, you spoke about consequences. I know that everything that you were out here doing was to help provide for the family. I believe that everything will work itself out eventually as long as you stay strong mentally and physically, but most importantly is staying strong spiritually. You know that I'm constantly praying for you and no matter what the situation, I will always be proud of you. I'm proud of the man that you've become, and I definitely will support you on the next journey once you're released. You have a purpose in life so be patient with yourself because once this storm is over, the sun will shine. Stay strong and remain focus.

Love, Mom

♟

Peace my brother:

As always, I fast and meditate that you are at peace, mentally and physically. As for myself, I'm striving to get by. I was happy to get a scribe and hear that you're holding your weight like a Megalith statue. That's what's up my brother. Just keep standing strong and you'll be home before you know it. We all make mistakes because we strive for perfection through our imperfections. Our environment along with our desires causes us to live the way we live. If we start surrounding ourselves around people that are pursuing legit avenues, then we would be compelled to get in where we fit in because we are able to adapt to anything that we put our minds to. I've enrolled into an online class through the University of Phoenix. I'm trying to get my Bachelor of Science in Business Accounting. I need to learn the right way to earn money for the future. I've been reading a couple books on business finance, stocks and whatever will show me another way of living. I've even completed a stock market course which taught me how to read and analyze charts. I'm going to go to Borders and get you a book called The Capitalist Nigger by Chika Onyeani. Dude is from Nigeria and he's explaining why we as a people are so fucked up and don't manufacture, produce or invent nothing that influences the economy. We're a nation of people who depend on everyone else to provide for us, from the loans to the food. Our culture doesn't produce anything. The book is saying that we need to look at the Jews, Arabs, Chinese and all the other ethnic groups that came to this country with nothing but in a matter of time took a large piece of this economy by establishing themselves with their trademark. It's time to step our game up my brother. Enclosed is a few dollars. It isn't much because we deserve millions.

Peace Blackman,

Trouble

♟

What up baby boy,

I hope that everything is good with you. As for me, I've been holding it together so that you'll have something to come home to. I know that many moons have passed by since the last time that I wrote but it hasn't been much going on out here to talk about. You're not missing nothing. These bitches are still turning tricks while these suckas is turning snitch. I hope that your eyes are focused on success because you're about to get a second chance at life. I saw your girl Rena the other day. She told me to tell you to write her and quit being a stranger. There's been a lot of niggas asking about you but I know that the majority of them are glad that you're locked up so I keep it pushing when I see them. They hate what they don't understand and fear what they can't conquer and when you were out here, niggas was scared to death. I miss you brah. It's not the same out here without you. Although the haters pray for your downfall, you can't let them stop you from handling your business. You have to expect the hate and embrace the obstacles because you were born to survive the odds. Spend this time to re-evaluate yourself because you're destined for greatness but only you can stop you from reaching your true potential.

Holla back,

Damon

What's wrong bae?

    It's 3:30 in the morning and I can't sleep, wondering why you haven't called or returned any of my letters. You know how much I value hearing your voice and receiving mail from you. You are a part of me and I can't imagine my life without your presence. I'm so scared out here by myself. I feel so unprotected like a deer in an open field. We've been through so much and I understand the trails that lay ahead but that don't make it any easier dealing with the pressure. When you don't communicate with me, I get frustrated. I love you unconditionally and when you love me back, I like the way it feels. I really appreciate everything that you've done for me and Princess. You deserve everything that you want in life and I'm willing to wait for you no matter how long that you're away. Everything will work itself out in due time. God would not put anything on you that He didn't think that you were able to handle so remain strong and stay encouraged. I hope that you're reading your Quran. Don't allow your surroundings to kill your spirit. Stay on your Deen and don't let this situation break you down because you're a diamond in the rough. Whatever it is that you're going through, let me go through it with you, don't shut me out. If you keep that anger bottled up inside, it's only going to turn into poison and poison shouldn't be in your system, especially in that type of environment. I know how you are and I don't want you to get into any trouble. Please write me back so I'll at least know that you're alright.

I Love You,

Keisha

After reading the letters, my spirits were lifted a little bit. It felt good receiving words of encouragement from my family and friends. It was during the hard times that the ones who cared about you held it down while the imposters faded away. I guess that the old saying is true (out of sight out of mind).

As I began to correspond to Keisha's letter, Sincere returned from the recreational yard drenched in sweat.

"Peace King!" he stepped into the cell.

"Peace!" I returned the greeting. "Did you get a good work out?"

"True indeed, I jogged for about two miles and then I hit the pull up bar for the rest of yard call. I don't know why you didn't come out with your boy?"

Sincere was from Brooklyn but was well known throughout the five boroughs. He was serving a twenty year sentence for robbery and attempted murder. Sincere was laid back and I liked his style. He spent the majority of his time reading and working out to help sustain his mind above the madness surrounding him. He was a very conscious black man who constantly educated me about our African Heritage and the treachery of the Europeans across the west. Well versed in politics, religion, philosophy, and law, Sincere was able to articulate when he spoke. He spent a number of hours in the law library, researching his case in hopes to find any loophole that would grant him his freedom. The administration revered him because he was a standup person who never backed down regardless of the circumstances. Although I didn't agree with all of his theologies, I listened whenever he spoke because generally, he was on point and his theories made sense.

"I just did some pushups a minute ago," I declared. "But I might go out there this evening and run a couple of laps."

"You've been saying that for two weeks now and I haven't seen you go out there and run a lap yet," Sincere shot back.

"That's my word," I laughed. "If I don't come out there this evening, I'll get out there in the morning and work out with you."

"Alright, I'm going to hold you to your word."

"Our word is all we got in here."

Sincere nodded in agreement. "Let me go and jump in the shower before these knuckle heads use up all of the hot water," he rushed out of the cell with his hygiene products.

It was time to offer Salat so I walked over to the sink and purified myself for prayer. As I brushed my teeth, I stared at the man in the mirror. I had come so far but still had a long way to go in making that transition from gangster to becoming a true believer in Islam. In my mind, I was ready to accept all of the responsibilities that came along with being Muslim but deep down in my heart, I still desired the life of the world. Ever since accepting Islam into my life, I've experienced serenity so why would I want to go back to realm of chaos and confusion? That was the question that I wrestled with on a daily basis.

As-salaam-alaikum, Ahki," someone greeted.

I turned around to see Musa, standing behind me, holding a prayer rug underneath his arm.

"Wa-alaikum-salaam-rahmatulah," I returned the salutations of peace.

"Are you ready to offer Salat?" he asked.

Musa was the Imam of the Islamic community inside of the prison. He was one of the most knowledgeable brothers on the compound, regarding the Deen so the Muslims went to him for advice and spiritual guidance. When I first got to the institution, Musa took me under his wing and educated me in the proper way to practice the religion. He taught me to speak Arabic and gave me the attribute Malik which translated to King in the Arabic language. Musa was five years my senior and had traveled a similar path which made it simple for him to identify with my struggles. He was serving a life sentence for a murder that he'd committed during a drug transaction that went bad. He was out of control when he initially entered into the system but once he found the Deen, he'd found peace within himself.

"I was coming to get you after I made wudu," I said, drying my face and hands.

"After you get yourself together, meet me in the chapel," Musa responded. "I'm going to go and round up some more of the brothers to join us for prayer."

"Insha Allah, I'll be there in a minute."

♟ ♟ ♟ ♟

When I stepped into the worship area, the muezzin was reciting the call for prayer. I fell into rank and stood shoulder to shoulder, heel to heel with my brothers in Islam, waiting for Musa to begin.

"Allahu Akbar!" he recited.

"Allahu Akbar!" we repeated in unison.

We offered four rakats for Asr salat then afterwards a few silent supplications were said amongst ourselves before dispersing back to our regular activities. On the way back to the tier, Musa and I took our time as we discussed a couple issues.

"What's on your mind Malik?" Musa questioned. "You seem to be a little distant today."

"I jive been buggin out lately, but I'll be alright," I replied.

"Why are you bugging out?"

"I don't know Ock, I just been stressing about some other stuff that's been going on in the free world."

Musa stopped walking and turned and faced me.

"Talk to me and tell me what's bothering you my brother."

I looked at him and took a deep breath. "The streets is calling me Ock and the voice inside of my head is getting louder and louder."

"That's the devil whispering in your ear, trying to get you to revert back to your old self."

"Don't get me wrong, I love this Deen and I know that Allah knows best but what am I supposed to do when I get out of here? All I know is the streets."

"That's the only thing that you want to know," Musa told me. "To change your self-perception, you must first change the way that you think."

"Every day that I wake up, I try to figure out my purpose, and the meaning behind my existence."

"You have to search within yourself," he declared. "That's the only way you'll ever know who you truly are."

A brief silence saturated the air as I allowed his words to marinate into my mind before he continued. "If you keep trying to cling on to the life of this world, you're going to lose it. I've been down for twelve years so I've seen all type of brothers accept the Deen. Some practice it to the utmost while others hang there kufi on the razor wire and forget about Allah as soon as they're released. Then when they get locked back up, they expect the brothers that never got a second chance to take them seriously. Their game is transparent, and I see right through them."

I could hear the anger in Musa's voice as he expressed himself.

"Some brothers are stronger than the others," I remarked. "You can't hold their mistakes against them."

"But a person who makes the same mistakes, expecting a different result, shows signs of insanity."

"What if a man is trying to feed his family?" I questioned.

"A man can't feed his family if he's incarcerated," Musa began walking again.

"You're absolutely right.' I agreed. "I don't know why I'm in such a hurry to get back out there in the streets when I know the end result is going to lead me back to prison if I don't get it right."

"If you don't get yourself killed."

"That thought has crossed my mind."

"I remember when you first got here," Musa reminisced. "You were a live wire with a short fuse just like the rest of us. Over the years, you've evolved into an intelligent young man and if you hold on to the Deen, Allah is going to do some miraculous things in your life."

"Alhumdu Allah!" I praised God.

"Do you know why I get so upset when I see brothers, claiming to be a Muslim but don't take Islam seriously?"

"Because you love the Deen!"

"And this may be the only opportunity that I have to practice Islam properly," Musa eyes began to water. "I might not make it out of here alive. I go to sleep and wake up every day with a life sentence on my back. All I got is Allah, so how do you think it makes me feel when I see a brother playing with the Deen like it's a game, coming back and forth to prison like it's cool".

By this time, the tears were flowing down Musa's face uncontrollably. I digested his words carefully because dying in prison was something that had never crossed my mind. Was I truly prepared for the test that awaited me once I was released from prison? Did I really want to go back to the life that I was living before incarceration? Over the years, I witnessed so many people fall victim and still hadn't learned my lesson.

♟ ♟ ♟ ♟

Sincere had his face buried into the USA Today when I returned from prayer. I picked up a section of the paper that he wasn't reading and began skimming the pages.

"The economy is hurting right now," I said.

Without looking up from the paper, Sincere responded.

"If these major manufacturing companies continue to go overseas, things are really going to get bad."

"Do you really think that it's going to get worse?" I asked.

"Hell yeah, it's going to get worse because it won't be any jobs for the people," he replied. "And if there aren't any jobs, the average working man is going to result to violence to feed his family."

"You think so?"

"I know so!"

Sincere set the paper down beside him and grabbed the chessboard.

"Do you feel like pushing the pieces?" he asked.

"You don't want to see me," I countered.

"It's only one way to find out."

I chose the black chess pieces and began setting up my side of the board as Sincere did the same with the white ones.

"Why do you always pick the black pieces?" he questioned.

"I like to see how you're going to come out."

"That's just how the Europeans want you think. They want to keep the black man on the defense and keep us wondering about what they're doing."

"It's not that serious."

"It is that serious," Sincere raised his voice. "Why do you think that the white pieces move first?"

I looked at Sincere and digested the jewel that he just dropped on me. He knew that he had the wheels inside my head turning.

"Can you see the signs?" he pushed his middle pawn two spaces.

Sincere loved playing chess; it was more than a game to him. He learned some of life's most valuable lessons through the fundamentals and enjoyed teaching the rudiments of everyday life through his tactics and strategies.

"Yeah, I see the signs," I moved a pawn forward.

"If you can understand chess, you can understand life. All you have to do is keep your eyes open."

By moving the knight into my territory, Sincere applied pressure. I countered by sliding one of my bishops into the cut like a snipper, hoping to catch him by surprise later on in the game.

"It's sixty-four squares on the board and you have to be aware of everyone just like you have to pay attention to everything that's going on around you in the streets. If you make one wrong decision, it can cost you your life or your freedom."

Sincere threatened my queen with his as he continued.

"And never revolve your game around a bitch because they come and go. You can always get another one if you mold her right," he pointed to a pawn.

After swapping out queens, I put his king in check with the bishop that I had placed in the cut earlier in the game. He blocked it with a pawn then castled after I countered attacked him with a knight.

"Pressure bust pipes but it also can make a diamond," he stated. "It's all about how you react when you're under pressure. There's only one King on the board and all the other pieces are soldiers and their job is to protect the King."

I studied the board and weighed my options, contemplating my next move. Thinking three moves ahead, I took a bishop with the knight that had invaded his territory.

"Checkmate!" Sincere glided his rook beside my king.

"Damn, I didn't see that," I yelled in frustration.

"That's why I told you to pay attention to everything around you; all sixty-four squares."

I looked at my alternatives on the board and seen where I had made my mistake.

"Damn, I slipped up!" I blurted.

"Slippers count," Sincere said. "But we learn more from our loses than we do we our wins. Remember that chess is just a game that we can start over but in life, you only get one shot to get it right and if you blow it, it's over."

Sincere and I exercised our brain power on the chessboard for the rest of the evening. For the better part of the night, he beat the breaks off of me. There wasn't any denying that his game was definitely better than mines; but the stronger the opponent, the higher my game elevated. Even though I couldn't beat him in chess, I took pleasure in the message that came along with defeat.

"Do you remember when I told you that there was only one king on the board?" he asked.

"Yeah, I remember."

"You're that king and all of those dudes that you surrounded yourself with in the streets are your soldiers. Your team is only strong as your weakest link and majority of those people that you had around you was only around because of what you had to offer, especially the broads. But the ones that are true to the game will stand tall with you win lose or draw. Be careful who you let into your circle because it's always the ones that are closest that can harm you because they know your moves."

I understood where Sincere was coming from because I had experienced deceit first hand. When things were good, everyone screamed that they would ride or die, claiming to be loyal. Now that the chips were down, the same ones who declared to be trustworthy weren't anywhere to be found.

♟ ♟ ♟ ♟

The next morning, Sincere had already left for the A.M. kitchen shift by the time that I awoke for Fajr prayer. After offering Salat, I read the Quran until it was time to eat breakfast. As I read Surah 103, I stopped to consider what the message was behind the verse:

"By the time, verily man is lost, except those who believe in monotheism and do righteous deeds and recommend one another to teachings of truth and of patience and consistency."

I had read and recited those words daily but for some reason, it seemed as if the Holy Quran was speaking to me; because I was lost and uncertain about the direction that I was headed. I wanted to believe that the only way that I would truly be successful was if I followed the Quran and the teachings of the Prophet Muhammad consistently, but there was something inside of me yearning for something else.

"Chow call!" The C.O. yelled through the tier.

Hearing the call for breakfast, I slipped into the single file line that was headed to the dining hall.

"Yo King!" someone summoned from the top tier.

Still in stride, I turned around slightly to see who had called my name. Once I seen Gip emerge from his cell, I slowed down a step or two so he could catch up.

"Hold up, I need to holla at you for a minute," he rushed down the steps.

I stepped out of line to see what he wanted. "What's good fam?" I asked as he approached. "That's what I'm trying to find out," he responded.

"You still got some of that Kush?"

"Yeah everything is still in play. What do you need?"

"I still got a couple of sticks of that presidential, but I got somebody that want to get a half ounce of that loud pack."

Gip was my eyes and ears inside of the prison. He kept me updated with the occurrences around the compound. Born and raised in the Central Park, one of Buffalo's most drug infested neighborhoods, Gip had the instincts of a seasoned hustler. If there was anything that someone needed inside of the facility, he was the person to see. It didn't matter if it was drugs, a shank, or a cellphone, Gip could make it happen as long as the money was right. Although we were from the same city, I watched Gip for several months before I approached him with a proposition. There was plenty of money to be made inside of prison and being that I had a female C.O. on the team, it was easy for me to get marijuana inside without being detected. The Muslims frowned upon the usage of drugs, so I offered Gip a 50/50 split if he distributed the monthly package and kept me off of the radar. He agreed to handle the day to day operation and deal with the other inmates as long as I was consistent with a reasonable number.

"Meet me on the yard when they call rec," I told him.

"A'ight, I'll be waiting for you near the pull up bar," he replied.

"That's a bet."

Once I returned from breakfast, I went back to my cell and sanitized my living quarters before exercising. One thousand pushups and five hundred crunches later, I jumped in the shower and performed ghusl for Friday prayer. Ghusl was a form of purification that every Muslim was obligated to administer to before Jumah Salat. Afterwards, I applied the scented oil that Musa had given me, during the month of Ramadan. As I stared at myself in the mirror, I began to appreciate the dedication that I spent on the pull up and dip bar. The hour's that went towards working out had my physic well defined.

Jumah wouldn't begin for another hour so I turned to Surah 18 (The Cave) inside of the Quran and began to read. The Cave was a chapter in the Quran that the Prophet Muhammad and his Companions recited every Friday. Following the tradition, I read the verses in Arabic. When I reached the 49th verse, I stopped for a brief moment and repeated the verse silently in English.

"And the book (one's record) will be placed in the right hand for the believer in the oneness of Allah and the left hand for a disbeliever in the oneness of Allah and you will see the criminal, polytheist and sinners fearful of that which they recorded therein. They will say: Woe to us! What sort of book is this that leaves neither a small thing nor big thing but has recorded it with numbers! And they will find all that they did before them, and your Lord treats no one with injustice." (Surah 18:49)

For the second time that day, I thought about the do's and don'ts of life. As someone proclaiming to be righteous, I understood the difference between right and wrong so why was it difficult for me to shun evil. Although prison was a controlled environment and the temptations were limited, I still searched for ways to cheat the system, knowing the odds were against me. I've been a gambler all my life but what makes a man want to roll the dice and risk his soul. Is it the love and respect that a person receives when they're on top? Maybe it's the power that they possess when calling the shots. Nah, the more that I thought about it, I had to agree that it was the money. Yeah in my case, it was definitely the money.

CHAPTER 28

THE NEW MILLENIUM

Happy New Year! The crowd screamed in unison as the clock struck 12:00 a.m. The Town Ballroom was filled to the capacity. Anybody who was somebody in the town came out to celebrate the New Millennium in style. Hustlers occupied the bar in multitudes, splurging and popping bottles. Gorgeous women strutted through the party in their most hypnotic outfit, attempting to entice a baller for a night of passion. Up in the V.I.P. there were buckets of champagne sitting on ice at every table. The sounds of Jay-Z cranked through the building as the Wolves stood center of attention, enjoying the scenery.

Nursing a double shot of Remy Martin, I observed my surroundings from afar; thinking about how much my life had changed over the past five years. At twenty-two, I felt like I had accomplished more than a person twice my age. Two years prior, I established a silent partnership with my brother Damon who operated a small restaurant uptown. I also invested in a couple rental properties throughout the city; one of them being a storefront that Keisha had converted into a salon. To someone on the outside looking in, it would've seemed like I was on top of the world but deep down inside there was a void that couldn't be filled.

Byrd staggered over, holding the Remy bottle and wrapped his arm around my neck.

"We made it my nigga!" he slurred. "We made it to see another year."

"And we're going to live to see many more.' I replied.

Over the years, Byrd had grown to become my closest and most loyal comrades.

"What's up with you?" he questioned. "Why you over here ducked off in the cut? Don't start that anti-social shit. You need to loosen up and get at these hoes."

"I'm straight."

He eyed me closely before he spoke again.

"I miss them boys too," he read my thoughts.

I examined the dance floor and swallowed the remainder of the cognac inside of the glass.

"It just doesn't seem right without them niggas," I grimaced from the warm liquid oozing down my throat. "They're supposed to be here with us popping bottles and all that shit that we talked about as shorties. They helped pioneer everything that we're doing and they're not here to reap the benefits."

Whenever I drank alcohol, I thought about TK, Jungle, and all of the fallen soldiers that we've lost to the graveyards and penitentiaries. Jungle and Shakim were found guilty of first-degree murder and sentenced to life in prison. My partner Trouble turned his life around after he almost lost it the day that he had gotten shot, trying to get at Vontae. Since then, he's settled down with the mother of his child and started a construction company. He still comes through the hood to reminisce with the crew once in a while, but he only sees the streets as a dead end. Then we were struck with another tragedy the day that Junior was decapitated in a motorcycle accident one morning, coming home drunk from the night club. As for the rest of the Wolves, they're still in the hood, chasing money. On TK's birthday, we all get together and throw a block party in his honor but things aren't the same without his presence.

"They'll always be with us," Byrd refilled my glass to the rim. "As long as we're out in the trenches, they'll continue to breathe through us."

Understanding the point that Byrd was trying to make, I polished off the drink and smashed the glass on the ground.

"This is for all of the gangsters that are not with us anymore!" Byrd shouted over the music.

He poured the rest of the Remy on to the broken glass disregarding that we were inside of a club. The spectators looked at us as if we were crazy as security moved in our direction to defuse the situation. Once they seen that it was Byrd and I putting on a spectacle, the bouncers pulled us to the side and asked if we could calm down. We agreed and made our way back to our section.

"Buy me a drink Byrd," a female said as we moved through the circus of people.

We looked up to see where the voice was coming from and noticed a short red bone, standing a few feet from us smiling.

"What's good Mya?" Byrd asked nonchalantly. "I haven't seen you in a minute, where you been hiding?"

"I've been looking for you," she responded seductively.

"You couldn't have been looking for me because I'm not hard to find."

"Well, what are you doing after you leave the club?"

"If everything goes as planned, I'll be doing you."

"Mmm hmm, we'll see," Mya turned her lips into a sneer. "You know how you be fronting."

"I got you boo," Byrd assured her. "Come and check me in the V.I."

Before we could step off, Mya stopped us short.

"Damn, can a bitch get something to drink?"

"Here," Byrd handed her the Remy bottle. "Go ahead and kill that."

As we walked off, Mya began screaming obscenities as she realized that the bottle was empty.

"You're silly as hell," I laughed.

"Fuck that bitch, she aint nothing but a tramp who always want something for free."

We joined the rest of the Wolves in the V.I.P. section and all eyes were on us as usual. We were looking fly as we posted up in our traditional spot. Slightly cocked to the right side of my head, I had on a Buffalo Bills cap to compliment the O.J. Simpson throwback jersey. The Roca Wear denim jeans added the right flavor to the all-white Air Force Ones, gracing my feet. I wasn't the type of hustler that longed for the attention that so many others yearned for. I wasn't into the bling and flashy jewelry, so my neck was bare and the only thing that was on my wrist were a few rubber bands. Byrd on the other hand was the complete opposite. He loved the attention. He had so many diamonds invading his jewelry, the colors of the rainbow reflected off of his pieces.

"Aye yo, what's up ma," Byrd shouted to the waitress across the room." Are you going to take my order or what?"

She stomped over with an attitude and began clearing off of the table.

"What do you want Byrd?" she spoke in a sinister tone.

"Don't come over here with an attitude girl," Byrd replied. "It's not my fault that yo ass had to work tonight."

"Don't start with me boy; I'm not in the mood for your bullshit. Now tell me what you want."

"You better be glad that I like you Sandra,"

She rolled her eyes up in her head, standing there with her hands on her hips. "Come on Byrd, I don't have all night to play with you. Are you going to order something or not?"

Byrd smiled as he exposed a large wad of C-notes.

"Bring me three bottles of Dom P and another bottle of Remy," he ordered.

Kim and Tasha were watching us from the bar. I acknowledged them with a wink of the eye, causing Kim to reciprocate with a naughty smile.

"Excuse me sweetheart. Do you see those two ladies over there at the bar?" I pointed, causing Sandra to turn around and look.

"Give them a bottle of whatever it is that their drinking," I added. "It's on me."

"Anything else?" Sandra asked.

"Nah, we cool," Byrd peeled her off.

She took the money and stepped off to fetch the liquor.

"Yo, what's up with shorty?" Polo asked, nodding at Sandra as he walked up. "Why she acting like that?"

"I was supposed to pick her up from work last night but I got caught up at the gambling spot," Byrd confessed. "You know how I get when I get to shooting dice."

"Don't nothing move but the money," Polo joked.

"Exactly!"

Right on key, the DJ began playing the song Get Money by the Notorious B.I.G causing the club to go crazy.

"If you're getting some muthafuckin money make some muthafuckin noise," he screamed through the microphone.

Voices exploded in the midst of the commotion as Sandra made her way back through the crowd, carrying the champagne above her head.

"That was my shit," Polo rocked his head to the beat.

"Yeah, niggas couldn't fuck with Big," Byrd countered. "He had the rap game on smash when this joint hit the streets."

"And we were getting a little bit of money when this song came out," I added.

Sandra set the bottles on to the table then handed Byrd his change.

"Don't insult me like that," he refused the money. "That's for you."

"Thank you but I'm still mad at you," Sandra pocketed the change.

Byrd cuffed her by the waist and pulled her in close. "I promise that I'm going to make it up to you."

She pulled away smiling. "Let me get back to work; I'll call you."

"Make sure that you do that. Don't be fronting."

Byrd and I were feeling ourselves. The sky was the limit and the world was for the taken. We had money, power, respect and enough women to go around. Minus the bullshit, life was good. Besides the fact that all of my friends weren't there to bring in the turn of the century with me, I couldn't complain. I was living the life that some people could only dream about.

Everyone in the club was vibrant. There wasn't a verbal or physical confrontation the entire night. People were enjoying themselves, drinking and dancing while others laughed and conversed at the bar. As the night progressed, I began to feel the effects of the alcohol. I staggered into the restroom, leaving the crew to attend to the extravaganza. As I relieved myself at the urinal, I felt the vibration from my cellular.

"Speak on it," I spoke into the receiver.

"Happy New Year's Boo."

I began smiling at the sound of Keisha's voice.

"Happy New Year's bae. What's up with you?"

"I'm waiting on you! Are you still at the club?"

"Yeah but I'm about to bounce in a minute."

"I miss you," she claimed in a sexy tone. "Are you coming over here when you leave there?"

"Yeah, give me about an hour," I slurred.

"Call me when you're on your way."

"Alright, I'll see you soon."

When I exited the restroom, Kim was standing in the foyer waiting for me. She pressed herself against me and placed her arms around my neck.

"Me give tanks for de bubbly star," she spoke in a drunken Caribbean accent. "It was well appreciated."

"You don't have to thank me," I told her. "I just want to make sure that you and your peoples enjoy yourselves."

"Me see you and your breadren in ere doing ya ting."

"We're not the only ones. You and Tasha are in here looking good as a muthafucka."

Kim spun around slowly in her alligator stilettoes, modeling off the red Donna Karen mini dress along with a DKNY hand bag.

"Ya like?" she struck a pose.

"I love it," I replied. "You look like a million dollars in small bills."

She giggled and fell back into the comfort of my arms. Kim and I had become well acquainted over time and she was definitely an asset to the team. Calling her a dime piece would be an understatement. Kim was Jamaican bombshell, a Caribbean princess to say the least. There were a number of hustlers competing for her attention, but regardless of the money they spent or the dreams they promised, Kim remained true to me. Besides being beautiful, she was smart, and she knew how to maneuver and manipulate her way in the streets. About a month ago, she pulled up on me at the park in an Expedition truck, sitting on twenty-two-inch rims. The vehicle belonged to a guy from the eastside by the name of Angelo who Kim had been dating. I excused myself from the conversation that I was having with Polo and walked over to see what she was talking about. She quickly handed me a set of keys and an address to Angelo's stash house. Kim had left Angelo at a hotel on the outskirts of town asleep. After having sex and draining him for his energy, she drove to the nearest hardware store and duplicated his keys.

After bringing them to me, she hurried back before he woke up and began getting suspicious. The following day, I sent Doo Wop and Melo up in the spot to search around. They discovered two bricks of cocaine and a couple of pistols. After gathering everything into a knap sack, they broke a window to make it look as if it were a breaking and entering.

"Can me come check ya tonight or do ye need to check in wit de wife?" Kim teased.

"I'm a grown man. I don't have to check in with anybody."

"Ya say dat now but luv makes da toughest rude boy go soft."

"So now I'm getting soft?" I laughed.

"Ya tell I if ya getting tender for da poon poon dat ya gurl give ta ya, cause me not seen ya in a week," she expressed.

"Don't worry baby, daddy will make it better," I squeezed her tight.

"So me guess me not leaving wit ya?"

"Yeah, we will slide out of here after I holler at my man," I assured her. "Go ahead and let Tasha know that you're leaving with me."

The admiring eyes stared as Kim sashayed her way over to where Tasha was dancing near the bar. Her ass bounced with every step that she took and the mini skirt, hugging her hips left little room for the imagination. I marveled at her bowlegged walk.

"I'm about to go and give her the business!" I thought to myself.

When I re-entered the VIP, I pulled Polo aside. "I'm about to bounce with Kim," I told him. "Let me hold your burner until tomorrow morning."

"You're going to leave me out here naked?" he quizzed.

"You already know that Byrd got his hammer on him in case something pops off."

Polo reached under his Averex Leather and inconspicuously passed me the Glock 40.

"Be careful," he warned. "It's already one in the head."

"I got it," I tucked it on my hip.

"What time are you getting up in the morning?"

"Why, what's up?"

"I'm trying to grab a big eight from you first thing on the A.M."

"Alright, just hit me up as soon as you get started and I'll swing through your crib."

"How much are you going to charge me?"

"I need twenty-eight."

"Come on fam, look out for me," Polo pleaded. "I got twenty-five."

"I need twenty-eight," I repeated. "I only got a quarter block left and I can't afford any shorts."

"Is it some butter?"

"Burn clean," I confirmed.

"Alright, whenever you get out and about come to my mom's building."

"I'll be there between nine and ten so make sure that you're woke."

"I'm going to be up and at it early," Polo said. "Just don't have me waiting for you all day because you know how you do?"

"Don't worry family, I got you," I gave him some dap.

I made my last minute rounds and conversed momentarily amongst the room while Kim stood across the bar impatiently. As I got closer to the exit, I locked eyes with her and signaled for her to follow me.

♟ ♟ ♟ ♟

"Oooohh fuck me poon poon... yeah.... just like that," Kim yelled as I stroked her from behind. "Oh shit... me feel it in me belly."

Her ass bounced up and down with every thrust.

"Damn girl, this shit don't make any sense," I reflected on how wet she was.

"Oh... please don't... don't stop."

"C'mere!" I instructed. "Put it in your mouth."

Without hesitation, Kim took me into her mouth and went to work immediately. I grabbed the back of her head as she slurped up the saliva, running down my scrotum. Kim was unmistakably a professional head hunter. She did her thing with skill; like it was a craft that she was determined to perfect. With the base of my organ in hand, she placed it in and out of her mouth at a steady pace and once her throat was relaxed, she took in every inch.

"Damn!" I groaned in pleasure.

Kim continued performing fellatio for the next ten minutes, stimulating me into a state of bliss. I began to tremble, releasing a load of semen down her esophagus. Tasting the flavor of the sticky fluids, she removed it from inside her mouth and ejaculated the remainder of the sperm onto her face. The sexual discharge left me drained as the consumption of alcohol settled in. Kim stood up from the bed and wiped her chin with the back of her hand. As she walked to the bathroom, I watched the outline of her nakedness move eloquently in the semi darkened room.

"King!" she called out from the bathroom. "C'mon and bave wit me."

"Here I come," I hollered back.

For the next three minutes, I laid there pondering.

"I might as well take a shower before I leave out," I thought.

Finally, I stood up and stumbled to the bathroom to join Kim in the shower. As the warm water from the nozzle beat against our bodies, I prayed that I sobered up long enough to make it home.

CHAPTER 29

THE DAY AFTER

Yo fam, where you at?" Polo screamed through the phone. "I've been waiting on you all morning. I thought that you were coming through between nine and ten."

The clock on the nightstand read 11:50 a.m.

"Damn, family that's my bad," I apologized. "I'm about to get up now. I'll be there in fifteen minutes."

I was still hung over from the night before. I rolled out of bed and quickly dressed in the same thing that I wore to the club. Ascending from the bed, Keisha observed me closely as I rambled through my pocket, searching for the keys to my car.

"Where do you think you're going? she inquired.

"I have to make a move real quick," I replied. "I'll be right back."

"All you do is run the streets and party with your friends. When are you going to spend some time with me?"

My head began spinning as I sat on the edge of the bed.

"Please don't start that shit," I rubbed my temples. "I already have a headache."

"Well maybe if you get some rest and quit jumping up every time that phone rings, your head wouldn't be hurting."

Keisha eased up behind me and started massaging my shoulders. "What you need to do is relax.

Between sentences, she kissed me on the neck.

"I'm going to go in the kitchen and fix you something to eat… then I'm going to give you a sponge bath… and after you finish soaking… I'm going to rub you down with oil… and if that doesn't make you feel better, I got something else that will get your head right," she added, reaching down the front of my pants.

True indeed, Keisha had stood by my side during the ups and downs. Our relationship had grown into something special over the years, but she still couldn't understand my commitment to the streets. She suffered many lonely nights due to my association with the underworld; and now that she was six months pregnant, she wanted me to settle down.

"Are you trying to seduce me?" I questioned.

"Is it working?"

"Mmm hmm."

Even containing an unborn seed in her stomach, Keisha was hard to resist.

"Check this out," I said, escaping her grasp. "Let me go handle this business and when I get back, you'll have my full undivided attention."

"Do I look like a fool to you?" she asked. "If you leave here, I might not see you again until the next day. Most of the time, I'm asleep when you come stumbling in here at five o'clock in the morning."

I slipped my hand inside of Keisha's robe and rubbed her belly, feeling the baby kick. "I promise you that I'm coming right back."

She opened up the drawer on the night stand, reached inside and pulled out my keys.

"Here," she tossed them on the bed.

"Why are you playing with my keys," I inquired.

"Just go!" she ordered with an attitude. "And you better come back."

"I'll be right back," I repeated with a smile. "And when I get back, I'm going to turn off the phone so that we're not distracted."

"I got to see that to believe it," she sneered.

♟ ♟ ♟ ♟

Yo Nas can't fuck with Jay-Z!" Melo barked.

"You must be crazy," Justice responded. "The god be spitting knowledge to you ignorant ass niggas. He be kicking actual facts; Jay be on some bullshit."

"Nah, Jay on that get money shit," Melo argued. "Nas can take that shit that he be talking about back to Africa because don't nobody want to hear that shit."

"If B.I.G was still alive, wouldn't either one of them niggas be eating," Doo Wop interjected.

This was the exchange of disagreements that I heard as I walked up the driveway. The young boys were always arguing about who they thought the best MCs in the industry were.

"What's up?" I stepped on the porch. "Where's Polo at?"

"He's in the house," Doo Wop established.

"Yo King, will you tell these boys that Nas is that illest nigga on the mic." Justice said.

"I could care less about them niggas," I told them. "Neither one of them is putting any money in my pocket."

"I heard that y'all niggas did it up big last night" he attempted to give me the blunt that he was smoking.

"Nah, I'm cool," I refused.

"Yeah, you must've been popped if you don't want to hit the smoke."

"I'm still on tilt from all of the Remy that we were drinking."

"You look like it," Doo Wop said.

"Yeah, it was a long night," I huffed. "After I go in here and holler at Lo, I'm going to go and lay it down."

"I need to scream at you before you leave," Doo Wop insisted.

"About what?"

"Go ahead and handle your business, I'll holler at you when you come out."

Out of all of the young boys, Doo Wop was the most thorough. Rain, sleet or slow, he was always the first one on the block and the last to leave. For years he had been on the sideline, watching and waiting for his turn. When the opportunity finally presented itself, Doo Wop took full advantage of the chance and handled his business.

I was engulfed by a fog of smoke when I entered the house. Shane was seated on the couch, smoking a blunt while bagging a pound of marijuana. He offered me the weed, but I declined.

"What time did you leave the club last night?" I asked.

"We chilled until the police came and shut it down." Shane replied.

"Why did they shut it down?"

"Do you remember the broad Shakila from Springer Street?"

"You're talking about shorty that pump weed for the dreads?"

"Yeah, her and her girl left a bitch leaking."

"For what?" I laughed.

"I don't know and I didn't stay to find out once the beast started spraying niggas with pepper spray," Shane said.

"I'm glad that I smashed out with my peeps before all of that shit jumped off."

"I figured that you snatched up a piece of ass when I didn't see you."

"That's all this nigga do," Polo stepped into the room. "If he could keep his mind off of pussy then I wouldn't be waiting around here missing money."

"My bad fam," I apologized.

"It's all good," he motioned me into the kitchen, "Let me see what you're working with."

He placed the digital scale on to the counter top as I retrieved the drugs from my pocket. When I balanced it on the scale, it read 126 grams. Satisfied with the weight, Polo handed me a wad of bills. He examined the product as I began counting the money.

"I didn't put anything on that," I told him. "That's straight drop."

"It looks like it's some fire," Polo remarked.

"You cool?"

"Yeah, I'm straight," he said.

"I'm going to get with you in a minute. I'm about to go to the building and lay it down."

"No doubt, I'll be out here. Swing back through if you come out?"

"That's a bet."

When I stepped back on to the porch, a light snow had begun to fall from the heavens above. Melo and Justice were still debating about the music industry while Doo Wop was next door, negotiating with a fiend. He looked up from the transaction that he was about to make due to the sound of my cell phone.

"Speak on it," I spat into the receiver.

"Where you at?" Keisha questioned.

"Girl don't rush me, I'm on the way."

"Could you stop at the store and get some rice to go with the chicken?"

"Yeah, I can do that."

"Can you also bring me and the baby some ice cream?" she asked politely.

"Bye girl!" I pressed the end button.

As I was ending the call, Doo Wop was coming towards me. "Do you still got some work left King? he asked.

"All I have is a big left."

"Let me get it."

"Alright, I'll be right back."

"How long are you going to be?" Doo Wop asked.

"I'll be back in ten minutes," I told him.

He counted out the money and handed it to me.

"Give it to Justice if I'm not here when you get back."

♟ ♟ ♟ ♟

Keisha was seated in front of the television with an attitude by the time I finally returned. She ignored my presence as she flipped through a Victoria Secret magazine. After setting the groceries in the kitchen, I grabbed the remote and plopped down next to her. Once I switched the channel, Keisha snapped.

"I was watching that!"

"How are you watching T.V. and reading the magazine at the same time?"

"You can really be an asshole sometimes, you know that?"

"Why, because I changed the channel?"

"You said that you were coming back in twenty Minutes," Keisha threw the magazine at me. "And here it is two hours later."

I blocked the book from hitting me in the face and chuckled. "At least I brought you and the baby back some ice cream."

"I'm serious King," she pouted. "Why do I always have to come second?"

"You don't," I defended. "I had to make another run and it took a little longer than I expected."

"See that's what I'm talking about. Why can't you put the streets on hold for me instead of putting me on hold for the streets?"

"C'mere," I gestured for her to move closer.

She scooted next to me and placed her head on my chest.

"Everything that I'm out here doing in these streets is for us," I rubbed her stomach.

"That's not true," Keisha argued. "I don't need all of the extra stuff. I'm satisfied with the simple things in life. All I want is you."

"And all I want to do is provide a better future for you and the baby."

"And I appreciate everything that you do but if God wants us to have it then he'll provide us with it."

"I guess it's supposed to just fall out of the sky, huh?" I snickered. "Nah, if a nigga want something then he has to go out there and get it."

"Whatever happened to working for it?

"Here we go again," I huffed. "You want me to go out here and work for someone for the next thirty years and then live off of social security until I die."

"It's better than being locked up for thirty years."

"Locked up?"

"Yeah, locked up," she repeated. "It's a chance that you'll go to prison for whatever it is that you're doing; and where does that leave me? Raising our child alone? Coming to visit you on the weekends and then explaining to our child why daddy isn't here? I don't want to live like that."

Ever since Keisha had gotten pregnant, I've been re-evaluating my situation, but her last statement really had my wheels turning. Prison had crossed my mind on many occasions and I understood that it came with the territory but thirty years in jail was something that I didn't want to experience. Caught between the ying and the yang, I juggled with a life altering decision.

"I'm going to chill," I spoke in a low tone.

Keisha raised her head to look into my face. "What do you mean, you're going to chill?"

"Give me another year and I'm going to stop hustling in the streets."

"A year?"

"One year from today," I confirmed.

"Do you promise?"

"I promise, but you gotta let me do me. You can't be stressing me out with all your emotional bullshit. My mind has to be focused."

"Alright, I'll give you your space," she smiled. "But you still have to spend at least one day out of the week with me."

"I can do that. Now can you take your spoiled ass in the kitchen and make me some something to eat? I'm hungry as hell."

For the reminder of the evening, Keisha and I enjoyed one another's company. We cuddled up on the sofa and ate ice cream while watching the movies she'd rented. I couldn't remember the last time that I had took a day to relax and I could tell from Keisha's demeanor that she was pleased to have me home for a change. We were expecting our first child, so her emotions were running wild. The life that I was living had her concerned. She spent a lot of time in prayer, invocating to GOD to change my heart. A million thoughts went through my mind as I held her in my arms. I knew that she deserved better and as I stared at the twinkle in her eye, I wanted to be the one that provided it for her. Although we were from two completely different worlds, our souls seemed to gravitate towards each other. I wanted to believe that I could change and settle down, but the pleasures of hustling were becoming more addictive than the drug itself. I dosed off, thinking of ways to expand and incorporate my dreams into a reality, so the question wasn't should I quit, but could I quit.

CHAPTER 30

DON'T TRY TO LIE NOW

"WHO IN THE FUCK IS KIM?"

I awoke to the sound of Keisha's voice screaming uncontrollably as she overlooked me, lying in the bed. In her hand, she held on to my cell phone with a tight grip and by the expression on her face, I could tell that it was going to be a long and complicated morning. In an attempt to gather my bearings, I sat up and placed my feet on the floor.

"What are you talking about?" I finally found the courage to reply.

"You know what I'm talking about?" she grimaced. "Now tell me who she is!"

The silence on my behalf confirmed the inner guilt that was conveyed on the surface.

"Don't get quiet now," she continued. "Answer the question."

"Yo, why are you going through my phone?"

"Are you fucking her?"

"You trippin!"

Keisha took a deep breath as she fought to hold back her tears. "You know what King at this point, I don't even care. If you want to be out there messing around with all of these non-descript hoes, go ahead and do you but leave me alone."

"Come here!" I attempted pull her towards me.

"No, get off of me," she snatched away.

"Come here, let me talk to you."

"No, there's nothing that you can say. I'm tired of you telling me how much that you love me and that everything that you're doing is for me and the baby. I'm starting to believe that all that is some bullshit because the only person that you care about is yourself. Everything that you're doing out there in them streets is to satisfy King. You're selfish and karma is a bitch!"

"What's that supposed to mean?" I asked her.

"It's exactly what it sounds like," Keisha tossed the phone on the bed as she walked out of the room.

I exhaled as I picked up the phone from off the mattress. The text messages from the last 24 hours between Kim and I appeared on the screen clear as day. Quickly leaping from the bed, I hurried into the living area behind Keisha.

"Yo, let me talk to you for a minute," I clutched her by the arm.

"Don't touch me!" she broke loose.

"Why you acting like that? I just want to talk!"

"What can you possibly say?" Keisha stared at me in disgust. "The best thing you can do right now is leave and give me some space! I don't even want to look at you right now."

With tears in her eyes, Keisha rushed back into the bedroom and slammed the door. Determined to resolve the issue, I attempted to enter but it was locked shut. From behind the door, I could hear her weeping softly. The pain that I had initiated due to my recklessness caused me to become uncomfortable as I listened to her snivel. With an uneasy feeling in the pit of my stomach, I slipped on an old pair of Timberlands along with a sweat suit and left the house.

♟ ♟ ♟ ♟

When I entered my mother's house, Ma Dukes was seated in the front room watching television. She immediately knew that something was bothering me the moment I walked through the door. As I took a seat next to her on the couch, she took notice of the ill-tempered energy in my body language.

"What's wrong with you?" she raised a brow.

"Me and Keisha had a little argument but it's all good!" I down played it.

"What you do?"

"Why you think that I did something. Why it couldn't've been her?"

"Because you're my son and I know the look on your face when you've done something that you ain't got no business doing."

I snickered, knowing all too well the look that she was referring to. "She went through my phone and found a text message from a broad that I know."

"Why was she going through your phone?" Ma Duke asked.

"That's my point exactly! If she wasn't looking for something, she wouldn't find nothing."

"No King, if you weren't doing anything, she wouldn't find anything. You want to run around here with all of these fast ass girls and then get an attitude when Keisha catches you. If Keisha is who you're going to be with, you're going to have to make a decision. If not, quit wasting that girl time and let her live her life."

"What about the baby?"

"What about the baby?" Ma Dukes said. "You're going to make sure that the baby is alright regardless if you and Keisha are together or not. You don't have to be with someone to take care of your child."

"But I don't want another dude around my kid!" I defended.

"Like I said, you got a decision to make. Do you love that girl?"

"Yeah, I care about her."

"Then you need to act like it and stop playing games because you're going to mess around and lose her if you're not careful."

"I hear you Ma but sometimes I'm not with it! I want to live my life without all the restrictions. I shouldn't feel like I got to answer to somebody about how I come and go! And when I don't do what they want me to, they get an attitude. All that emotional stuff is draining."

"You see that's the problem! You want the benefits of what comes with being in a relationship, but you don't want the responsibility that it brings. Boy, if you're not Caesars son!"

"Ma, why you always do that?" I sneered.

"What?" she frowned.

"Compare me to him," I contested.

"Because you act just like him to the point where it's déjà vu. And that's not a bad thing because your father was a good man, he just made some wrong decisions at times and you have those same characteristics."

"Give me an example?"

"First of all, y'all have a problem with authority and second you both like to run around, chasing these loose females that don't care anything about you when y'all got a good woman at home."

"C'mon Ma!" I breathed heavily. "You sound like you're taking her side.

"I'm not taking her side; I'm just telling you the truth." she chuckled. "You're putting Keisha through some of the same nonsense that I had to tolerate out of Caesar. She's is a good girl but there's only so much that a female can take."

Ma Dukes had become my voice of reason whenever Keisha and I were at odds. She was always able to bring a balance and have me look at things from another point of view. Her comparison between me and Pops was a strategic way to get me to identify with the hardships that she suffered, concerning my father's lifestyle. She knew that I was uneasy with the mistreatment that she had to bear; so why would I place Keisha in a similar dilemma, knowing what my moms had gone through.

"I understand what you saying Ma, but you and Pop's situation was a little different," I reasoned.

"How so?" she waited for a response.

"Y'all were married!" I declared. "Keisha and I don't have any papers. We can walk away whenever we choose to."

"You're absolutely right but let me tell you this: When a woman loves a man, I don't care if they're married or not, she's not going to just let him just walk away without a fight. You and Keisha are about to have a child, so you'll always be connected in one way or another. And although a baby can't keep you in a relationship, you should always make sure that woman is taken care of properly if she's taken care of your child. That's the responsibility of a real man."

"That's a fact!" I agreed. "Shorty got my seed inside of her, so I got to make sure that she's good. I'm just not with all of the drama! I can do without all that"

"Well quit doing stuff that's going to cause a problem," my mother stated. "You're still not looking at the part that you're playing to bring the drama!"

Seconds later my phone chirped with the sound of a bell, alerting me that I had received a message. I looked down at the mobile device and chuckled as I read the text from Keisha.

I can't believe that you would play me like this after all that we've been through. It's all good tho because shit is about to change once I have my baby. I'm sick of your ass! You ain't shit! You can go ahead and keep fucking that bitch just stay the fuck away from me. CLOWN!!!!

After reading the message, I shook my head in frustration. I couldn't believe that I forgot to erase the tread between me and Kim. How could I be so careless? I made several attempts to call Keisha but was sent directly to the voicemail. The distress caused by my recklessness had her in her feelings. I just hoped that the anguish that she was subjected to wouldn't have an effect on the baby.

CHAPTER 31

SILK

A few weeks had passed by and I still hadn't spoken to Keisha. Although I extremely missed being in her presence, my pride wouldn't allow me to reach out and call. Time healed all wounds, so I figured that she would extend the invitation to talk whenever she was ready. Plus, the time a part gave me the opportunity to concentrate on my affairs in the streets without interruption. In order to get to the bread, I had to be laser focused and not allow my personal life to interfere. Every day it seemed like the stakes were being raised and the risks that I had to take in order to survive in the game were more dangerous. Checking my rearview, I circled the block before parking on the side of Fosters Bar and Grill. As a precaution, I cocked the Ruger, placing one in the chamber as I grabbed the duffle off of the seat and exited the vehicle. The smell of fried fish and collard greens greeted me at the door as I entered the bar. A feeling of nostalgia took me back to a place that I remembered as a kid. Except for the new faces occupying the place, everything still looked the same.

"Hey Nadine, is Silk around?" I approached the lady behind the bar.

"Yeah, he's in the back," she quickly responded. "You need to talk to him?"

"He should be expecting me!" I told her.

Nadine picked up the phone and called Silk. She looked at me and nodded as he instructed her from the other end of the line. Once the call ended, Nadine pressed the buzzer, unlocking the door to the private room, permitting me to enter. The office space was extravagantly furnished with a Lexington Leather Sofa across from a brownstone Madison bar cabinet against the far wall. From the ceiling hung a plasma television which was used as a security monitor to survey the premises. On the floor laid an aristocrat carpet that felt like you were walking on air with

each step. Silk stood up from behind his glass desk and greeted
me with a firm handshake.

"How's it going King?" he said. "Have a seat."

I did as directed as Silk made his way over to the bar
cabinet and poured us both a drink.

"What are we looking like?" he handed me the glass of
liquor.

In return, I gave him the small duffle bag that I was
carrying.

"I need three of em," I told him.

For the past couple of years this had become a normal
routine. Silk had some of the best cocaine in the town and none
of the local supplier could compete with his prices. He only
administered to a small alliance of clientele which permitted him
to operate under the radar. Majority of the hustlers that he dealt
with were relationships that he had built for over twenty years.
The only reason he even considered doing business with a
young nigga like me was because of the correlations with my
Pops.

"Alright, I'm going to have Marco meet you at the car
wash on Main and Northampton at nine o'clock tomorrow
morning," he proclaimed. "Make sure that you're on time!"

"I'll be there first thing in the A.M.," I assured him.

"How's your father doing?" Silk took a sip of his drink.

"I haven't been up there to see him in a minute but he's
good!"

"Tell him that I asked about him the next time you talk
to him."

"I'll make sure that I tell him."

"On another note, we need to talk," Silk sat on the edge
of his desk.

I took a drink from the glass as I searched his face
closely. The gravity in his voice was stern, so I assumed
whatever it was that he wanted to talk about was substantial. So,
I prepared myself.

"What's good?" I questioned with a raised brow. "What
you want to talk about?"

Silk took another sip from his drink, gathering his
thoughts.

"Why do you hustle?" he finally spoke.

"Huh?" I was caught off guard by the question.

.   "Why do you hustle?" Silk repeated. "Why do you risk your life in these streets every day?"

"I do it for the same reason that everybody else do it; for the money!"

"Is it really for the money or is it for what the money can do for you?" Silk tested. "Because some of these niggas do it for these bitches, others do it for the fame and then you have those that don't know why they do it, they're just trying to be accepted by any and everybody that'll accept them. You see when me and your father was coming up, it took a special type of person to be a hustler. You couldn't just wake up, watch a music video and go on the block and start pumping. It was levels to this game and you had to get permission from those that controlled the neighborhood before you started doing your own thing. You might've had two or three hustlers in the neighborhood that was really getting down for theirs, now you got a hundred niggas on one block, fighting over the same dollar. Renegades! No structure! And in order to thrive in this way of life, you need some type of order, otherwise you're just another nigga who only exists for the moment, waiting to get killed or go to jail."

"That's deep!" I said.

"Nah King, that's real!" Silk countered. "Have you ever thought about the probability of the people that make it out of the streets successfully?"

"What you mean?"

"I want you to think about everybody that you know that ever hustled in the streets, rather they sold dope, robbed, pimped, whatever their hustle was. Then I want you to think about all of the hustlers that you know that made it out successfully. I'm talking about, they got their money and walked away clean."

An unnerving silence submerged the room as I sought my mind for the answer. Silk sat on the desk, staring at me with a blank expression, anticipating my reply.

"I can't name anybody that I know who made it out successful," I admitted.

"So, what makes you think that you're any different?" he grilled me.

"That's a good question."

"Well, I got news for you my friend," Silk continued. "You're not different. You're not any different than anybody that came before you or the ones that will play the game after you. Now there is a few that do get lucky and slip through the cracks, but it's not many. You got to know when to hold and when to fold young fella."

"Let me ask you something!" It was my turn to ask the questions. "From the outside looking in, it seems like you're doing pretty well for yourself, so why don't you walk away while you're ahead?"

"Listen here King; I sold my soul to the devil a long time ago," he chuckled. "I couldn't stop if I wanted to. There are too many people that I feed who depend on my hustle. I accepted my fate a while back and I'm okay with the decision that I've chosen. I'm going to embrace whatever they give me when my time comes. It's inevitable! And we're not exempt from those consequences."

"I often have thoughts of leaving but I haven't reached my number yet."

"And you'll never reach that number because that's how the devil works. Nothing is ever enough! And when you do obtain that amount that you're comfortable with, another obstacle will always be around the corner waiting for you. It takes discipline to get yours and get out. The problem with our people is that we have no discipline. We're greedy! And greed has always been our down fall."

Silk spoke like a true scholar when it came to the rudiments of the game. He had a way of articulating himself which made me think and I couldn't help but wonder where he was going with this conversation.

"You need to be coming up with an exit plan!" Silk continued. "You have a good head on your shoulders with the world at your fingertips. You got options! Don't let these streets pull you in to the point where it's your only alternative. You still got a chance King. Don't be like me and your father and wake up old, wondering where the time went!"

"This ain't my end game Unk, I got a plan!" I told him. "I've been investing in some other things to clean my bread up. Me and brah got the restaurant and I got a few houses that's beginning to generate some income but it's not enough to support the lifestyle that I've grown accustom to."

"Well then maybe it's time to sacrifice and downgrade your lifestyle in order to cash out in the long run. Remember, it's the turtle who won the race."

My mind was whirling in a thousand directions when I left Silk's office. There was something valid in the information that he conveyed to me. He spoke from experience and could relate to the road that I was exploring because he had traveled a similar path. Keisha and Ma Dukes were always encouraging me to leave the streets alone and I understood their concerns, but they couldn't connect with what I was going through. The picture that Silk painted was more vivid because he could identify with the difficulties that a young man faced daily as he scuffled to find his way. He was just trying to provide the navigation so that I didn't crash.

♟ ♟ ♟ ♟

Early the next morning, Marco was waiting in a parking space in the far-right corner when I pulled up to the car wash. I checked my watch and noticed that he arrived twenty minutes earlier than the prearranged time. As expected, he was seated on the passenger side of the vehicle, surveying the surrounding area. After parking the vehicle next to his, Marco gestured for me to jump in the car with him.

"What's good fam?" I greeted as I slid into the driver seat.

"Business as usual, player," he returned, motioning me to drive through the car wash.

Without another word, I did as I was instructed as Marco raised the volume on the stereo system. He spoke in a low pitch as I drove on to the conveyer track and into the high-powered jets of water mixed with detergent.

"There are three bricks in the trunk underneath the spare tire," he informed. "Once you get it to where it's going, park the car on Wyoming and Pembroke near the train tracks."

"Where do you want me to leave the keys?"

"You can leave them over the sun visor."

"Alright, cool!" I said.

"Make sure that you put your seatbelt on and be careful," Marco advised.

Once we exited the tunnel, he quickly departed and hopped into a tinted out Sedan that was waiting for him as the attendants approached to dry the vehicle. A light chuckle escaped my mouth as I thought about Silk. I had to admit, the system that he implemented to remain off of the radar was smooth and I respected the precautions that he took to conduct business. It was a science attributed to his success and why he was able to last so long in the game. The sound of my cell phone broke me out of my thoughts. I tipped the attendant with a five dollar bill then answered the call as I pulled out of the station.

"Hello?" I picked up after a few rings.

"Where you at?" Keisha responded.

"I'm out handling some business, what's up?"

"Why haven't I heard from you?"

"The last time that I seen you, you didn't want to hear nothing that I had to say."

"I didn't want to hear the lies that you were about to tell me."

"What the fuck is you talking abo…" I caught myself and took a deep breath.

I could feel my blood about to boil but I wasn't about to allow Keisha to take me off of my square this early. I had a full day ahead of me so her shenanigans would have to wait until later.

"Listen babe, I'm not trying to argue with you," I resumed. "I'll stop by the house later when I'm finished handling my business, okay?"

"I'm not arguing," Keisha said. "I just want to know why I haven't heard from you. It's been two weeks and you haven't called to check up on me."

"Babe, I've been busy and I wasn't trying to be around all that negative energy; but I'll be over there when I get done doing what I'm doing."

"Oh now you too busy huh? You probably over there busy with your little bitch! I swear on everything that I love when I catch that hoe, I'ma set her ass on fire!"

"You buggin!" I shook my head. "Let me get off of this phone while I'm driving. I'll be over there in a minute to talk to you."

"Yeah okay, I ain't showed you buggin yet," she spat. "But I'm going to bug out on you and that bitch when I find her!"

"You sound crazy!" I snickered. "You're pregnant, talking about, setting somebody on fire. You need to go sit yo ass down somewhere and chill before you fuck around and have a miscarriage on some bullshit."

"Fuck you, you bitch ass nigga!" Keisha screamed with venom on her tongue.

"Now I'm a bitch ass nigga," I let out another chuckle. "You know what I'ma talk to you later!"

I ended the call as Keisha continued to shout out more obscenities, attempting to get beneath my skin. Seconds later the phone was chiming off again, causing me to develop an attitude.

"What!" I answered in a harsh voice.

"Oh, now we're hanging up? Keisha matched my tone. "Is that what we're doing? You're hanging up on me now?"

"Why are calling, fucking with me?" I exhaled. "It's too early for this shit."

"Because I feel like it!" she returned.

"I thought that you didn't want to argue?" I spoke in a more controlled manner.

"You know what, you're going to keep playing with me and get exactly what you're looking for!"

"And what's that?"

"You'll see!" Keisha declared. "It ain't no fun when the rabbit got the gun!"

"So what, you threatening me?"

"Nah, I'm not threatening you but like I told you before karma is a bitch!"

"Whatever man, I aint stunting that shit."

"You don't got to be stunting it, but I got your number though!"

"Are you done?" I asked sarcastically.

"Ooh, I HATE YOU!" she yelled right before hanging up.

"She bugged out!" I huffed and tossed the phone onto the passenger seat.

CHAPTER 32

COOK UP

"Hello?"

"What up, King?"

"What up, who this?" I questioned.

"You don't know my voice nigga, this Polo," he verified.

"Oh, what's good Lo?

"Coolin, where you at?"

"Over here with Byrd, what's good?"

"I need to come and holler at you, did you get some more work?"

"What the fuck wrong with brah, you know that these phones are filthy!" I barked with an attitude.

"My bad fam," he apologized. "Where y'all at so I can pull up."

"We're at the spot on Stockbridge," I told him. "Stop at the store and get a Dutch Master on your way."

"Alright, I'll be there in a minute."

When I ended the call, I turned to Byrd and shook my head.

"That nigga trippin," I told him.

"Why, what happened?" Byrd replied from the kitchen.

"Just talking reckless on the phone like this shit that we doing is legal. Niggas is getting way too comfortable around here. I'm about to switch some shit up."

"That sounds about right."

For the better part of the day, Byrd and I had been cooking and bagging up the product, getting it ready for the streets. The fumes from the cocaine were strong, lingering throughout the kitchen into the other areas of the apartment. Similar to a chemist, Byrd stood over the stove, mixing the contents of the oil and baking soda together. It was magic, the way he twirled the fork around the pot like a wizard with a wand, making an extra seven grams appear on every ounce that was cooked. After it dried, I proceeded to package the drugs into eight balls, ounces and big eighths, obtaining an additional 252 grams per kilo. The process was exhilarating and draining all in the same. The potential profit margin caused us to be enthusiastic although the procedure it took to get there was a little tedious.

"Here's the last of it," Byrd announced, setting a slab of crack on the newspaper to air out.

"You're really a beast with this shit," I responded, examining the drugs.

"I know my way around the kitchen a little bit," he chuckled.

Byrd skills were A1 when it came to cooking up the work. Out of everyone in the crew, he was the only one that could bounce it and still keep it raw. Still analyzing the creation that he produced, I held a piece up to the sunlight, beaming through the window.

"It's like glass," I marveled. "You're going to have to teach me how to chef it up like you."

"If I do that, you might try to X me out," Byrd joked.

We both chuckled slightly, knowing that his statement disclosed a hint of truth. Any ability that a person possessed to earn them some additional bread made them an asset. A rule of thumb that we learned early was to play our hand close to our chest, so I respected Byrd's train of thought. While we were in the middle of wrapping everything up, there was a knock at the door, causing him to reach for his pistol.

"Chill, that's probably Lo, coming to holler at us," I said, rising up from the table.

Byrd tucked his gun but remained on point as I went and peeked through the blinds. On the other side of the door, Polo stood there on the swivel, nervously looking up the street in both directions

"What's good brah?" I opened the door, allowing him to enter.

"Peace King," he greeted me with dap as he passed through the threshold.

"Did you grab a Dutch?"

"They didn't have any more Dutchies, so I grabbed you a Swisher Sweet."

Polo handed me the blunt then walked deeper into the apartment where Byrd was placing the packaged crack into a book bag. They greeted each other with the hand shake that they had made up when they were kids.

"What's popping Bee?" Polo took a seat.

"Shit, about to go home and lay my ass down," Byrd replied. "I had a long night then I had to get up this morning and handle this wit brah. I'm tired as hell."

"Alright, if you get into something later on, holler at me."

"I ain't doing nothing, but I'll give you a jingle later to see what's poppin!"

Byrd got up from the table, taking the backpack with him. Once he was gone, Polo came into the kitchen where I was rolling up the blunt.

"How much are you going to charge me for a quarter joint?" he inquired.

"I don't even know why you ask me that," I said. "You already know what I want."

"I know, but it's not for me so I need a little room to play," Polo negotiated.

"How much room, you need Lo?"

"I'm at least trying to clip me a nickel."

"You're killing me."

"C'mon fam, I got the bread on me and everything," he pulled out the money.

"How much is that?" I questioned

"Fifty-five hundred."

"You're killing me," I repeated.

"Damn, King let me win sometimes."

"You a funny nigga, man. You lucky I love you," I expressed with a grin.

After retrieving the work from the freezer Ziplock, Polo and I made the exchange. He quickly checked the merchandise before slipping it into his jacket.

"Appreciate you brah, I'll get with you in a minute," he began moving quickly.

"You alright brah?" I studied him closely.

"Yeah, I'm cool. Why you ask me that?"

"You seem like you speeding my nigga, slow down."

"Nah, I'm good. I'm just trying to go and bust this move real quick."

"Alright, twist that lock on your way out," I told him.

As Polo made his way towards the door, I fired up the blunt to relax my nerves. It had been a busy day and I couldn't wait to settle down for the evening. The essence of the smoke took me back to the conversation with Keisha earlier that day. Maybe I had been a little inconsiderate, concerning her feelings? She had sacrificed a lot for our relationship and for me not to take her emotions into consideration was selfish of me. I picked up the phone and dialed her number only to receive the voicemail after a couple rings. Moments later, my phone began ringing with her name flashing across the screen.

"What up!" I answered nonchalantly.

"You called?" Keisha responded with a hint of an attitude.

"Yo listen, I don't want no beef with you and I apologize for being an asshole. I'm willing to do whatever I need to do to make it up to you."

"I appreciate your apology but you're going to have to show me with your actions. I'm tired of you of disrespecting our relationship."

"What you mean?"

"The girls calling your phone, you staying gone for days and me not knowing where you are is beginning to be a little too much for me."

"Okay, I'm going to try and do better," I promised.

"You always say that," she returned. "I need you to quit trying and do it.

I could hear the exhaustion in her voice as she spoke. I took a deep breath as I contemplated my thoughts.

"Alright, I got you," I agreed. "I'm going to get it right."

"We'll see!" she exhaled.

Suddenly there was a loud bang, causing the front door to come crashing down. Before I could react, there were a number of plain clothes officers, barging in with their weapons drawn.

"Get Down… Get Down!" they yelled. "Put your hands where I can see them."

"What's going on?" I responded fearfully. "I didn't do nothing!"

"Shut up and get on the ground!" they continued to shout.

I cautiously adhered to their commands with my hands behind my head. A million thoughts raced through my mind as they proceeded to rummage through the premises, searching for drugs and weapons. Everything was moving in slow motion as they placed the steel handcuffs around my wrist.

"You have the right to remain silent," A detective specified. "Anything that you say can and will be used against you."

"What did I do?" I questioned.

"You have a right to an attorney," he continued.

As I listened to him read me my rights, I couldn't help but wonder what crime, I was being penalized for. It was a good thing that Byrd had took the majority of the work with him when he left otherwise it might've been lights out. The couple grams that they found weren't enough to keep me forever. As they escorted me out of the house to a nearby patrol car, I noticed Polo in the backseat of an unmarked vehicle. My heart skipped a beat as the puzzle was beginning to gel together. The possibility of one of my comrades setting me up had always crossed my mind but experiencing it was something different. The betrayal of one of my closest friends was a feeling that was unexplainable. I gathered up enough strength to smirk at him in disgust as they sat me in the back seat of the squad car. He couldn't even look me in the eyes, all Polo could do was lower his head in shame.

CHAPTER 33

THE COUNT DOWN
(Present)

"That's crazy!" Gip shook his head. "It's always the one's that you least expect who end up being a rat!"

"Tell me about it!" I replied.

"Where's your man at now?"

"I don't know. Ain't no body seen him since that shit happened."

"Damn, I know that shit fucked you up?" Gip emphasized.

"I was sick," I told him. "That shit still bothers me somedays, but it's cool because he has to look himself in the mirror and live with that every day."

"Believe that!"

As Gip and I walked around the track talking about the day that I got arrested, I examined all of the prisoners that were on the yard. I wondered how many of them were imprisoned by similar circumstances. I searched each man's face as I past and saw an indication of stress mixed with the anger that had built up due to the years of confinement. Like most people in the penitentiary, I had become accustomed to the hostile environment, but on this particular day, I was subdued by an eerie feeling. The energy was weird and although the sun was shining, there was a greyish cloud, hanging in the sky. There were hundreds of inmates on the yard, participating in any and everything you can think of from exercising to drug distribution. As we strolled by the guys on the basketball court, Gip had a look in his eyes as if he was possessed. Without warning, he pulled a four inch blade from his pants leg and attacked one of the inmates observing the game. He shoved the knife in and out of him, three or four times before the guy collapsed on the court. It all happened so fast. Before anyone could respond, Gip dropped the shank and fell back in line with me around the track. Moments later, the prison alarm blared throughout the jail and a substantial number of guards stormed the rec-yard in a haste dressed in combat gear. They yelled obscenities, instructing everyone to lie face down on the ground, attacking anyone who didn't comply. The guy who had gotten stabbed was quickly given first aid and rushed to the infirmary to stop the bleeding. For the remainder of the afternoon, the entire facility was on lockdown without any movement. Everyone on the yard was questioned about the incident but kept quiet about what they had witnessed. By the time the security restriction was lifted, the day was over. Later on that night, the entire jail was talking about the violent episode that had occurred. The victim was a kid from Syracuse who went by the name Swag. The word around the compound was that he had been breaking into lockers and stealing people's commissary. One of the Bloods had administered the hit and paid Gip an ounce of weed and few packs of cigarettes to put in the work. A man's life is worth less than a hundred and fifty dollars, I thought to myself as I walked the tier. As usual, Sincere was at the desk reading when I entered the cell.

"Peace!" he greeted, looking up from the book.

"Peace!" I returned the salutation.

"What happened on the yard?"

As Sincere anticipated my answer, I searched my mind for the correct response. In my heart, I felt that he had already knew the answer to the question but wanted to see if I was going to tell the truth. Over the years that I spent sharing a cell with him, Sincere had become something like a mentor, preparing me for life outside of prison. He had a habit of testing my intellect and asking rhetorical questions to see where my head was at.

"It got real in the field," I finally replied.

"And what part did you have to play with it getting real?" he continued to probe.

"I didn't play a part at all; I was just there when it went down. I didn't even know Gip was going to pop off like that."

"I don't even know why you rock with dude? You're going to mess around and get some time added on, fucking with that clown."

"I didn't even do nothing!" I defended. "I can't control what homie do."

"But you can control who you choose to be around," Sincere said.

"That's my man though!"

"Why, because y'all from the same city? Know a few of the same people? That's some kid shit. You have to be able to measure a man, not by where he's from but who he is and that nigga is a clown! He moves completely different from how you move but you're going to get yourself caught up in his bullshit if you're not careful."

"How you figure that?" I frowned.

"You're guilty by association," he refuted. "His issues can become your issues. When that boy gets out of the hospital, him and his crew is going to want revenge and it's a possibility that they're going to get at you due to your affiliation."

"I'm not worried about that nigga or his crew," I defended. "They already know that I'm about that action and will do whatever."

"But why would you put yourself in that position?"

"We're in prison and I can't escape these four walls, so what do you want me to do. Be a hermit?"

"You go home in less than a year King and it's plenty of brothers that would love to be in your shoes. Me being one of them and if I was you, I wouldn't be doing anything except preparing for my freedom."

"I thought that's what I've been doing?" I said with a hint of confusion.

Sincere nodded in agreement.

"Don't get me wrong, you've definitely transformed into a different person from when you first walked through them gates and I'm proud of you. But you still have some work to do?"

"We all got some work to do, ain't nobody perfect!"

"You're right, but I'm not asking you to be perfect." Sincere professed. "I'm advising you to make good decisions. You're loyal to default and that's going to be your downfall."

"How am I loyal to default?" I stepped deeper into the cell, taking a seat on the bunk.

"You're devoted to everyone's cause but your own. At some point and time, you have to be selfish and focus on yourself. When you were in the streets, I'm pretty sure that you held your entire crew down when shit got real. But how many of them has held you down since you been in here?"

"Not many!"

"You see what I'm saying? You can't continue to come to people's aid and allow them to use you until you're useless."

"I feel what you're saying but I can't change who I am."

"You don't have to change who you are, just change the objective. The same energy and confidence that you put in everyone else needs to be directed towards you and your family. Before you know it, those gates are going to crack and you're going to be a free man and the habits that you create in here is going to carry over into the streets. I'm not trying to tell you how to live your life but get into the habit of aligning yourself around the right people. Your support system is going to be a key factor to your success."

Sincere and I elevated our conversation well into the early hours of the morning. I processed the wisdom and transcribed the discussion into the depths of my mind. A surge of thoughts flowed through me as I listened to him speak. He expressed how much that I reminded him of himself when he was younger and didn't want me to make the same mistakes that he had. After Sincere had fallen asleep, I couldn't stop the brainwaves from vibrating inside of my head. I thought about how I had ended up inside of prison and how most of my friends abandoned me during this vulnerable time. When I was free, I thought that the good times would last forever and that we would always be family but I guess I was wrong. I thought about everyone who I had disappointed from Ma Dukes and Keisha to Coach Pete. I could've been anything that I chose to be but the allure of the fast life had distracted me from my true purpose and now I'm lying in a cage, living with regrets. A glimmer of hope engulfed me as I thought about my release date and how I intended to get acclimated back into world. I wasn't going to waste my potential any longer on meaningless activities or people that didn't benefit me in any way. I had a family that depended on me to come home and be the King that I proclaimed I was. I wasn't going to be a product of the system and be subjected to modern day slavery anymore. Once I was released, I planned on remaining free, not only physically but free from the shackles that society placed on our thinking. As I drifted off to sleep, I continued to impregnate my mind with thoughts of getting my life together.

The following morning, I was awakened to the sound of the steel gates cracking open throughout the tier. The jangling from the C.O's keys could be heard throughout the cellblock as he walked the unit, waking everyone up for breakfast. I rolled out of the bed and quickly brushed my teeth. Sincere was already up in his routine, sitting at the desk reading a book. He acknowledged me with a slight nod of the head but continued focusing on the literature in front of him.

"Are you going to eat?" I asked, spitting the toothpaste into the sink.

"Nah, I'ma fall back," Sincere replied. "They don't have anything good down there."

"Alright, I'll be back."

When I stepped out onto the range, I was approached by a guy from my hometown by the name of Ron. He had just come back to prison on a parole violation due to a dirty urine. I never understood why people would risk their freedom to get high. Ron was a wannabe and always had a story to tell, so when I acknowledged him coming in my direction, I prepared for the trivial chatter.

"You heard what happened to your boy?" Ron asked in a tone just above a whispered.

"My boy who?" I responded with uncertainty.

"Ya boy Gip," he confirmed. "He's in the hole for the stabbing that happened on the yard yesterday."

"Are you for real?"

"Dead ass!"

"What happened?"

On the way to the chow hall, Ron gave me the rundown on how the goon squad had ran up in Gip's cell and hauled him off to segregation. The administration had played the video tape back and witnessed the brutal act that he had committed on the basketball court the day before. My thoughts went back to the conversation that I held with Sincere about how my association with the dudes from my city could lead to trouble. I was relieved that my name hadn't been mentioned but knew that I was on the radar more than likely. For the next few weeks, I tried my best to maintain a low profile but the places to duck off to were limited. Gip had sent word through a kite that I should take precaution and stay on point at all times because it was a war brewing. Although I had nothing to do with the beef, my connection with him made me target. I was on the countdown to go home and wanted to avoid any type of confrontation but wasn't about to allow anyone to do me any physical harm. Everywhere I went, I kept a bagger close by just in case it popped off. A little over a month had gone by before the drama came to a head. It was a Thursday afternoon and I was in the law library, assisting another inmate with his case when Swag and a guy from his crew entered. This was the first time since the stabbing that we'd crossed paths and I was ready for whatever was about to transpire. A malicious grin spread across his face as we locked eyes. Swag nudged his partner, nodding as they headed in my direction. Nervously anticipating my next move, I exhaled deeply as the person who I was helping advised me to think before I acted out. Going against my better judgement, I disregarded his advice and stood up in Swag's face. Before I could say a word, his affiliate caught me with a hard right to the jaw, knocking me against the wall. After regaining my balance, I flew into a blind rage. All I could see was red as I charged at them forcefully. The next couple moments were a blur. All I remember was the four of us rumbling throughout the library, crashing into bookcases and shelves. Within minutes, the response team charged the premises, carrying us off to the hole.

Segregation was another world inside of a world that existed in the prison. The shadowy lights barely reflected off of the dark grey walls, giving the unit a murky ambience. The cells reeked of funky armpits and ass, due to the lack of showering that was permitted. It was pure mayhem once entering this restricted area. The cells were either freezing cold or extremely hot, producing a miserable environment for the detainees. All day and night, loud banging and screams could be heard on the block, making it difficult to sleep. Everyone was confined to a cell for twenty-three hours a day and the isolation of the hole caused some of the inmates to develop mental issues over time. Others used this time to cultivate their mind and build their physical exterior. Being subjected to this atmosphere was draining and it took a strong person to overcome the psychological effects of solitary. There were many days where I felt as if I was going crazy but I wasn't about to be consumed or broken by the system. The entire time that I was on keep-lock, I was concerned that I wouldn't be released on time due to the altercation in the library. To keep myself occupied, I wrote letters and read everything that I could get my hands on to escape the harsh reality that had me afflicted. Some days I would just lie on my bunk and listen to the madness that was taken place around me. A few weeks into my stint, the guy in the cubicle next to me killed himself because the guards wouldn't allow him out of the cell for the mandatory hour that we were permitted. Prisoners were always causing themselves bodily harm. It became the norm and the officers didn't seem to care. They were only there to collect a pay check so they could get back to their families. We were just a number to them and they could care less if we lived or died. As the weeks passed, I began formulating a strategy for my life after prison. The biggest regret that I had was not being present in my child's life. Seventy five percent of the African American household was being led by the black woman and the penal system played a major role in those statistics. I began imagining how I would do things differently once I was released. I was going to be the best father to my daughter. The love and affection of both parents was instrumental to a child's development and I planned on doing everything in my power to nurture that relationship. I just needed to get my freedom back.

CHAPTER 34

MY TIME IS COMING

120 days was more than enough time to get my mind right and once I was released from the hole, I was ready to conquer the world. I had accumulated four months of hair on my head so the first thing that I did was hit the barber shop and get a cut. By the time I reached general population, I was looking forward to building with Sincere. I knew that he would have a critical opinion about the incident in the library because he had foreseen it before it happened. I stepped into the cell and to my surprise he wasn't there. The book that he was reading was cracked open on the desk alongside a yellow notepad. I picked it up and curiously scanned the title which read, The Autobiography of Malcolm X, a narrative of a Detroit bred hustler turned Muslim. Like so many men that were incarcerated, I had read the story a time or two and was inspired by the transition that the ex-con had made into society. Knowing a person from the streets can redeem himself while serving time in prison was something that encouraged me to keep pushing. Malcom AKA Malik El Shabazz was the perfect example of what a criminal could do if he changed his thought process.

"They finally let you out huh?" Sincere walked into the cell.

Setting the book back in its place, I spun around, greeting him with a pound as he approached.

"Yeah, they couldn't hold the kid forever," I told him, humorously.

"What's the plan now that you're out of the hole?"

"I plan to get right. Sitting in that room by myself everyday gave me time to reflect on everything that I've been doing wrong and it's time to switch some shit up."

"It's easier said than done," Sincere protested.

"That's a fact!" I agreed. "Everything that you said was going to happen, happened. Sometimes it takes a person to go through the fire for them to smell the smoke but I get it now!"

"Do you really get what I've been trying to teach you or are you just running your mouth like the rest of these fools in here?"

"Nah, I get it and I'm done wasting my time on the things that serve no purpose in my life."

"I believe that you can do it as long as you're in this controlled environment but what are you going to do when you get back to the hood with your boys? When the blunts are circulating and the broads are coming at you from every direction?"

"Stand firm on my square!" I emphasized.

"That shit sound good but when things aren't going your way and your bread looking funny, that's when the real test is going to come. That's when you're going to see what you're really made of."

"Listen brah," I looked at Sincere with intensity in my eyes. "I'm tired! I'm tired of losing and I'm tired of putting myself on the line for everyone else except for me. It's time for a change and I don't care how tough it gets, I'm not going back to who I use to be. I'm not going back to the streets unless it's to help somebody else find their way out. I don't care if I have to work two jobs, cut grass and cash in bottles; I'm not coming back to prison once they let me go. It's a million and one hustles out there and I refuse to be limited to something that could possibly cost me my life."

A smile spread across his face as Sincere nodded in approval.

"That's what I'm talking about," he said. "You keep thinking like that and there's no doubt in my mind that you're going to be successful."

"I don't have a choice; I got a kid that needs my direction and leadership."

"You have a nation of black males that need your direction and leadership," Sincere corrected. "Just like Malcolm X, you can give a voice to the voiceless and be an example for these young warriors struggling to find their way."

The one thing that I admired about Sincere out of the many was his ability to look past the present moment into the future. His outlook on life was always on a broader scale. He spoke with confidence and the drive that he fashioned was beginning to rub off on me. As my release date drew near, the anxiety thickened. I couldn't wait to get out and put my plans into action. I immersed myself into studying and maintained a low profile. I couldn't afford to get mixed up in anything that may have delayed me from going home, so I fell back from all negative energy. Most of the people who I'd associated with understood why I had distanced myself but there were others who assumed that I was acting funny. Either way, I didn't care what anyone thought or had to say, I was going to live my life on my terms, free of false entitlements. It had taken years for me to come to the conclusion that I didn't owe anyone anything.

The following weekend, I was exercising when the correctional officer told me that I had a visit. After finishing my set, I quickly showered and got dressed, anticipating who had come to see me. When I reached the visitation room, Ma Dukes was seated twenty yards from the C.O's control center. A warm smile stretched across her face as I approached the table. We embraced with a long hug before taking our seats.

"Hey son!" she began. "How you been doing?"

"I'm good, taking it a day at a time," I replied. "What's up with Brah?"

"He's not doing nothing but working and raising his kids."

"Tell him that I asked about him."

"He was supposed to come up here with me but his job called him in."

"No doubt, what else is going on?"

"You tell me what's going on," Ma Dukes grabbed my arms. "Look at you, getting all big and stuff."

"I'm trying to get it right before I come home," I laughed.

"Speaking of home, when are you getting out?"

"I got ninety-seven days and a wake up!" I confirmed.

"I know that's right, but what are you going to do once you get out."

"I got a couple things lined up but first I'm going to start by getting a job. One of my friends owns a construction company and he said that he has a spot for me when I come home so I'm going to see what that's about and make it work!"

"I hope so King because it's not anything in those streets but trouble," Ma Dukes stressed. "I worry about you all the time and I just pray that GOD watches over you."

"I'm going to be alright this time around," I promised. "I'm done running the streets, selling drugs. That's not how you raised me and I just want to show you that everything that you taught me wasn't in vain."

Ma Dukes let out a sigh of relief as my words resonated into her mind. She smiled but her gaze revealed a woman that had seen and suffered a lot. The crow's feet in the corner of her eyes symbolized that she was aging rapidly due to the years of stress. It was at that moment that I realized how much of a substantial role that she played in my development and how lost I would be without her.

"Ma, is everything okay with you?" I asked in a concerned manner.

"Yeah, I'm fine!" she avowed.

"Are you sure?" I pressed. "It seem like your energy is off a little bit."

"I'm a little tired but I'm okay."

"Have you been going to your doctor appointments?"

"Don't worry me. Just worry about getting out of here and getting your stuff in order. I'll be fine!"

"For real Ma, you got to make sure that you are taking care of yourself because I don't know what I would do without you."

Ma Dukes took a deep breath and considered her thoughts before she replied.

"Back when your father shot me, I thought that I was going to die," Ma Dukes reflected. "The only thing that kept me alive was you and your brother. I remember lying in the hospital bed, praying, and asking God to allow me to live long enough where the both of you didn't need me to take care of y'all anymore and I believe that HE answered that prayer. You and Damon both are smart and strong young men so if something were to happen to me, you'll be able to figure it out."

"C'mon Ma, don't talk like that!" I grumbled.

"I don't plan on going anywhere, anytime soon but I'm not always going to be around," she accentuated. "Death is promised to everyone so I've always tried to provide you with the tools for you to fend for yourself."

"And you've done a great job!"

"Aww son, thank you!"

"Nah ma, thank you!"

"For what?" she questioned.

"For never giving up on me!" I answered. "And I promise that I'm going to make you proud when I get out of here."

"I'm already proud of you King," Ma Dukes placed my hand inside of hers. "You are wise beyond your years and you've taught me a lot about life. Just because you're incarcerated doesn't mean that I'm not proud of you. Everyone makes mistakes and I believe that you're going to utilize your errors, get out and do some great things. The choice is yours!"

For the remainder of the visit, Ma Dukes and I discussed everything from religion to what was going on in the family. She said that my daughter Princess was growing fast and had a similar personality as me. In return, I vowed to implement some of the same principles inside of my child that she had instilled in me. She expressed her concerns about me coming back to the same environment that had stolen my innocence so long ago and advised for me to remain patient during the transition. I reassured her that I was finished with the life in the fast lane and my main priority was to become a better person. The expression on her face was priceless as I articulated the obligation to my family.

"God is the best of planners," I explained to Ma Dukes. "And I believe that this was all a part of The Most High plan to get my attention so HE could cultivate me."

"Okay son, it sounds like you got it figured out," she smiled.

"Not yet, but as long as I remain focused on Allah, I'll figure it out."

"Well, Jesus Christ is still my Lord and Savior but if Islam can keep you on the right track, I will respect and support your decision to be Muslim."

Suddenly the guard made an announcement over the PA system, informing the room that the duration of the visitation was over.

"Do you need anything?" Ma Dukes asked as she stood to leave.

"Nah, I'm good. I can live off the land until I get out."

"Alright, give me a hug."

I stood up and embraced my mother closely. The smell of her perfume took me back to a time when I was a little boy in her arms. When we released, I exhaled deeply as I watched her make her way through the security doors. An enormous portion of me wished that I was going with her, but I knew that my time was coming. I knew that my freedom awaited me on the other side of that exit.

CHAPTER 35

NOW YOU'RE READY

The week before being released, the anticipation of getting out had my temperament in a vibrant state. It was a Friday afternoon and the sun hung in the sky, shining brightly. It seemed as if the grass was greener and the birds were chirping a little louder than usual as I left out of the building where we recited the Jumah prayer. The sermon that the Imam lectured, during the Khutbah had me filled with confidence. I felt as if the words in his message were speaking directly to my spirit as he touched on the importance of knowing your purpose in life. He expressed how the obstacle's that's endured prepares us for our destiny and as long as we follow the example of the Prophet Muhammad, Allah would make the path easy.

"That was a good message," I stated as I walked up behind Musa.

At the sound of my voice, he turned around slowly, allowing me to catch up. A welcoming grin appeared across his face as I approached him.

"As Salaam Alakium!" Musa greeted. "What's good with the brotha?"

I properly returned the salutation of peace as I joined him on the walkway back to the housing unit.

"I'm glad that you enjoyed the Khutbah my brotha" Musa addressed my original statement. "If I said anything that was useful, it was from Allah and give him the credit, but if there was anything that I said that was false, may Allah forgive me for my shortcomings."

"You definitely dropped a jewel or two that I'm going to take with me to the streets and apply it," I told him.

"That is right!" Musa recollected. "This time next week, you'll be going to the Mosque and offering the Jumah prayer a free man. It must feel good?"

"I've been dreaming about that day for a long time and I can't wait to get my life back."

"I'm happy for you Ahki, and I pray that you do the right thing with the blessing that Allah has given you. Don't go out there and forget about the hell that you had to endure in here. The bondage that a lot of brothers are still going to have to sustain after you're gone."

"I promise you that I'm going to stay grounded and focus on doing the right thing."

"And what's the right thing?" Musa questioned.

"I'm going out here to get a job, take care of my family and stay out of the way," I quickly replied. "I'm not trying to get caught up and find myself back in here with these police telling me what to do."

"Hold firm and stay true to those words. A lot of brother's go home and fall back into the same routine that got them jammed up in the first place. Be the difference and don't allow the environment that you're going back to, pull you back in. I believe in you and if you continue to believe in yourself and stay on the right track, Allah is going to open some doors and bless you beyond your imagination."

"Thank you Ahk!"

"If you really want to thank me, go out there and give us a voice. Let society know that there are some brothers who change their lives while serving time and prison. Break the cycle and give us some hope because hope is the only thing that some of us got in here."

The pitch in Musa's speech indicated a genuineness that was absent in the prison population. I could hear the sincerity in his voice as he encouraged for me to be an example for the brothers that would remain in the struggle long after I was released. Years of frustration had assembled inside of him and the only thing that kept him moving forward beside his belief in Islam was the passion he held for the fellow Muslim to do better. It was people like Musa who I planned on setting an example for. It was brothers like him who I wanted to make proud. A tear escaped the corner of my eye as I thought about all of the young black males that may never get the chance to experience life on the other side again. We were losing our men to the penal system in multitudes and the numbers were rising every day. We were becoming an endangered species due to the black children lost to the cemeteries and prisons across the country. 81 percent of the murders committed in America occurred in the urban community making it likely that the crime was committed by another black man. It's alarming to know that it is more black males in correctional facilities than on college campuses. I understood why Musa was so passionate about the conditions of our people.

The following day, our conversation was still heavy on my heart as I laid on the bunk, staring at the ceiling. On the bed beneath me, Sincere sat analyzing the pieces on the chessboard in front of him. Playing the game of the Asian strategist by himself was a preference that he established early in his sentence. By studying the board from both sides, Sincere was able to see the perspective from every angle.

"You kind of quiet up there!" he acknowledged. "Is everything good?"

"Yeah, I'm straight, I'm just thinking!" I replied.

"Well since you're thinking so hard, are you trying to get a game in?"

"Yeah, we can get one in!" I rose up.

When I hopped down from the bunk, we began setting up the pieces to the chessboard.

"You seem a little distracted," Sincere analyzed. "What's on your mind?"

"It ain't nothing, I'm good!" I told him.

"Are you sure?"

"Yeah, I'm Gucci. I was just thinking about a conversation that I had with one of the brothers yesterday."

"Don't let that be the reason that your game is off because I'm not trying to hear no excuses."

"Nah, it's not going to be any excuses, I'm focused!"

"Okay, we're about to see how focused you are."
Sincere pushed the first chess piece.

He eyeballed me with a cunning glare as I countered his move. For the next ten minutes, we exchanged pieces, aiming to position ourselves into a victory. I switched from my normal reserve style of playing to a more aggressive strategy which caught him by surprise.

"I see you've been practicing!" Sincere stated as he studied my last move.

"Nah, I just had to change my game up and come at you with a different approach!" I declared.

"I see!" he nodded his approval. "I'm impressed but you still got a lot to learn."

Sincere threaten my territory with a knight, forcing me to move my bishop back in order to protect the king. As he counteracted, I weighed my options, calculating the move that he would try to attempt next. He was always thinking four steps ahead so I premeditated all the possibilities that would place him in the best situation.

"I see what you trying to do!" I told him. "That shit ain't gonna work!"

"Study long, study wrong!" Sincere shot back with a chuckle.

Finally, I gathered up the audacity and did something that was totally unexpected. I boldly pushed my queen on his side of the board and took one of his pawns.

"You know that you can't play without your queen," he said.

"I cant allow myself to stay attached to nothing if it's not putting me in a better position."

Sincere quickly swapped out, opening a passage for me to bring my rook down and put him in check.

"Everything that looks good ain't good for you," I replied sarcastically.

With his back against the ropes, Sincere examined the squares, trying to figure his way out. Realizing that there was nothing that he could do to stop the checkmate, he knocked his king over and surrendered willingly.

"Good shit" he shook my hand. "I didn't see that coming."

"About time!" I returned with a smile.

In all the years that we've been together, I was never able to defeat Sincere without him giving me some type of an advantage. He looked back down at the chessboard and deliberated on where he had gone wrong before, staring up into my eyes.

"Now you're ready for the world!" he finally said.

"What you mean, I'm ready for the world?" I asked a bit confused.

Sincere snickered and continued to stare at me with a firm glare in his eyes.

"The entire time we've been building, I've been preparing you for the free world. I know that you look at chess as just a game but you can tell a lot about a person from the way that they play. Your game has elevated to the next level and as long as you apply what I've been teaching you, you'll stay ten steps ahead of the competition. I've always told you to protect the king on the board and that same rule still pertains when you hit the bricks. There's going to be all types of people coming at you from every direction and you need to look at every angle, every possibility that could be harmful or helpful. Use your head to out think these niggas and persuade every piece around you to put you in position to win. At the end of the day, it's about winning, and you can't win if you're in jail or dead. Look around you! We're surrounded by these steel bars and concrete brah! This ain't life, this ain't living. This shit is for suckas and I'm the biggest lollipop in this bitch because I allowed them to trick me off the streets and take me off of the board. So, where my game ends, yours is about to begin."

CHAPTER 36

WELCOME HOME

The following week at eight o'clock in the morning, I walked out of the prison gates a free man. Other than the state issued clothes that were on my back, the only thing that I left with was the letters from my loved ones and the Quran. The six hour bus ride was therapeutic as I absorbed the sceneries of the rural areas and small country towns on the way home. I thought about everything from what I wanted to eat to the first person I might see once I got to the city. The feeling of freedom was surreal. No chains or shackles around my wrist or feet. No more guards escorting me to my destination or breathing down my neck, watching my every move. I had the liberty to walk in to a store and purchase a bag of chips or drink a cup of ice water if I decided to. It was the small things that people felt entitled to that we took for granted. My mind went back to Musa, Sincere and all of the brothers who I had built a relationship with while serving my time. A sense of compassion lingered in my heart as I thought about them and how they may never get a chance to undergo the moment that I was feeling right now. I felt as if I had an obligation to do right by them and every other prisoner that had influenced my life. As the Greyhound approached downtown Buffalo, the voice of the bus driver snapped me back to the present moment as he spoke over the P.A. system.

"Welcome to the Nickle City," he announced. "The temperature in the city of Buffalo is seventy-nine degrees and the time is now 1:49 p.m. We will be approaching the terminal shortly. Thank you for riding Greyhound."

Once the bus was parked, I grabbed the few belongings that were in my possession and quickly made an exit. As I walked through the station, I took in my surroundings. Everything seemed to be moving at a fast pace. Everyone was either on their phone or engaged in some type of electronical device. From what I could see, the hustle and bustle of life was technology driven and everyone was up to speed except me. I stepped outside, allowing the afternoon sun to smack me in the face. Just as I was about to begin walking, a silver S550 with tinted windows pulled up and stopped in front of me. Seconds later, Byrd hopped out with a Cuban Linx, dangling around his neck as the iced out Rolex shined on his wrist. He approached with a couple playful jabs to the body before embracing me with an enormous hug.

"Welcome home baby boy," he said. "I see you done got all swole and shit."

"I had enough time in that muthafucka. I had to do something to relieve the stress," I told him.

He looked at me astonished at how big I had gotten from lifting weights.

"Damn, it's good to have you back!"

"It's good to be back!" I glanced over at the car that he was driving. I see life has been treating you good since I've been gone."

"A lot of things have changed since you've been gone but we'll talk about that later. Hop in so we can get you cleaned up because that state shit is not a good look."

Although it felt good riding shotgun in a Mercedes Benz with my right hand man, a part of me was conflicted. I hadn't been home for more than a New York minute and was already putting myself in jeopardy. I had love for Byrd but I knew that he was still in the streets hustling and that wasn't the energy that I wanted to be around. I thought about Sincere and how he said that everyone was going to come at me from different directions and as the music pumped softly, I wondered what was Byrd's angle.

"Why did you catch the bus?" Byrd turned the song down. "You know that I would've came and got you."

"I know, but I needed time to think," I replied.

"You don't think you had enough time to think in prison?"

"I had more than enough time to think, but I wanted to spend my first moments free alone in my thoughts. So I could get some clarity before life kicks in."

"What, you done found Jesus or something brah?" Byrd looked over with a grin. "Talking about you need some clarity."

"I need my mind to be clear!" I said. "I can't come out here speeding!"

"You've been through a lot King and not once have I heard you complain. It takes a strong dude to overcome what you've been through but we're in position now, so whatever you need, I got you!"

"Good looking fam! And I appreciate everything that you did for me while I was in the bing. That shit meant a lot to me."

"I didn't do anything that you wouldn't have done for me. That's what brothers do!"

"No doubt!" I nodded in agreement. "So what's been going on in the hood?"

"It ain't nothing going on but a bunch of young boy's wilding," Byrd declared.

"It's like that?"

"Man, them young niggas got the game twisted. They're playing the game without the instructions. I'm talking about, the rules is all the way missing. I stay the fuck out of them little niggas way. You'll fuck around and have to kill one of them."

"It sound like the young boy's got you under pressure," I laughed.

"You'll see when one of them crack babies run up on you and do your dishes," Byrd refuted.

"Nigga's ain't doing nothing that we weren't doing when we were their age," I said.

"Nah, these little niggas is different!" Byrd responded as he merged onto the expressway.

After taking me shopping and getting something to eat, Byrd drove through the city, showing me how much things had changed since I'd been away. I was taken back by how the town had transitioned. The place that I once considered home looked unfamiliar to me. Where profitable storefronts and businesses once dwelled, there were run-down or abandoned buildings inhabiting the streets. All throughout the neighborhood residential housing was replaced with empty lots and trap houses. The vibrant corners where the hustlers use to congregate day and night looked like a ghost town. The only thing missing was the tumbleweed turning over in the street.

Everything was in disarray. Drug dealers were now dope fiends. The dudes who use to get chumped off were now the ones terrorizing the town, robbing everything moving. Even college kids were chasing the hustle, writing counterfeit checks and swiping credit cards. Shit was crazy. Before taking me home, Byrd pulled up on the block and parked. I incredulously shook my head as I observed the madness that I'd helped create. It was like everyone was living in the twilight zone.

"So what's the plan now that you're home?" Byrd asked in a cool like manner.

"I have a few things in mind, but first I'm going to start by finding a job," I told him.

"A job?" he cringed.

"Yeah nigga, like a real nine to five," I chuckled.

"Brah, niggas is going to set you out; you don't have to get a job. We're eating right now and if parole is what you're worried about, we got that covered. My man Flip got a call center downtown and I already talked to him about putting you on the books. You don't have to worry about nothing, I got you."

"What do you expect me to do Bee? Come out here and push packs on the corner, trying to pick up where I left off? Do you expect for me to put my life on the line for a neighborhood that don't give a damn about me? Is that what you want me to do?"

"We don't move like that anymore!" Byrd disclaimed. "I realize how much you have lost and sacrificed for the hood. You're one of the OGs that helped start this shit, so you wouldn't have to touch nothing."

"I love you like a brother Bee, but I'm not on that type of time anymore," I looked him in the face. "We're not eighteen anymore and I'm not going to act like I am. I'm done!"

Byrd stared me back in the eyes to see if I was joking or not.

"You're serious huh?" he responded in a disbelieving tone.

"I'm dead ass."

"I'm not even mad at you brah. You got to do what you got to do!"

"Thanks for understanding fam!"

After Byrd and I clapped hands, I exited the car. Walking away from that vehicle, I felt as if I was leaving my past behind. Although the streets of uptown Buffalo molded me, I couldn't allow it to cultivate my future. I had suffered too much to go back to who I use to be and even if I wanted to return to the savagery, I couldn't. I had learned who I was as a black man in America. No longer could I participate in the destruction of my community. No longer will I poison the minds of my people. The old me was dead. I had buried him inside of a 6x8 coffin. The world was about to get introduced to a King, entering the next chapter of his life. A man in search of a new beginning.

THE END

Made in the USA
Columbia, SC
10 January 2019